Charlotte Mayweather, the penniless and illegitimate dependent of Drymote Estate, struggles to find her place in the world after the death of her uncle leaves her unloved and alone. When Edward Cotterhugh first arrives to claim his new inheritance, the heir of Drymote seems intent on nothing more than careless frivolity, much to the chagrin of his father, who will stop at nothing to see him embedded in good society. Charlotte quickly learns that Edward's insouciant attitude hides a far darker past, though. As Edward learns to confront his ghosts, Charlotte fears that she is losing her sanity as her mother did before her. Together they must unravel the mysteries of Drymote upon All Hallow's Eve, before it is too late.

This book is a work of fiction. Names, characters, places, and incidents either are products of the author's imagination or are used fictitiously. Any resemblance to actual events or locales or persons, living or dead, is entirely coincidental.

The Heir of Drymote
Copyright © 2021 Beth Fuller
ISBN: 978-1-4874-3230-0
Cover art by Martine Jardin

Published by eXtasy Books Inc or
Devine Destinies, an imprint of eXtasy Books Inc

Look for us online at:
www.eXtasybooks.com or www.devinedestinies.com

The Heir of Drymote

By

Beth Fuller

DEDICATION

For Pete, Ezra, Teddy and my parents.

CHAPTER ONE

Shelter – there must be shelter somewhere.

Charlotte Mayweather peered dismally around the wild and rambling grounds of Drymote Estate, trying to blink the rain out of her eyes. Hydrangeas, their mop heads drooping under the onslaught, bobbed in silent agreement around her and the Michaelmas daisies swayed with the winds, but nowhere seemed to offer any sanctuary from the sudden downpour.

Nobody knows I am out here. Nobody is coming to help. The realisation chilled Charlotte's skin as thoroughly as the rain did, leaving her shivering and miserable. The climb up to Drymote house was too steep and too far to run to, even if she hadn't twisted her ankle when she fell. She clutched at that ankle now, sprawled upon the ground, trying to rub the throbbing ache away as the pebbled path tattooed indentations on her skin. Her respectable mourning blacks were now mud-dyed brown and she had lost her second-best shawl somewhere out there amongst the bushes when she had raced the storm for shelter and lost.

She tutted under her breath as she surveyed the damage. Her dress had scarcely been respectable as it was, old, meticulously mended, slightly too small. She had hoped to make it pass muster for Albert's upcoming ball with some cheap glass jewellery and some old velvet ribbons, but there was no hope of that now.

Is that really my most pressing concern? I will not be attending the dance at all if I have joined Uncle John in the grave.

1

Charlotte gritted her teeth and forced herself to sit up.

I never should have left the house today. Again, the hydrangeas bobbed in agreement. She scowled at their sanctimonious faces.

"It's a little late for recriminations now," she told them sternly. Unsurprisingly, they did not reply.

She huffed out a damp breath and wiped her hair out of her face, smearing little kisses of mud across her forehead. The truth was she felt like she could no longer breathe in the silent, grief-stained halls of Drymote, still wearing their mourning wreathes, crowned in crêpe at the door. These days it felt like she could not breathe anywhere where the wind was not howling and the skies were not an open call for freedom.

Still, she could not help but curse the feet which had led her through the extensive gardens. She had spent the day meandering down pathways, past the glass-houses and the lake, through the walled garden and the orchard rows to the farthest depths of the garden's limits, down to the hidden, lurking corners where Uncle John had fallen prey to the eccentric fashion of follies.

And yet, perhaps one of those buildings might yet suit her purposes now, for she could hardly sit out there in the rain all afternoon. The staff would certainly think her eccentric if she did. *No, they will think me mad. Rich old Lords like Uncle John can be eccentric – penniless, illegitimate wards are only ever mad. Perhaps they will even send me away to the same asylum my mother died in.*

Charlotte shuddered, and it was not merely for the rain seeping through to her very bones. She could think of nothing worse than the beckoning madhouse. Better by far to die out in the open skies than locked away, chained to a bed, force-fed by an orderly.

She squinted through the dense flower beds, trying to acclimate herself after her fall. The Hermit's Retreat, though by far the smallest of John's follies, was also the nearest, so it was in that direction that she began hauling herself. Another flash of lightning seared across the shrouded sky, burning the clouds white.

She limped onwards, her ankle whimpering with pain every time she put her weight to it. Her old mourning dress, a remnant from Aunty Ursula's funeral a few years back now, was weighed down with the waters that clung to it. She left a sweeping trail of mud in her wake as her sodden skirts kissed the pebbles and earth. She looked around for aid, but the howling world around her remained endlessly empty. The few gardeners — those who had remained at Drymote after Albert had inherited it and purged Uncle John's old loyalists for cheap agency hires and untrained foundling maids — were clearly bottled away in the gardener's bothy, drinking hot toddies and planning the planting season for next spring. She could not say she blamed them.

"Who would be fool enough to come out in this weather?" she muttered and laughed at her own imprudence, but it was quickly cut short. The ground beneath grew slippery as she staggered across it, her booted feet sliding upon the grass, chewing up chunks of mud with every slippery footstep. She fell again, adding a litany of bruises to her impending hypothermia, and though she tried, she found she could not regain her feet this time. She gritted her teeth.

"They don't call you stubborn for nothing, Charlotte May-weather," she told herself fiercely. "You are going to make it to that folly if it is the last thing you do."

She could not bear to put the weight upon her foot again, so she rolled up onto her knees and began the painful crawl down that final twist of path. Pebbles and twigs stuck to her palms and scraped her knees even through her petticoats. She was sure she looked ridiculous. Perhaps the rain was a blessing after all. She could only imagine how much they would mock her if anybody was to see. She forced herself onwards grimly, and when the cave-like temple came into view at last, Charlotte could have *wept*.

The Hermit's Retreat was small, a single one-roomed building, decorated within and without in small white shells studded upon the walls, and a mosaic of pebbles upon the floor and upon the ceiling. There were no windows in it, and for that she was glad, for they would only have let the rain come howling in, nor was there a door, just a small opening in the foremost wall which she dragged herself through still on all fours. Out of the worst of the wet, she collapsed grate-fully to the floor, dripping and exhausted. She closed her eyes, letting her breath come trembling through her icy lips, her fingers massaging the pain throbbing from her ankle, the only place upon her whole body where heat was humming, it felt.

And her eyes leapt open at once, as a cough emanated from above her. A pair of boots stared at her. She stared back for half a moment and then pulled herself upright with a yelp to see the tall outline of a man lingering in the shadow of the corner. She had been so eager to escape the rain that she had not seen anybody hiding within.

He cocked an eyebrow at her, and she felt her whole body turn to flame, even as her gaze skated over him. She did not recognise him. He was not one of the house staff, nor the garden men. Fear at once coursed through her, as though she had been struck by the lightning still intermittently zig-zagging through the greys and blacks outside. She struggled up to her feet, but the man stepped forwards, holding out his hands in a placating manner, a somewhat smug smile lingering on his lips as his gaze raked over her dishevelled appearance.

"Pray, do not. You will only do yourself more mischief."

She ignored him, though she did need to lean upon the wall to take control of both her feet. She was all too aware that he had just watched her crawl into this folly on her hands and knees, probably much to his amusement.

"Who are you?" She tried to sound as imperious and commanding as she could, given the circumstances. The mud bespattering her clothes showed up all too clearly with each lightning flash outside, and the white light reflected off the rainwater still pooling beneath her feet. "What are you doing in my uncle's house?"

The stranger smiled. He had an arrogant face, she thought. It was well-formed and handsome, but it carried that knowledge all too clearly in the tilt of the chin and the straight and haughty nose. His lips twitched up in one corner, a smirk more than a smile. His hair clung to his head too, drenched with the rain that had caught them both, and droplets sprayed about them as he flicked it subconsciously off his forehead. *Those eyes . . .* The thought drifted lazily through the back of her mind, even as she sought to quash it. His eyes were so dark they seemed almost black. She felt her skin burning even hotter, if such a thing was possible.

"This is your uncle's house, is it?" The man looked around at the Hermit's Retreat, his stare lingering scathingly upon the shells adorning the walls. "I cannot say I think much of his decor. Nor for his guest quarters. Why, there is not even a bowl to wash up in." He grinned again, what he presumably thought was a charming and disarming smile. "You belong to that fine old house up there, then?" he asked.

He turned and stared out of the little doorway, his gaze fixed upon the sheets of water all but hiding the gardens from view. The trees, their boughs weighed down with water, blocked even the topmost roofs of Drymote from sight. She stared as well, as if she might find a way home.

"They said in the village that the lord, forgive me, your *uncle,* was dead, though."

The words were callous, thrown at her with all the unfeeling lightness of a stranger, and they stuck in her throat.

"Yes," she said with quiet dignity. "You have heard right. Lord John Cotterhugh has been dead a month past." Had it really only been a month since Uncle John's weathered hands touched the leaves and flowers of his beloved garden in benediction? A month since his fingers last plunged beneath the earth as if he were rooted there too? She swallowed and forced back the treacherous tears blinking to her eyes, unwilling to expose herself to yet more ridicule before this stranger. "It is his brother, Albert, who owns Drymote now." Uncle John had died intestate, the abruptness of his own mortality taking him unawares, and everything had gone to Albert by law. Uncle John had not even left her so much as a token to remember him by.

"Ah, I see. And your uncle, Albert—"

"He is *not* my uncle," she interrupted with a vehemence that surprised even her. She blinked and swallowed the anger which rose to her throat. "At least, that is, there is no blood to bind us." *And little inclination on either side to forge a relationship without it.* "Aunty Ursula, John's wife, was my mother's sister. It was she who was my blood-kin. They took me in when my mother died, and when both Ursula and John followed her to the grave, Albert kept me afterwards through charity." Charity! How that word stung her lips! She pressed them together as if she could take the pain from the words that way. Something flickered in the stranger's eyes—pity, or contempt? Neither one was ideal.

"I see. Well, would this Albert prosecute me for trespassing upon his lands? I was passing by when the urge to wander them came upon me, and then the rains came upon me too, far too suddenly for me to escape. A punishment from the fates for my temerity, perhaps? Or was it you, you old denizen, that summoned such storms to haunt me?" he asked the mural of the glowering Greek god upon the ceiling. The mural frowned down at them sternly from beneath a flowing beard of grey pebbles, and the man beside her twinkled at Charlotte merrily, a lopsided, conspiratorial smile lingering upon his lips.

"I am sure that he would remind you that these woods are not public land." *That is putting it tactfully. Albert is a stickler for his rights.*

"All land is public land if you are brave enough."

"Ah, the poacher's motto."

The man grinned and did not try to deny it. He was empty handed, at least. The sudden rain-burst must have interrupted his hunting.

Charlotte crossed her arms, about to summon some rebuke to knock the arrogant stranger off his pride, but as she stopped leaning against her arm, her knee buckled beneath her.

The stranger darted forwards and caught her around the waist and gently guided her towards the pebbled floor.

"May I test your ankle? We must see if it is sound."

Charlotte hesitated. It was hardly appropriate to let a stranger examine her, but her ankle was badly hurting. She could feel it swelling up inside her boot even now, throbbing with pain. She gave a sharp jerk of the head, and he was already undoing her laces before she had finished nodding. She gave a gasp of pain as he took her foot in his hand and rolled it about expertly.

"It is swollen and badly twisted, but it is not broken. You must rest with it elevated for a day or two."

Charlotte frowned at him. "You are a medical man?"

He spoke with all the confidence of one, and yet she had never known a doctor take to poaching before. The stranger laughed. "I fear not, but I have been in my fair share of scrapes. One learns how to patch oneself up in time."

She did not find that hard to believe. He had the aura of a man who attracted trouble. His eyes sparkled again, and she became abruptly aware once more of how dishevelled she looked. *And here I am giving myself all the airs and graces of an heiress. He must think me a fool.*

"Thank you for your advice," she said stiffly. "I will surely take it, when I can."

She tried to get her boot back on, but found it impossible. The man laughed.

"Take it now then. Here." He caught her foot in his hands and, sitting down upon the pebbled floor, he rested it atop his own leg to keep it high. She felt herself blushing, but he scarcely seemed to notice.

He rested his back against the shells of the wall, and together they added to the dampness of the floor, their two muddied capes dripping amongst the pebbles as they regained their strength. A soft silence swam between them for a moment as the thunders rolled outside, and, despite the winds and the weather, the little hut felt almost warm as they were cocooned within it. His hands still rested upon her foot, as if he had forgotten they were there, and it was an action at once so intimate and comfortable that she almost forgot that they were strangers and it was wildly inappropriate. *He does not think of it as anything other than a medical fact.* And yet she scarcely could remember the time anyone had touched her so casually or confidently, as if they had a right to. If it affected him in any way, he did not show it. The anonymous Greek god stared lifelessly down at her with untold scorn.

"I think the rain is lessening," the man said softly, still staring out at the world beyond the doorway. "Let me fetch someone for you."

"There is no one left to fetch." She could not keep the bitterness from her voice. Once upon a time she would have had John to worry about her, or even Fletch, the head gardener who had both lived and worked here for thirty years, but he had been ousted from his home without so much as a by-your-leave when Albert took over. Charlotte had protested, pleaded, cried and stormed, but she could not change Albert's mind.

Poor Fletch. He had let her climb up on his work bench when she was only a sprout herself to poke sunflower seeds into pots and water them in with his heavy cast-iron watering can, chasing her out of Uncle John's glass houses with a mock ferocity if she ever ventured in there unsupervised. To lose them both so close upon the heels of one another was cruel, and to have them replaced with the carelessness of Albert was even crueller.

The poacher quirked an eyebrow at her.

"Albert will not notice your absence?"

"Not today. Today, *Lord Cotterhugh*" — she stressed the word for the impertinent poacher — "would not notice if the skies turned purple. He is too busy awaiting the arrival of his only son and heir."

The stranger smiled. "Ah, and is that such a propitious occasion?"

"It has a rarity value. Edward has not visited us at Drymote since he was a child. The only likeness we have of him is a painted miniature from when he was a boy, with a cherubic smile upon his chubby cheeks. I imagine he is rather different now." Probably squat and balding like his father. And a somewhat spiteful smile twitched at her lips as she imagined the dashing heir everybody swooned over waddling up the path to Drymote as Albert's copy, save thirty years of life. She turned to see the poacher was watching her with amusement, and she blushed again. "This can scarcely be of interest to a stranger such as yourself."

"On the contrary, I find it all very intriguing. Tell me more of the denizens of Drymote."

"There is little more to tell. Edward will inherit Drymote Estate after his father passes, and Albert wishes him to be here now to learn how to run it properly. That is all."

"There are no scandalous rumours to report? How

disappointing."

"Oh, there are scandalous rumours aplenty, but I am far too sensible to listen to them."

The rumours had trailed through the half-empty halls of Drymote long before the announcement of his upcoming arrival had. Edward had abandoned his degree at Cambridge, where he had been all but ready to take a first. Edward had travelled all across Europe, disappearing and reappearing sporadically every few months. Edward had won a duel against a celebrated Italian pistol master. Edward was a renowned lover and a romantic. If Edward were half as large as his reputation, he would be too tall to fit through the doors.

She wondered if he was going to be as insufferable as Albert. She was not sure she could handle two of them. Albert had made it his business to make her life a misery since he had inherited Drymote, tucking his toes into the master bed scarcely before Uncle John's corpse had cooled in it. If Edward was as cruel as his father, perhaps she would move down to the Hermit's Retreat permanently. *Perhaps I too could take to poaching with this handsome stranger . . .*

His eyes sparkled at her as if he could read the thoughts from her mind, and she felt her skin turning to burgundy. She struggled to her feet, a gasp escaping from her lips as she placed her weight tentatively upon her ankle once more. He got to his feet too and offered her his hands, but she ignored them.

"Forgive me, I should not be alone here with you. As you have noted, the rain is slowing now, and I must return to the house to prepare myself for the arrival of Albert's son. If you had any sense, you would leave, too. If any of the gardeners caught you poaching, they would be duty bound to report it to Albert."

He leant forwards, his eyes sparkling ever more brightly, close enough that his breath whispered over her damp and chilled skin, warming it through. Charlotte felt a shiver run through her, and it was not earned by the cold. *I must not succumb to his temptations. He knows full well what it is he does.*

"What of you? Will you report me to Albert—forgive me, that is, *Lord Cotterhugh*?"

She hesitated and took the boot from his hand to buy herself time. She ought to, she knew, but she could not deny that she was reluctant to do so. She forced her foot back into it, crying out slightly as the wet leather chafed against her swollen skin. He watched her, and she could feel his gaze upon her still.

"Well?"

"It . . . it would not be . . . gallant of me to injure a man who has done me good," she said stiltedly. "No, I will not tell Albert today, I am sure he would not like to be bothered about it on the day of Edward's arrival, but if I should see you in these grounds another time, I cannot promise so much again."

"Oh, you will certainly see me in these grounds again, now I know it is inhabited by such fire-spirited nymphs."

She scowled at him and he laughed loudly. "For now, I will content myself with accompanying you back to your door. You would not deprive me of your company for some little while longer, I am sure."

She opened her mouth to protest, but he held up his hands to stem the flow of words escaping her.

"No, do not fight me, I am quite decided. Would it be *gallant* of me to let an injured lady limp her way to the doors alone?"

She scowled fiercely.

"You mock me, sir."

"No, I merely tease you, there is a difference. Besides, I have a hankering to see this house and the entitled little lordling who will inherit it. The point is moot anyway, as your foot has swollen too much to allow you to hobble home alone."

This, at the very least, was true. She felt her head spinning as she tried to place her weight upon it.

"Come," he said persuasively. "I have no rabbits with me, nor any blood upon my hands to give me away as a poacher or pilferer. We will say that I was passing by the borders of this oh-so-private land when I heard you fall and, being the heroic man I am, came hurrying to the rescue. Surely they will not prosecute me for that?"

She hesitated. Albert would rebuke her for such errant behaviour, but in truth she was not looking forward to the long and damp stagger homewards alone, and she could hardly crawl all the way up those slopes. "It is a risk," she said warningly.

"Ah, but it is my risk to take, and after all, what is life without a little adventure?"

She strongly suspected it was the call of such adventure which tempted him to it, and not the overwhelming allure of her company. He was a man for whom the pleasure of life was the risking of it, she thought. "I thank you then, and will gladly accept."

He reached down and tried to put his arms around her waist, but she batted him away.

"What are you doing?"

"You cannot walk. Let me carry you."

"You will not carry me across the fields! I do not know you!"

"I will not be impudent, I promise it upon my honour — if you can trust the honour of a poacher and thief." The thought seemed to amuse him. "You are such a slight thing, I doubt I shall even notice the weight of it, if that is what concerns you."

"That is not what concerns me, sir," she snapped. "I will not allow myself to be carried. I was given two feet and I will use them."

He rolled his eyes but offered no more arguments. He proffered his arm instead, and she threaded her own through it, wincing as she limped out into the world once more. The air was fresh, the storm blown through it having washed away the cloying closeness that had been oppressing her all day. Were her clothes not clinging to her, muddied and sodden, and her ankle not still throbbing with pain, Charlotte thought she might even have enjoyed it.

The man looked around the grounds as they made their slow and laborious journey back to the house looming up the hillside above. "These gardens are very fine."

"They were my uncle's pride and joy. Even on his death bed, he was entreating me to take care of them." She felt tears prickling at her eyes, even before this stranger, and looked away lest he saw them there.

Uncle John's words came calling back to her as he'd lain ashen-faced and fast-failing in his bed, clasping desperately to her hand, his words falling into delirium and rambling. *Your future is held safe in these gardens, child. Remember that when I am gone. My love for you is bound fast in the same stones that hold my love for Ursula. You must remember, you must recall it, your happiness and security will be found in these gardens.* He had stared hard at her even as his strength had failed and she had promised to recall it, only to soothe the troubled ailments of his mind. He had all but lost his wits by the end, falling into paranoia, seeing ghosts and conspiracies everywhere, and she had often thought that she had lost him even before he died.

No, my uncle is not lost. He is still here, as deep-rooted as the trees he once grew.

She did not want to return to the cold and empty halls of Drymote where Albert now reigned. She did not want to wait upon the arrogant presumption of the new heir. She would gladly have lived out here beneath the wild and whipping winds and the endless skies forever, if she could have.

Alas, she could not. The real world came crunching up inevitably to meet her as they rounded the final corner and made their way up the long and sweeping driveway. She sighed and drew herself back into the present moment.

"I am within sight of the doors now, you ought to go whilst you can."

"You are ashamed to be seen with a man of no name and no estate?" he ventured with a grin.

"I would prefer not to lie, and I do not know how I can explain your presence without either injuring you or telling falsehoods."

"Ah, I think that neither will be necessary, in fact," he murmured as the doors above them were thrown open. Albert stood there, gaping at the two of them.

"Go," she whispered. "Quickly, before it is too late."

But it was already too late. Charlotte extracted her arm from her benefactor's as Albert came hurrying down the steps, his patches of baldness glinting in the grey and leaden daylight.

"Sodden! Absolutely sodden! You will catch your death of cold. And late! Do you even know the hour? We were so worried about you!"

Charlotte stared at him. She did not think Albert cared enough to worry about her well-being. She stared even harder as Albert thrust his arms around the man next to her, squeezing him tightly.

"Why did you not take the carriage I sent for you? You have not grown any better since the last time I saw you. In fact, I declare you grow positively worse."

"Forgive me, Father. And you too, Miss Mayweather." The man grinned, turning to face her with an irascible smile and a small bow. "I fear I forgot to introduce myself properly upon our first acquaintance. Edward Cotterhugh at your service."

CHAPTER TWO

Charlotte stared. The words did not seem to penetrate her mind at first. It was only as Edward grinned wider that the truth sank in. She took a step back and nearly fell to the floor again as her ankle gave way.

"Father, Miss Mayweather needs to rest. We met out on the grounds and she slipped as the rains turned the grass to mud."

He knows my name. He has always known who I was. She scalded a deeper shade of burgundy yet.

"She should not have been out there this afternoon anyway." Albert glowered, gazing at her muddied, torn and still dripping dress with scorn. "I expressly told her that we were awaiting your arrival. She should have been about the house ready to receive you."

"She did receive me, with all the courtesy you could expect and then some," Edward protested with another wicked grin. "But come, we will not argue about such things. Let us all get in and get warmed and clean. Miss Mayweather, will you not allow me to see you to your rooms?"

But she shied away from his proffered hands.

"Thank you, but I can see myself to my room from here." Her scowl negated the politeness of her words somewhat.

"You will never manage the stairs upon that ankle," Edward warned, but Charlotte merely turned her nose into the air and hobbled past. She gritted her teeth together hard to stop the cry of pain escaping her.

"Miss Mayweather, I really must insist, you will do untold

damage to it if you continue using it." He reached out for her, his fingers warm as they brushed against hers. She closed her hand into a fist instinctively, but she could still feel their phantom presence there. She did not reply, nor did she even deign to look at him as she continued her laborious progress past.

"Leave her, son. You will never find a woman more stubborn or more ungrateful if you searched the whole of Christendom. Leave her to her pride, and come warm yourself by the fire."

Edward did not make an immediate reply. She could feel his gaze burning into the back of her as she dripped painfully up the long and winding staircase, her frozen fingers clinging desperately to the banister. One of the new maids, her hands full of clean linens, her harassed hair escaping underneath a mop cap, pushed herself up against the wall as Charlotte hauled herself upwards. The maid did not say anything — even foundling maids knew better than that — but she could not hide the look of shocked approbation at Charlotte's appearance.

Charlotte gritted her teeth. She had not realised quite how long this staircase was before. It was already half-decorated for the upcoming ball. The evergreen wreaths being wound around the spindles would probably have started wilting by the time the ball actually rolled around, but Albert was not known for his patience.

Charlotte hobbled to her room and shut the door. The silence within was soft and inviting, enveloping her warmly in its safe embrace. She collapsed onto her bed, groaning almost as much as her mattress did, and closed her eyes as mortification washed over her. Her ankle was throbbing, but it did not hurt half as much as her wounded pride. *I called him a poacher! He watched me crawling through the mud like a wild woman. I gave him far too free an opinion of Albert!* She picked up a pillow and held it over her scalding face as if she could smother the memories.

If I never leave this room again it will be too soon. Laughter rose up warm and welcome through the quiet house from the lower rooms, and she could not help but think it was aimed at her. The creak of the door echoed through the room, and Charlotte sat up quickly to see Maud standing there with a jug of water in her hands.

"Lord Cotterhugh wishes to know if you will be joining them for dinner, Miss Mayweather?" The squat, plump maid asked, bobbing into a small and somewhat disapproving curtsey, her gaze roaming freely over the damp dress Charlotte still wore.

"I just don't think I could face it, Maud," Charlotte told her. Maud set the jug down by the ewer and murmured,

"Very good, Miss. Shall I help you dress for bed then?"

She stripped the muddy mourning dress off Charlotte efficiently, scarcely before Charlotte had answered, and laid it over the back of the chair by the fire to dry. The maid took her leave without another word.

Charlotte sighed. No matter how warm or friendly she behaved, Charlotte just could not break through Maud's icy and proper reserve. Maud, and the butler, Roberts, were the only servants to have come with Albert from his last household. In a very real way, Maud was Albert's maid, not Charlotte's.

I should count myself lucky that Albert lends me the use of her at all. I could very well be in her place, if it was not for his begrudging beneficence.

Charlotte arranged her aching ankle on a pillow and tried to settle down to rest for the evening, but sleep would not come to her, even as the bats started flittering outside the glass and the clouds shrouded the moon. Her leg grew stiff and aching from being held so still through that long, quiet night. She was still awake at the first tinge of morning, the dawn seeping mockingly through the heavy curtains, prodding at her aching and irritable body. She lay listening to the house coming back to life through the walls of her room, hearing the skittering feet of the serving staff hurrying about, Albert's easily recognisable shuffle, a strong, confident tread which must surely belong to Edward, and she remained in her bed through it all, hidden away.

There was a knock at the door, no doubt Maud come back to oust her from the bed by force, but when she called out, "Enter!" Charlotte found Edward standing there instead, his hands laden with a breakfast tray. The morning sunlight streamed in through the window and caught on his curls. He had not outgrown them, as many children did. They lent him a roguish, boyish air, aided in part by that lopsided grin he treated her to, even now. He looked bright and cheery this morning, in no way discomfited by yesterday's misadventures.

She blushed, struggling up into a sitting position in the bed. "Mr Cotterhugh, I hardly think this is appropriate!"

Edward simply closed the door behind him with his elbow and brought the tray forwards for her.

"You did not come down to breakfast, and you will not heal unless you eat. Forgive the personal remarks, but you do not have enough weight to drop. We could lose you behind a garden rake."

She stared at him, caught by surprise. It had been something that John had said often, but she had not expected to hear such homely phrases from a cosmopolitan city-man like Edward.

He laughed, apparently mistranslating her expression.

"Have I shocked you with my impudence? Well, never mind. Say you will forgive me and have some tea and toast."

He had also plucked a Michaelmas daisy from the garden, she saw. Her fingers stole it from the tray top and she lifted it up to her nose, breathing in the scent deeply. Uncle John would have considered it sacrilege, for he always held that flowers belonged in gardens, not vases, but she could not deny that she was pleased to receive it. Edward took the flower from her hand and replaced it with a small plate of toast. She resisted the urge to roll her eyes, but obediently took a bite, and Edward nodded in approval, twirling the stem between his fingers absent-mindedly.

"They say that Michaelmas daisies represent farewells," she told him in between mouthfuls. "Are you intending to leave so soon?"

"Would that please you?" he asked dryly, perching himself upon the edge of the bed. Charlotte found she was all too aware of his presence there. There was an invisible weight to Edward that seemed to pull everything into its orbit, as if she were tilting towards him, an effect she suspected he had on a lot of women. *And I am sure it is an effect he knows about and uses to the uttermost.* She did not know what to say, so she took another bite of toast instead.

He laughed. "Ah, you are still cross with me. No, no, do not deny it." He grinned as she opened her mouth to protest. "Your face betrays you even if your words are entirely proper and polite. I doubt you are even aware that you scrunch up your pretty little nose when you are angry, and purse your lips tightly, even as you try to hide it. Your voice is an actor's, but your face does not know how to lie, I fear."

Her fingers fled to her face. He was right. She had not realised she had been pulling such expressions. She scowled. "For future reference, I and my *pretty little nose* do not appreciate being patronised."

Edward laughed again, long and loud. "You are a stone, woman, unflinching and unyielding. I shall enjoy you immensely."

He will enjoy ruining you, he means, she told herself, even as her stomach fluttered treacherously at the compliment. Perhaps it felt that she had received so few that even one so ironically given was one to be treasured. *He is not serious. He does not know how to be.*

"Enjoy me?" She heard herself say sceptically. "That seems unlikely. Most men do not *enjoy* my harridan's tongue."

"They are men of little discernment then, for there is nothing half as pleasurable as a battle well fought. I confess, when I heard John's ward was still at Drymote, I came expecting some timid little waif bobbing and curtseying meekly around the house, and instead I found a dragon guarding the gates. Believe me, it was an exchange I was happy to have made. I would like to be friends, if you would permit it."

She looked at him suspiciously. "Friends?"

"You are aware of the concept, I take it, though with a tongue like that, I am ready to believe you have little personal experience of such things." He twinkled at her, and his laugh rang out once more as she scowled at him. "Come, Miss Mayweather, you have no other kin. Would it be so very wrong to find friendship with me?"

How can he want to be friends after yesterday's debacle? And yet, she found she wanted to believe him despite her better judgement. "I will not be seduced by your charms," she warned him. "I have heard of your reputation."

"I would not dare try it. A woman who chases off poachers without even a pistol to her name is a woman who should not be underestimated."

She pursed her lips. "I think this friendship is going to consist of you teasing me a great deal," she said dryly.

"Oh yes, certainly. I hope that you will grow to find it as diverting as I do, in time." He grinned. "Say then that we will be allies, for I will surely need an ally for this ball tomorrow."

The ball . . . she had almost forgotten about it. Her glance fled to the tattered mourning dress hung over the back of her chair and her heart sank down to her stomach. She could hardly go in that! Society thought little enough of her as it was.

To her chagrin, she found that Edward's gaze had followed

her own. She said the first thing she could think of to draw his attention back to herself, away from her shameful poverty.

"Do you really need allies for a ball? It is a party, not a hanging."

"Is it not? I feel I am the condemned man everyone is coming to gawk at upon the gallows." He grimaced theatrically, and she could not help a breath of laughter despite herself.

"Do not let your father hear you say so. He has spent a great deal of energy and expense arranging it. I hear that the whole neighbourhood is aflutter with it. They are all quite excited about your grand introduction to Birchton society."

He raised an astute eyebrow at her. "You do not approve of balls at Drymote?"

Charlotte shrugged with a valiant attempt at nonchalance, trying not to let the pain which pulsed through her every time she thought of it escape to the surface. *It is Albert's house now, he may do as he wishes.*

"My uncle died scarcely a month back. It is hardly proper to host a party in a house of mourning."

Edward leant forwards until his hair tickled her cheek, and tucked the stolen flower behind her ear.

His breath was a whisper as it ran across her skin, and she felt her cheeks tingling. She squeezed her hands together tightly by her side, willing herself not to blush.

"I think you care too much for propriety, Miss Mayweather."

Her stomach clenched and her breath tightened in her chest, but she wrestled both back under control with sheer willpower alone and turned to face him instead. Their stares were glowering only inches apart, their noses almost touching, their breath playing together with every hiss and hush, and for a moment everything she had been about to say fled her mind.

Get a grip on yourself, Charlotte, she told herself firmly. You do not want to end up like your mother. You know what

Aunty Ursula always said—*it is a slippery path for young women. Once they are lost, they cannot be reclaimed. First disgrace, then the madhouse, then death. You must care for propriety, your reputation is the only shield you have left.*

She swallowed, forcing the moisture to her lips with difficulty. "I cared deeply for my uncle, and I care still for his memory."

"Well, I cannot believe John would have wanted his memory to make you so miserable. Or perhaps the idea of enjoying yourself is anathema to your character, Miss Mayweather?"

She reared away, her cheeks beetrooting, hot and uncomfortable.

"How could I enjoy it when they will all stare and laugh at me? When they see me there in my old and patched dress and whisper behind their hands that I am nothing but a social climber, hoping to steal a husband?"

"You do not know they think such things, and even if they do, what of it? You care too much for their opinions."

Perhaps it was the truth, but it was easy for him to say. He was the heir to Drymote, rich and powerful, handsome and charming. He could afford to rise above the world's approval and approbation. He did not know the sting of the world or the way it murmured calumnies in her wake. She glared at him, but she could feel the tears rising to her eyes nonetheless.

"I thought you came to make friends," she said. "Is it a habit of yours to treat your friends so ill?"

He scalded, his lips thinning until they were naught but a bitter slash across his face. His breath was coming in sharp and uneven, but he got to his feet, bowed curtly before either of them could say any more and marched off without another word. The door slammed shut behind him, and she let out a bitter breath. That was unkind, she chided herself. *You need to better recall your place here. He is the heir and you are the charity-case.*

"Well then, he should be less infuriating!" she muttered to herself, but she could not help a guilty squirm of conscience anyway.

"Where is that blasted boy?" growled Albert, glaring around the dinner table. The rabbit-pie and vegetables stared invitingly up at Charlotte, but she merely murmured something demurely and folded her hands over and over in her lap. Albert rubbed at a blotchy red sore on his hand absentmindedly, his face growing redder and crosser with each passing moment. Charlotte was almost sure that the erratic bald patches which littered his head had grown bigger since Edward's arrival yesterday. *Perhaps he has literally been tearing his hair out.*

"And he gave no word to you as to where he was going?" Albert snapped at her for the fourth time since they had sat down.

"No." For the fourth time. *Edward stalked straight out of the house when he left my chambers this morning and he has not been back since. I did not intend to wound him so deeply . . .*

Albert threw up his hands in frustration. "Well, we might as well eat then, I suppose."

He did not bother saying grace, a piety he only upheld when they had guests to impress, but dug straight in to the food sourly, and they began the meal together in silence. The dinner table had sometimes been a quiet affair with Uncle John, too, for he tangled himself up in his own thoughts all too often and did not rise from them even in company, something Aunty Ursula had often chided him for in loving exasperation. This felt different somehow. The old silences had been comfortable and homely. These were stiff and awkward, and Charlotte felt very aware of herself as she ate, the chink and clatter of the cutlery seeming over-loud in the otherwise empty room.

She cast about for something to say, merely to break the

painful quiet. "The flowers are doing well this year. The autumn has been unusually mild. The gardeners think we will have plenty to decorate Drymote with for the ball tomorrow."

"We will not, if you insist on stealing them," Albert snapped. One hand was massaging his temple, and she suspected that he had fallen prey to one of the frequent headaches which plagued him, but, with her own temper flaring, she found she could not sympathise much with him.

"I have not stolen anything!"

"Do not prove yourself a liar as well as thief. You are still wearing the evidence of your crimes."

She scowled at him in confusion, and he nodded to her hair. Her hand fled up to the flower wilting behind her ear guiltily, and she took it down at once, crumpling its faded petals in her lap. She had forgotten it was there. She could only imagine what snide remarks Maud was making to the other servants in the gossipy back halls and attic bedrooms.

"I'm sure we can spare one flower," Edward said, coming into the room behind her with the worst possible timing. "Especially seeing as Miss Mayweather pays much more care and attention to that garden than either of us can claim to." He threw himself nonchalantly into a spare seat at the table and, though she did not turn to look at him, she could feel her cheeks scalding. How on earth would he interpret her keeping the bloom? She longed to tell him it had been nothing more than an accident, but she felt that would only make it worse. He was already busying himself about his dinner and did not seem to notice her discomfiture.

Edward did not seem to be about to admit that it was he, not Charlotte, who had plucked the flower. She pressed her lips together but did not bother to defend herself.

"That is not the point," Albert began hotly. "Those flowers are the property of Drymote Estate, and they belong to the *owners* of Drymote Estate."

Edward raised an eyebrow, his laden fork paused halfway to his mouth. "Come now, Father, are we really going to be that petty?"

"It is not petty to uphold the law."

"Let he without sin cast the first stone, hmmm?"

"Do not quote the scriptures at me, son. I do not recall the last time I managed to drag you into a chapel. It makes all the neighbours gossip, and it quite damages all the hard work I have put into securing their necessary good opinion for your successful parliamentary career."

"I already know I am beyond salvation, Father, I do not need some sanctimonious do-gooder reminding me of all the ways I have fallen short. And I assure you, I have no desire to have a successful parliamentary career."

"It won't happen again, Albert," Charlotte said quickly as Albert's face reddened and his jowls began to quiver. The two warring men both turned to her. "The flowers will be left to grow."

"Not even so much as an apology," muttered Albert mutinously. He threw his napkin to the table and glowered at them both. "You will excuse me. I find my digestion troubled by such unpleasant, argumentative and all round disagreeable dinner companions." He got to his feet and stormed from the room.

"He says more than he means, Miss Mayweather," Edward said as the door banged upon its hinges and Albert's stomping footsteps faded across the hall. "His medicine increases his paranoia until he believes the whole world to be conspiring against him. He does not intend to make you feel an outcast here."

A small frown puckered her brow.

"His medicine? I did not know he was ill. I hope it is nothing serious."

Edward rubbed a weary hand over his face, and for a

moment the façade of the careless young gentleman slipped.

"It is fatal. A long, slow and drawn out death, and he bears it badly. It is the reason I came home."

Charlotte looked across to him and she felt the breath go out of her chest in one long, stuttering exhale at the look upon his face. He was smiling, but there was no humour in it. She felt her hands grow limp in her lap, the wilted flower still lingering there in the folds of her skirt. She longed to reach out to him but her hands stayed stubbornly there in her lap.

"I am so sorry," she said quietly. "I didn't know. Is there anything I can do?"

"I doubt it, unless your saintliness extends to miracles as well as preaching." He smirked at her, his usual insouciance returning as quickly as it had fallen, but he also ran a hand through his hair, disarranging his curls.

He does that when he feels uncomfortable, Charlotte thought distantly. He probably was not even aware that he was doing so. The knowledge felt strangely intimate somehow.

Edward shrugged a little when she did not speak. "He wishes to see his legacy secured before he passes from this veil of tears. It has become somewhat of a fixation of his. Please do not take it personally."

Charlotte stared down at her fingers as they entwined themselves together in her lap, the faded petals strewn across her skirts. The dress was no longer damp, and the maids had done their best to brush out the dried mud, but it still looked the worse for wear.

"Uncle John did not say his brother was dying," she said quietly and Edward barked out a bitter laugh.

"I'm sure that was at my father's request. He has somewhat of a . . . *personal* disease. Syphilis," he mouthed at her across the table, and illumination dawned all at once. Charlotte felt herself blushing again. She had not imagined the fussy little

Albert to harbour venereal diseases.

Edward just shrugged. "It is a painful way to go by the end, and the cure is as bad as the malady. Not that mercury is a cure, of course, but it extends his life expectancy and mitigates against some of the worst effects. The whole thing bears heavily upon him." He sighed heavily.

It bears heavily upon you, too, Edward Cotterhugh, Charlotte could not help but think. Once again her fingers longed to abandon their propriety and stretch across the table to hold his. Once again, they sat thick and lifeless in her lap.

Edward looked up at her, his dark eyes flickering by the glow of the dinner table candles. "I know he can be hard to live with. Please try to think kindly of him when he is at his worst."

"Yes," she said distantly. "I will." She lost herself to her thoughts for a moment, and when she looked up she found Edward's gaze was still fixed upon hers. She was struck again at the colour of his eyes. They were a midnight blue that almost seemed black in the evening's light. She could not tell what he was thinking. She blushed once more and looked down at the table.

"I am sure Albert is not the only one who can be difficult to live with. I know that I often overstep my boundaries. I would like to apologise to you for the things I said this morning," she told her dinner plate. "I said much more than I intended to, Mr Cotterhugh. I should remember my place better. Please forgive me."

Edward just laughed. "No, I will not forgive you for that. I never want you to *remember your place.* This is your place. Drymote is your home as much as it is mine, more so, perhaps. I never want you to feel less than its mistress."

But she was less than its mistress, as Albert never missed an opportunity to remind her. When Edward wed, his wife would be Drymote's true mistress, and Charlotte would be evicted from the only home she had ever known.

"Thank you," she said stiffly. "It is good of you."

"Say then that we will be friends, as I asked of you this morning. You never did give me an answer, recall."

"Yes, if you wish it."

He breathed out a laugh. "I do wish it, very much so."

"Then oblige me by not giving me any more flowers, they only cause trouble." She gave him a wry smile, and his laugh grew louder until it filled the entire dining hall.

Charlotte had almost entirely forgotten she was miserable by the time she returned to her own chambers that night. Maud followed her in to brush her hair for bed and help her out of her dress.

"If you please, Miss Mayweather, there's a parcel for you on the bed."

Charlotte looked up, and followed Maud's curious gaze to the large box sitting temptingly behind the bed curtains, bound in ribbon. Charlotte crept over, her fingers snatching at the small note tucked beneath the velvet band.

For the ball tomorrow. I seem to recall your last dress got quite ruined in the rains. Edward.

She stared at the fine, curling handwriting, feeling mortification creeping over her slowly but surely. *This must be where he's been all day, organising this gift in the village. Did he think I had been hinting, earlier?*

Maud read the note over her shoulder and let out a scoff of disapproval. Charlotte stared at her and Maud pursed her lips.

"Begging your pardon, Miss Mayweather," she said haughtily, "but nothing good ever comes from letting a man buy you gifts. They start expecting things. And you know what gentlemen are like . . ."

Charlotte felt her skin scalding at Maud's self-righteous disapproval. "Thank you, Maud. That will be all."

Maud dipped into another curtsey and swept from the room.

Charlotte glowered after her. Maud and Albert were one of a pair, with their fussing, sanctimonious disapproval and high and mighty airs. Charlotte opened the box.

Within it was a beautiful violet dress, light and flowing muslin and tulle, embroidered with black flowers. Miss Jenkins, the dressmaker of Birchton, kept some dresses ready-made in her little parlour shop as patterns for her clients to choose from. Edward must have bought one for her to wear.

She held it up against her body and regarded herself in the mirror. It required a little taking in, perhaps, for Charlotte was scrawny and had not the curved figure society cherished, but it was not a bad fit. She did not think she had ever owned a dress so beautiful, even if it was in mourning colours. She felt a lump growing thick in her throat as she stroked the fabric with gentle fingers. In the bottom of the box was a matching violet ribbon and some black artificial flowers for her hair. *He has even thought to get accessories.*

She stroked the fabric in wonder, feeling the muslin rustle and whisper against her fingertips. She would not look like a poor relation in this. She would not stand out in her faded blacks amongst the peacock colours of the county belles. *But will they think me over-dressed? Will they think me aspiring beyond my position in such fineries? Or worse, what if Maud is right? What if Edward expects something for his munificence, or the county thinks I've paid for it with something other than money . . .*

"Edward is right, you care far too much for the opinion of strangers," she told her reflection sternly, and she could almost hear his laugh, echoing through the recesses of her mind.

CHAPTER THREE

Charlotte found the reflection in the looking glass was beaming back at her as she lingered before it. The night fell deep and dark outside the windows and the noise of the ball downstairs was already beginning to curl its way, smoke-like, up the stairs, but she found she could not tear herself away from the stranger in the mirror. Charlotte would never be beautiful. Her hair was too fine and straight, refusing to keep its curls for long no matter how she bound it in rags of a night, her face and body too thin and bony, her frame too petite, but in this dress she might almost pass for pretty. She ran her fingers across the skirts softly. *Miss Jenkins is a miracle worker.* The violet ribbons and black flowers nestled like a secret promise in her fair hair. She could scarcely tear herself away from the looking glass, and in truth, she did not want to. Downstairs would be full of gossiping matrons, competitive belles, scandalous young men and over-opinionated older men. Up here in the quiet of her chambers, there was nothing but her and her reflection.

One pretty dress and I am already growing vain. What would Uncle John say?

Very little, probably, unless she sprouted foliage and flowers, in which case he might take an academic interest. She smiled fondly at the memory of the absent-minded old man pottering around the place. It had not been the same since Albert had arrived.

Still . . . poor Albert . . . Syphilis was a nasty way to go. and despite Albert's best efforts, he would not be able to hide it for long. Although it was uncouth to discuss the French Disease in the presence of a lady, even Charlotte had heard some of the awful rumours about that malady. The way one's nose fell off in the final stages, branding the infamy of such a disease for all to see, and the horrible twitching spasms that wracked through the body, wrenching it out of one's control until the poor patient, inching painfully towards death, had to be *chained* to the bed like an animal.

Perhaps that was why Albert was so desperate to see her ousted from Drymote? Perhaps he wanted her gone before he could no longer hide his demise? Those sores that scarred his body and the erratic patches of baldness were only the first skittering stone-falls of the avalanche. It was only going to get worse, and when it did, it was going to get worse quickly. The slow tumble would become a hard fall towards the grave.

Perhaps too, that was why he paid so much for such a lavish attraction as this ball, when he would not pay coin for the workers' wages. He was seeking out a little joy against the bitter backdrop of his own mortality. She should not begrudge him that.

I will think more kindly of him. I will certainly try to, anyway.

She grabbed Aunty Ursula's Indian Lace shawl. It was very fine, far too fine to be worn usually, but tonight was a special occasion, and it finished off her outfit very well. *I look like an imposter, dressing up as someone I am not. Well? And what of it? Tonight, let me be the beautiful stranger. Tomorrow I will go back to being the penniless orphan.*

She spent one last look at herself in the mirror and then gathered her skirts up to sweep from the room. It was a full skirt, bundled with petticoats, and it made her feel a good deal grander and statelier than she usually did. Holding on tightly to the banister, only limping slightly, she made her way across to the top of the stairs.

Voices were already murmuring about below, but she found she was not the only one lingering above. Edward was lurking by the window of the hall, staring morosely out at the carriages still rattling up the driveway. He was resplendently clad in an expensively embroidered waistcoat and cravat, his black curls swept back off his face. She felt herself swallow. Whatever else one said about Edward, no one could deny he was handsome. Tall, broad-shouldered, dark-haired and dark-eyed. He could have stepped straight out of an oil painting.

His gaze met her reflection in the mirror-dark window and he did a double-take, whirling around to stare at her, his eyes wide. He let out a little laugh. "Well now! I scarcely recognised you without the mud! Who are you, and what have you done with the wild woman of Drymote?" He hurried across the landing to stand beside her.

She bobbed into a curtsey, wincing a little as her foot ached upon her. No doubt a night of dancing would not do it any good, but she scarcely cared.

"Where have you been hiding? I have not seen you at all today," she chided playfully. "I wished both to thank you and to reprimand you. You should not be spending your money on me."

His gaze raked her body again, taking in the black and violet dress she wore. "I assure you that you do not need to thank me. I am *amply* rewarded by seeing you in it."

What would have been gallantry on another's tongue was insinuation upon his, and well he knew it.

"Besides," he added, "You were direly in need of it. You certainly would not catch yourself a wealthy husband tonight in your old mourning blacks."

"I am not sure I wish for a husband. I value my independence too highly, and the law does not provide much security for married women." Even if she did have any money or property to her name, it would all belong to her husband by law if she wed. The law does not provide security for penniless spinsters either, she reminded herself. You must choose the lesser of two evils.

Edward just laughed. "I do not think I will allow you to marry, even if you wished to. I enjoy your company too much to give it up to some other scoundrel. You must stay here for my amusement, if for nothing else."

I will not amuse him forever. He will tire of me as soon as his next plaything comes along, and I will be alone again, as I am always alone.

"Jesting aside, you look enchanting, Miss Mayweather. Promise you will save a dance for me, for I fear your dance card will be filled up all too quickly, and I am too jealous to allow these neighbourhood cads to monopolise you for themselves."

His eyes were glimmering, and she could not tell if he was teasing her again or not. She glanced downwards to avoid his gaze. "Oh, well, you know what they say, Mr Cotterhugh, fine feathers make fine birds."

"You do yourself a disservice, but I will not waste my breath by pressing the issue. Already I have learnt of your stubbornness, and I see I will not persuade you to take a compliment."

She laughed and threaded her arm through his. "You give them too easily for me to value them much. Come, it would never do for the guest of honour to be late to his own party." She began the long and painful descent down the well-bedecked stairs, leaning upon his arm a little more heavily than she would have liked.

Edward groaned, a long and heartfelt groan, as he accompanied her down the stairs, her little hand tucked tightly into the crook of his arm as if it belonged there.

"I do not feel in the mood for frippery tonight. If we hurry, we can sneak out of the door without being seen whilst our guests are occupied. Let us escape out to the Hermit's Retreat and live there alone with our good Greek friend watching sternly over us and no other cares at all."

"Being the heir comes with duties and responsibilities, Edward," she said with mock sternness.

Edward stopped and looked at her.

She felt the old familiar blush creeping over her as his eyes shone. "What is it?"

"I believe that is the first time you have used my Christian name."

Charlotte felt her cheeks scald deeper. "Forgive me," she began, pulling her arm free from his, but he cut across her, grabbing her hand and replacing it by force.

"There is nothing to forgive. I like it. Promise me that it is the only name you will call me from now on."

"I can make no such promises, for I am sure there are many other things I could call you," she muttered, but she found a smile lingering on her face anyway.

The hall beneath was already far too warm, despite the continual opening and closing of the great front doors by the footmen. Several of their neighbours whispered as they saw Edward and Charlotte descending the stairs together, and Charlotte was a little disconcerted to see that their gazes lingered on her just as much as on the prodigal son.

"I am not the only person of mystery that intrigues them tonight," Edward whispered to her wickedly. "When I went to the village I heard them all talking about the hermit of Drymote and how cloistered she had been under her eccentric uncle's care. They think you quite the prisoner here, Charlotte, and have woven some extraordinary romances around your isolation. Miss Jenkins was all a tizzy to think that she would be dressing the Lady of Shalott."

"But that isn't the least bit true! Uncle John never forced me to stay here. Nobody else wished for my company!"

Edward shook his head at her in disbelief. "I think you do not see yourself very accurately at all. Tonight, perhaps, you will learn better."

He did not release her hand, but led her straight through to the ballroom, where the musicians were already playing and quadrilles were formed across the floor. Colour filled the room and for a moment, Charlotte almost felt giddy. The candles flickered, the heavy scent of the fresh-plucked autumn roses hung tantalisingly in the air, and there were more people than she had ever seen gathered together in one place before.

"I think my father overdid the invitations, rather. There is scarcely room to breathe in here."

"Come now, do not tell me the cosmopolitan Edward Cotterhugh is overawed by a country ball," she teased. "Not he who has been to the bustling halls of London and Europe?"

But despite the teasing, she found herself a little overwhelmed as well. It was typical of Albert, she could not help but think. He was so desperate to cultivate a good opinion abroad that he tried to woo everyone at once, but tonight these guests would leave whispering about how Lord Albert Cotterhugh was so uncouth that he did not even know how to organise a ball properly.

Money does not buy class, Uncle John would have sniffed, as he did whenever he forwarded any opinion on the society he had shunned, and Charlotte felt the same coil of sadness winding around her stomach that she always did whenever he popped into her mind. *Grief is a long and winding road.*

She turned to see Edward was watching her silently as she lost herself in her own thoughts, as if he could read them from her eyes, or perhaps he just enjoyed the rarity of her silence.

He raised an eyebrow at her, as if asking whether she was finished with her reflections. "You often do that," Edward murmured to her, his glare fixed penetratingly upon her face. "Retreat into your own thoughts."

She felt herself blushing. "Forgive me. I have been

accustomed to being alone here."

"I do not think that is a problem which will bother you much longer. My father is determined to fill Drymote with eligible young belles and match-making matrons for as long as it takes until I finally settle down. Cast your eyes in any direction, and you will see a dozen who are dying for an introduction."

"Have a care, Edward. If your head swells any larger, it will no longer fit through the ballroom doors."

He laughed long and loud, his eyes sparkling again. Say what you would about Edward, he knew full well how to laugh at himself.

He made no move to leave her side, even as the band struck up for yet another song and a gaggle of ladies paraded past arm in arm trying to catch his attention. Miss Penny Armitage, the daughter of a retired half-pay captain, had a large feather stuck in the back of her hair. It wagged and wobbled with every sashaying step, like a snake under a charmer's flute, and Charlotte couldn't help staring at it, as though she had been hypnotised. Edward's dark eyes did not flee to it at all, though. Their focus stayed fixedly upon Charlotte's own face, and she found herself blushing all the more for it.

Albert appeared abruptly, fighting his way towards them, flushed and sweating through the crowd. He tried his best to hide his ire, but his smile was tight and forced and his eyes were hard as he struggled to maintain his manners before the cream of the county. With his handsome kid gloves hiding the sores on his hands, and the flush of heat hiding the pallor of his skin, it was impossible to tell that he was ill. None of these people would ever guess he had the French Disease, Charlotte thought distantly. He did not greet Charlotte, or even bother to glance in her direction.

"Edward come, you must meet our closest neighbour, Miss

Bletchley."

Edward rolled his eyes good naturedly, but bowed to Charlotte and accompanied his father out across the crowded ball room. Charlotte watched them go. Her ankle was throbbing, though the night was but young, and the heat of the room was beginning to tell upon her, so she sank gracefully into an empty chair against the wall and watched the assembled company instead.

Miss Bletchley was enchanting. She was everything that Charlotte wished she could be in her secret heart of hearts, Tall and yet softly curved, poured into a flattering ballgown offset in light sky blues, like a child of the summer itself. Her hair was flame-red and in perfectly formed ringlets, set off with a cluster of white flowers crowning her head. She dimpled prettily as she smiled, her gaze glancing up at Edward beneath long lashes, her cheeks rosying into ladylike pinks instead of the horrid burgundy blushes Charlotte always fell prey to. She made a fine pair with Edward, she innocent and maidenly, he charmingly roguish, the two of them exceedingly striking. Charlotte looked away sharply. *Unless I am very much mistaken, the next mistress of Drymote is already here.*

"They make a handsome pair, do they not?" A familiar voice said beside her. Charlotte blushed. She had not realised she had been watched. Mr Harris, the curate, did not seem to notice her discomfort. His gaze was also resting upon the couple on the other side of the room, laughing merrily together. Their happiness seemed to sparkle like candlelight in the heavily scented room.

"Mr Harris, good evening. I did not see you there. In fact, it has been a while since I saw you last, in a non-official capacity, at least." He had not been to dine with them since Aunty Ursula passed, in fact. Uncle John had never bothered inviting visitors round to their dinner table. He preferred the isolation of his own thoughts. The memory of his stubbornness and self-imposed exile warmed her with a melancholy nostalgia, even tinged as it was with sadness.

"Yes, and we so little get the chance to chat after the Sunday service. My time is taken up by other, more voluble, parishioners." He smiled at her with that same, gentle smile he was so known for. *So different to Edward's lopsided, arrogant smirk.* "How have you been faring since Lord John Cotterhugh's passing?"

"It has been a time of adjustment, of course, but Albert and his son have been . . . kind to me." *For shame! Surely it is a cardinal sin to lie to a clergyman? I suppose Edward has been kind, if one can count his peculiar type of teasing as friendliness. Albert, on the other hand . . ."*And how are you enjoying the evening so far?" she added aloud.

Mr Harris turned to look at her, dragging his gaze away from the couple across the hall with difficulty.

"Oh, very much so. I was very keen to see Drymote again. I recall Lady Cotterhugh's kindnesses when I first came here very well." Mr Harris' eyes crinkled sympathetically. "You must miss her a great deal, even now."

Charlotte smiled back. Mr Harris was a young man, for a clergy. He had scarcely sprouted whiskers the first time he had come to pay a call at Drymote, and she recalled how Aunty Ursula had taken him under her wing.

A mother's heart without a child to hold, that was how Uncle John had always described his wife. And, on some of his less tactful days, he had added, *the best thing your mother ever did was die, child. Ursula was so glad to raise you for her own.* It had cut Charlotte deep the first time he had said it, but she had learnt to take it in the spirit it was intended in the end. Yes, Aunty Ursula had had a mother's heart, and poor Mr Harris had been so young, awkward, and ungainly that Aunty Ursula could not help but mother him.

Charlotte smiled dryly. She had been awkward herself at their first encounter, a stilting, blushing sixteen year old, dressed in her first adult gown and trying to play the good hostess as he talked earnestly about complex theology she did not understand across the dining room table. Aunty Ursula had teased her gently the following day about her new beau.

Mr Harris was not unhandsome, in his way. He had thick, bouncing brown hair, an open countenance and perpetually earnest expression, but Uncle John had said the curate placed him in mind of a Labrador, and Charlotte could not unsee it now. It did not incline her to romantic daydreams about him. Mr Harris was a good man, an honest man, a *reliable* man and, though she ought not to admit it, even to herself, a painfully predictable one. There was very little in him to excite or stimulate.

She turned to look at Edward instead again, and found that he had gone. She scanned the crowd hurriedly, but she could not see him with any of the pretty young women of the surrounding villages. A wave of foreboding crept up on her. *He should not be missing. Not on a night dedicated to his arrival.*

She rose to her feet with a quiet plea to be excused. Mr Harris looked at her, a little startled.

"You are not leaving already, Miss Mayweather? The evening is scarcely half-over."

She bobbed into a curtsey, wobbling uncertainly upon her throbbing ankle. "I fear I must. I injured myself the day before yesterday, and the pain is coming back upon me now. I must rest my foot before it falls worse."

"May I assist you in any way?"

"There is nothing that can be done but rest and time, I fear, but thank you for your kindness." And he *was* kind, she had always found. She did not know why that made her feel so terribly sad. *It would solve a lot of my problems if I could only train myself to love someone like him.*

Of course, one could marry without love—plenty of marriages were built on nothing more than respect, honesty and kindness and were none the less happy for it. She had grown surrounded by the unfathomable well of Ursula and John's love though, one that would never run dry no matter how deep they plunged into it, whose waters bubbled up anew in every season and trial and she could not imagine marrying for any less — no, not even to escape Albert.

She smiled at Mr Harris, bobbed into a curtsey and hobbled away.

Edward was not in the outer hall, either. Charlotte's frown increased. She grabbed at Maud, who was whispering in the doorway with another servant, their stares fixed on the ball within that they were not permitted to attend.

"Maud, have you seen Mr Cotterhugh?"

"He went to take some air in the rose garden." Maud's gaze lingered insinuatingly, and Charlotte felt herself blush, but she pulled Aunty Ursula's shawl up around her shoulders anyway and swept out into the night after him. She could hear the servants whispering together behind her back as she left.

It was dry but chilly. The cold seemed to have a scent of its own as it lingered there in the air, clinging to her skin and skirts. The moonlight danced high above the estate, painting everything an eerie silver and there, striding between the battered lavender and stripped back rose bushes with a powerful gait, was a shadow of a man. She gathered up her skirts, threw all propriety to the wind, and hurried down to meet him.

The crunch of his booted feet on the gravel echoed through the night, mingling with the muffled melodies of the house drifting through the French windows towards them. Save for the fact that he was thirty years younger and far better dressed, it was almost like having Uncle John back again. *A Cotterhugh man out there amongst his estate.* Charlotte sighed. Perhaps she was selfish to have rued his coming. Drymote needed an heir, after all, and Uncle John was not returning. Why should Edward not have it, just because it meant that she would have to leave? Drymote was the important thing, its continuation and preservation, not her own little happiness.

As she drew closer, she heard him whispering furiously.

"Leave, before I call the footmen to throw you out by force."

The moonlight fell upon a stranger standing beside Edward with a thick mop of dark hair and a curling lip. When he spoke, she found to her astonishment that he had a thick Italian accent.

"You prefer to leave the dirty to work to other men now, do you? Will you not draw your pistol on me?"

What on earth is an Italian man doing in the sleepy little parish of Birchton? Whoever he was, his presence did not seem welcome to Edward, who was glowering at the stranger and growled out,

"I will send for the magistrate."

The stranger sneered once more. "Come now, Cotterhugh, I cannot believe you wish to involve the law. But then again, it's one law for you and one law for the rest of us, isn't it?"

"Go!" Edward shouted, pushing the man hard.

The man just laughed, then slipped off into the night, his laughter still echoing in the moonlight.

Charlotte stepped forwards uncertainly, and Edward's head whiplashed up to face her. Even by the light of the moon, she could see that he was red-faced and fuming.

"Edward, whatever is the matter? Who was that?"

"Nothing," he growled, running a hand through his hair, disarraying it, and for a moment a wild fantasy of running her own fingers through his hair appeared before her mind's eye.

Edward blew out a breath, his shoulders slumping as he wrestled himself back under control with what was obviously a great force of will.

"It was nothing, Charlotte," he said again. "Just uninvited guests gate-crashing the ball. I did not want to bother my father with it. Such things always plague him, and his tempers are not equal at the best of times upon his medicine." He ran a hand over his face. "Lord above, I hate these things," he said bitterly. He shook his head and blew out another breath. "Forgive me, I am being a bore. These nights always bring out the worst in me. Tell me that you, at least, have enjoyed yourself this evening."

"Yes, very much so."

"And danced every waltz and quadrille with eligible young bachelors?"

She blushed.

"I am not a good dancer. I have forgotten the little that Aunt Ursula taught me when she still lived."

"Nobody has asked you to dance?" he asked, and he sounded genuinely surprised, though he shouldn't. Even in a pretty dress, she was still a penniless daughter of disgrace. "Well, that is such a waste." He bowed and held out a hand to her formally. "May I have the pleasure, Miss Mayweather?"

She stared at him for a moment, thinking she had misunderstood, but he did not retract his hand.

"You wish to dance? Out here?"

His eyes were sparkling, though the tensions still lingered in his hunched up shoulders, and she thought perhaps he needed this, it was not just an act of charity.

"Please, Charlotte."

She bit her lip and then put her hand into his. It was just as warm as she remembered. His hand fell around her waist and he began twirling her gently through the rose bushes to the whispered echoes of the music still drifting out from the halls. Her skirts swished around her as smoothly as the melody did.

"I thought you said you did not know how to dance?" he teased her. "You are certainly doing your aunt's tutelage proud."

Charlotte did not know what to say to that, so she held her tongue. *Aunty Ursula would have loved to be here tonight, she had always loved dancing.* Sometimes Charlotte thought that Aunty Ursula only taught her how to dance in the first place so that she could whirl about the ballroom, too. The memory of the two of them laughing around the empty hall, skirts flying around them in time to their echoing glee, crashed upon her so suddenly it hurt. *Drymote was once a place of joy. I would give anything to see it become so again.*

Edward's gaze did not leave hers, but she found she could not tell what he was thinking.

"You should return," she whispered reluctantly as the song came to a stop and their footsteps unwillingly stilled, too. Though they had stopped dancing, he did not take his hands from about her waist.

"Perhaps," he confessed, "but I find I do not want to."

His eyes were so large and dark that she could see her own reflection echoing back in them as she stared up at him.

He leant forwards, as if he were about to say something, his lips a breath away from her own, making her chest tighten painfully, but they were both startled by a sharp call behind them.

Albert stood watching them. Edward let go of her at once, and Charlotte felt her skin burning in the moonlight.

You have done nothing wrong, she reminded herself firmly, but it was difficult to recall it, under Albert's stern gaze.

"Miss Bletchley is looking for you, Edward," Albert snapped.

"I doubt that. She did not seem to be particularly enamoured by my charms, Father."

"Perhaps she would be if you did not storm off into the night when you ought to be entertaining your guests."

Albert scarcely had a right to chide anyone else for their bursts of temper, Charlotte thought, but she held her tongue.

"I had something I had to deal with."

"I can see that," sneered Albert, and Charlotte felt her

blush deepen.

Edward narrowed his eyes but merely held out a hand to Charlotte. "Well? Shall we then, Miss Mayweather?"

"It is late. I am sure Charlotte would rather be abed."

"Father!" Edward began, outraged, but Charlotte lay a restraining hand on his forearm, eager to stop a fight from breaking out.

"No, Albert is right. I am over-wearied, and, in truth, my ankle pains me still. I fear I have done too much too soon after my fall. I will go to bed. Thank you both for a pleasant evening." She bobbed a curtsey and took herself back into the house alone as the two men bickered out there in the gardens behind her.

The Cotterhughs are all out of sorts this evening. Thank goodness I am a Mayweather and above such things. Nor does that seem likely to change at any point soon.

She sighed and took herself back up the stairs to her bedchambers alone.

CHAPTER FOUR

Charlotte woke to the muted sounds of scuffling around her room. She peeled her eyes open blearily and fumbled a hand through the bed-curtains to see Maud there by the dresser. Charlotte blinked.

"Maud? What time is it?"

Maud hastily stopped her tidying, dropping the artificial hair-flowers back onto the dresser table. She bobbed into a curtsey. "Lord Cotterhugh asked me to rouse you early today, Miss. Dr Farringham is coming to pay you a visit this morning, and you must be ready to receive him."

Charlotte struggled out of bed, wincing as her ankle, still swollen and throbbing, pained her.

"Dr Farringham?" She blinked stupidly, the sleep still settling in the crevices of her mind. "I don't know a Dr Farringham. We have always been attended by Dr Mendle."

"When Lord Cotterhugh is paying for the consultation, he decides which physician you will see." Maud sniffed haughtily, and Charlotte could feel scalding shame rising in her cheeks, the humiliation of being the impoverished burden already blistering her ego. The lady's maid pulled out the seat of the dressing table and waited impatiently beside it. Charlotte sighed, but obediently limped her way over and sat down.

"Besides, it is an honour. Dr Farringham is Lord Cotterhugh's personal physician," Maud said, pulling the hairbrush through Charlotte's hair, tugging at the tangles none too gently. "It is very generous of him to arrange a consultation for you, merely because you hurt your foot, and it was very generous of Dr Farringham to fit you in on such short notice, for Lord Cotterhugh only requested it of him last night. But then, Dr Farringham owes Lord Cotterhugh a great deal, I believe." Her voice was unusually warm, and Charlotte could not help staring at her through the mirror's reflection.

"You are fond of Albert, I think," she said gently. Maud scalded, tilting her head skywards. The maid could only have been six or seven years older than Charlotte was. She must have been some thirty years younger than Albert. *It cannot be a romance?*

"I have been in his service a long time, and he has always been very good to me. He is always very good to everyone. It is not surprising that he should earn some gratitude."

And there it was again, the unspoken reprimand for Charlotte's own ungracious attitude, her own disgraceful lack of gratitude.

Maybe I have misjudged him? Maybe everyone else sees him more clearly than I do?

"You are right," she conceded with a sigh. "It is generous of him, and wholly unnecessary. I am sure it is nothing which a little time and rest cannot fix. Rest is the only cure for the poor, as Fletch used to say."

Maud stared at her in scandalised horror, as if asking how Charlotte had the audacity to proclaim herself poor in the presence of a servant, and Charlotte could not help but smile. There was something almost Albert-ish about Maud's approbation.

She sat still whilst Maud arranged her hair for her and fetched the old black dress she was to don once more. She could not help a small sigh as she saw it. It was so very old and forlorn.

"Perhaps I will wear the violet ribbons again today," she mused aloud. "I know it is not a special occasion, but after all, why can one not wear ribbons any day of the week?" It would take the sting out of reverting from the fairy-tale princess back to the workaday drudge anyway.

She looked around her dresser top, but could not find her new ribbons. She frowned, pulling open the drawers and rummaging through the ornament box. She looked beneath the table and the chair, but it was nowhere to be found.

Maud was holding up a green ribbon instead. The evergreen of the holly bushes, it had wrapped her birthday present from Uncle John last year, she recalled, and nobody had thought that he would not live to see another. It blurred slightly before her eyes and she shook her head.

"No, green is too vibrant, and I am still in mourning. I know I had those violet ribbons somewhere."

"You were not wearing them when I undressed you for bed last night, Miss Mayweather. They must have fallen loose when you were in the gardens."

There was a sniff and definite hint of approbation lingering in Maud's tone, and Charlotte felt herself bristling at the insinuation.

"Thank you, Maud," she snapped. "That will be all."

"Very good, Miss. If you wish to rest here, Lord Cotterhugh has instructed me to show Dr Farringham up to you when he arrives."

It was not the job of a lady's maid to do so, but all the servants were working far beyond their duties these days, for Albert employed as few of them as possible.

The house was dismal and cold without the continual bustle of them about the place, footsteps echoing on tiled floors, empty grates in unused rooms casting shadows. Cold and vast, a mortuary and a crypt. The Hermit's Retreat was a warmer home than these empty, judgemental halls, she thought, remembering the snugness of the two of them there, hiding away from the rains, her foot in his hands, his eyes on her face. There was an intimacy there that was not found in

Drymote any longer. *The house is being abandoned, with us trapped inside it, buried alive.*

She looked up and saw Maud was watching her impatiently.

"Dr Farringham is to see me in my bedroom?" she repeated with a frown. "Why not the parlour or the drawing room?"

Maud shrugged. "Lord Cotterhugh wished to afford you some privacy. He did not want to cause his son undue consternation on your account, I believe."

Maud was a good deal too much in Albert's confidences, Charlotte thought darkly, but she took herself back to bed obediently anyway.

Perhaps it was for the best. She was not all that adept at resting when she ought to and she could not deny that her ankle was still aching every time she moved it. She propped it upon a pillow and lay back to stare at the canopy of the bed above.

I do not need a lot of fuss. The thought drifted dreamily through her mind as she sank back into sleep, but she could not deny it was a kind thought all the same.

A knock at the door roused her from her doze, and Maud walked in with a gaunt, cadaverous man, *a bag of elbows,* as Uncle John would have pronounced him, in a sombre black suit and an even more sombre expression. *He looks more fitted for an undertaker than a doctor.* She hoped it was not an ill omen. Still, she smiled her best smile and welcomed him in. He held up a silent hand to stop her from rising from the bed and lowered his impressive black leather bag to the floor with a quiet *thunk.*

"It is this ankle which is injured, I assume," he said, raising it from the pillow where it rested.

She could not help but wince as he rotated it first one way and then the other. He hummed under his breath.

"It hurts to put weight upon it?"

"A little. It was getting better I think, but perhaps I tried it again too soon. It was swollen up once more this morning and it has not gone down again since."

He hummed again. "Tell me, have you had any other symptoms? Have you had a fever? Has the affected area felt hot to touch? Have you had any swelling or stiffness in any other joints?"

"No," she murmured, feeling foolish. "I really think it just needs a little rest. I fell badly upon it and then walked too much afterwards, that is all. I do not need so much attention."

Dr Farringham hummed a third time, a frown upon his face.

Dr Farringham must think her the worst kind of fool. Still, whatever his opinions were, he kept them to himself. The good doctor was clearly not a man given to volubility.

"Well," she said nervously. "What is the verdict?"

"As you are not the one currently employing me, Miss Mayweather, you will excuse me if I reserve my pronouncements."

He stood up.

She stared at him. "I . . . what? Excuse me? You will not even tell me what is wrong?"

"I understand that Lord Albert Cotterhugh is acting as your guardian. I assure you, I will give him all the necessary instructions. Good day."

He was out of the door before Charlotte could do anything more than gape wordlessly at him. Dr Farringham was probably of the school which thought too much knowledge rotted a woman's brains. *No wonder Albert likes him.* She herself definitely preferred the plump and amiable Dr Mendle.

Still, as I am not the one paying for consultation, I suppose I must take what I am given and be grateful for it. Besides, Albert is not of a reticent disposition. It will not be long before I hear all.

Sure enough, almost as soon as the crunch and rattle of carriage wheels sounded upon the gravel outside, Albert was in the doorway. He crossed the room to her bedside and sat down, steepling his fingers together thoughtfully. The sores running across the backs of his hands, cracked and weeping, looked more painful than ever.

Perhaps he should have taken Dr Farringham's consultation for himself—only, she reminded herself, there was no cure for the French Disease. All that could be done was already being done.

Albert looked up at her, and there was a rare glimmer of regret lingering in his pompous eyes.

"Charlotte, you must prepare yourself, for Farringham's diagnosis was not positive," he said with a small frown. "You have done untold damage to your ankle by your stubborn and persistent use of it."

Charlotte felt her heartbeat fluttering.

"I am sorry," she said with as much penitence as she could muster. "I will rest it better now."

"That will no longer be enough."

Charlotte could only stare at him in horror. "What do you mean?"

"You have wrought permanent damage to your ankle. You have weakened it beyond measure, probably by dancing upon it last night," he added sourly, her and Edward's transgressions clearly still foremost in his mind.

Her expression did not change, though she felt the panic mounting within her in a crescendo, as arctic as the stormy seas. "But Dr Farringham does not think I will not walk properly again, surely? Not for so little as a twisted ankle."

"He thinks it is certainly a possibility. He has prescribed you a regime of exercises and a permanent prescription of muscle strengthening vitamins. You must take them thrice daily if you are to have any chance of recovery."

The thought could barely penetrate. She shook her head numbly.

"No," she said. "No. No. That cannot be true. I am scarcely twenty-one years old, I cannot lose my independence so soon." *Never to be able to walk around the grounds unaided again. To have to consider whether I could brave a wet path alone. To hobble and limp and lean upon another's arm for the rest of my life, and all for the sake of a wet afternoon's walk and a little stubborn pride, I have doomed myself forever.*

She looked up to see an unusually sympathetic expression on Albert's face.

"If you take the strengtheners as you are prescribed and diligently do your exercises, you have hope yet. It will be a long road to recovery, Charlotte, but you are not without optimism entirely."

"I cannot afford such medicines," she said distantly. "A permanent regime of vitamins? I have no funds to afford such things." *I am going to lose the use of my foot, and all because I am too poor for the treatment.* She would have to leave. She would have to find work — any work at all — to afford such long term care, or, if she could not bear to leave her home for the wild unfeeling whims of the world she was so untrained to deal with, she would have to live as an invalid for the rest of her life. *What a choice to make.*

Perhaps I should go out as a governess. Albert had been hinting, rather unsubtly, at such for a while now, and yet Charlotte scarcely felt that her own education allowed for such a thing. Uncle John had been more inclined to encourage natural curiosity than formalised learning. When she had been a child, he allowed her to traipse after him as he pottered around the gardening, quoting the Latin names of plants at her and pointing out their interesting genotypes, or setting her loose in the library to explore the colourful maps of the Great Atlas, almost as large as she had been, as her interests had taken her, rather than setting her a governess of her own to teach her French, Greek and Music. She could read, of course, and write, but her education was certainly patchy, and she did not feel fit to bestow it upon another.

Albert sat upon the edge of the bed.

She looked at him.

He sighed in a long-suffering way. "Perhaps, for the sake of my dear brother's memory, who, I know, was very fond of you and, indeed, often regarded you as his own daughter, I could make some adjustments to our family finances and find the money for your medicines."

She clutched at him desperately, hope swelling within her. "Truly?"

"He would not wish to see you lamed, I know. And, despite what you think of me, I am no monster."

She felt her cheeks scalding at the accusation. *Perhaps I have been a little unjust in my estimation of him.* She had let her anger and her grief colour her perception of his character, and here he was offering her generosity. She resolved shame-facedly to think better of him from now on.

"Thank you," she said as humbly as she could.

"It will be no little expense," he warned. "And it will be no small inconvenience to us to arrange it."

"I am very grateful for it, indeed."

"How grateful?" he said sharply.

Charlotte stared at him. "I — well — very grateful."

"Then show your gratitude, Charlotte. You must oblige me with a favour in return."

Maud's words came swimming back to Charlotte. It seemed Dr Farringham was not the only one who owed Albert a great deal.

This is what he does, she realised. He traps you and uses you, and forces you into gratitude which he can spend against you . . . and yet, what other choices did she have? She could not go lame, not if there was another alternative.

"How may I help you?" she asked carefully. Albert considered her and she could almost see him phrasing the words in his mind.

"Edward has taken to you, it seems."

"He has been very kind to me."

"Yes. He is young and flighty. Reckless. He thinks little further than his own amusements and does not consider the longer-term ramifications of such things. He will grow out of it, of course, but I would not like to see him entangled in anything permanent because of one foolish mistake in his youth."

Charlotte felt herself burning beetroot once more. "I do not know what you are insinuating," she said stiffly. "But I assure you, Edward has not . . . he has been . . . there are no entanglements between us."

"Good. I would like to see it continue that way. If you wish to receive the medicines you require from my hand, you will ensure that it does."

Charlotte clenched her fists. "I do not appreciate being blackmailed, sir."

"It is not blackmail. It is reciprocal kindness."

"Edward does not think of me that way anyway."

Albert laughed, and she felt the cruelty of it sting deeply.

"Oh, I know *that*. Yours is not the character nor, frankly, the appearance to captivate him. But he likes the challenge of it, and whilst he is amusing himself with such petty and, to his eyes at least, harmless flirtations, he is damaging his future prospects for more serious matches."

"Miss Bletchley," whispered Charlotte, and Albert nodded.

"I will be frank with you, Miss Mayweather, for I think yours is a personality which appreciates honesty. My brother was not good with money. When I inherited Drymote, the finances of the estate were . . . less than optimal."

Charlotte frowned. "Truly? But Uncle John so rarely spent money." Not that he was a miser, she thought miserably, only that if it did not blossom or sprout he was not interested in it.

They did not buy expensive clothes, or hold lavish balls, they did not have thoroughbred horses in the stables or keep an expensive gig and carriage. He did not even wager on dogs or boxing. The only thing he spent money upon was the little needed to eat and drink and, of course, the garden.

"I fear you did not know my brother as well as you thought you did," Albert said dryly. "To be perfectly honest with you, unless something drastic happens, Drymote will have to be sold to pay off our debts. If Edward marries Miss Bletchley, her money will rescue the estate. If she is frightened off by his flirtations to you, flirtations which will have no ultimate outcome for anybody involved and which he does merely to pass the boredom of his little country life which is so different from the busy cosmopolitan lifestyle he is accustomed to, we will all be doomed."

Charlotte felt herself blanching.

"He does not care for you," Albert said persuasively. "Ensure that it stays that way, and I will ensure that you remain upon your own two feet. There is no downside for anyone here. It is only your stubborn pride that is rebelling from this fact, Charlotte."

Perhaps he was right. Perhaps, unladylike though it was to admit it, she had been enjoying Edward's attentions. She had been enjoying this half-fantasy that someone like him could be interested in someone like her.

She squeezed her eyes closed to stop the tears within them from falling.

"I assure you, sir, Edward would no more think of me as a wife than he would the gardener's daughter. I cannot make him wed where you wish him to, but I will make sure that Miss Bletchley is under no illusions as to his relationship with me."

Albert patted her hand familiarly. "I will see to those pills for you," he said. "Dr Farringham is a good man. You are lucky I insisted he see you. If we had left it any later, it might have been too late entirely."

Charlotte could only smile weakly as Albert let himself out, but she couldn't help but wonder if he meant too late to save her ankle, or too late for Edward's reckless heart . . .

CHAPTER FIVE

"Maud? Have you seen my shawl? The good Indian Lace one that once belonged to my aunt?"

"No, Miss."

"Are you sure? It was there upon the chair."

"Are you calling me a liar, Miss Mayweather?" Maud's quiet voice was chilling despite its polite tones.

"Of course not."

"I am happy for you to check my rooms, if you believe I have taken it."

"I wasn't accusing you of anything," Charlotte snapped in frustration. "I just need to find it. Help me look, please."

She rummaged with increasing desperation through her belongings, strewing them across the rooms whilst Maud waited demurely, watching her.

"There is your old wool one here, Miss Mayweather. Will that do?" She held out a faded, bobbled shawl that had seen better days. It was far more suited to a poor dependent than the luxurious Indian Lace one was.

Charlotte could have cried in frustration. *Is it not enough to have lost Aunty Ursula, must I now lose her clothes too?*

She could picture Ursula's smile in her mind, the way her hands always stroked Charlotte's fair hair gently. *Come now, child, there's no use crying over clothes, is there?*

"Yes, Maud, it will have to do," she said. "Thank you," she added belatedly, aware that she was taking her foul temper out on the maid and it was not her fault.

Maud bobbed a small curtsey and made her way towards

the door.

"Lord Cotterhugh said as to be sure to remind you to take your medicines, Miss Mayweather," she added over her shoulder, pulling the door closed behind her. Charlotte rolled her eyes. *Even when he is doing a good deed, Albert is an insufferable nag.*

Still, she obediently pulled out the pill bottle from the box on her dresser and tipped one out. The small white pill sat innocently in the palm of her hand, staring at her in the bright morning sun. Albert had been as good as his word and had procured them for her very quickly. He had sent them via Maud just that morning as she came to dress Charlotte for the day ahead. *He must be determined indeed to keep me out of Edward's good graces to have found them so soon.*

Now that the time had come to take it however, she found herself dreading it. She sat at the dressing table, her gaze fixed upon the tiny tablet nestled in her hand, the room silent now that Maud had once more taken her leave.

Is this who I am now? An invalid tied to the pill bottle?

"Don't be ridiculous, Charlotte. You know it will do you good," she chided her reflection in the looking glass firmly. She swallowed it in one swift movement, before she could change her mind.

The pill was bitter and large. She gagged upon it as she tried to wash it down, but at last she managed to swallow it. A small dry sob threatened. *And I must take these thrice a day for the rest of my life?* The prospect seemed far too daunting, and for one moment, she wished for nothing more than to lie down and cry.

She was interrupted from her wallowing, however, by a knock at the door.

Edward popped his head around, some jaunty remark upon his tongue, which fell away as he caught sight of her face.

"Charlotte? Whatever is the matter?"

She rubbed her face clean and forced a smile to her lips, slipping the little pill bottle into the ornament box on her dresser hastily before he should see it. She did not need more pity now.

She did not reprimand him for approaching her in her bedchambers this time. She thought there would be little point. Clearly, Edward was determined to make a scandal of her reputation amongst the servants. She could only trust to their discretion that they would not spread such calumnies abroad. She could imagine only too well what Maud would say, with her scrunched up disapproving expression on that plump, red face. Charlotte sighed.

"Nothing at all, Edward. May I help you in any way?"

He grinned his best, rakish grin, but it was gilded with a brittle edge of concern still.

"Certainly you may. I find myself wearied of country life already. I have traipsed through these grounds from top to bottom and back again already this morning. Yesterday I undertook to explore the library, and the day before that I even attempted the attics, searching out mysteries and secrets, but Drymote is no Udolpho's Castle, I fear. There is very little excitement to be found in the country. Give me some occupation, Miss Mayweather, before my brain rots entirely."

She rolled her eyes at his hyperbole, but limped over to him, threading her hand through the crook of his arm so she could rest her weight upon him. Her ankle complained with every jolting footstep, but she gritted her teeth and bore it. She would not become an invalid now. She would *not*.

"I have promised to go down to the chapel today. The parishioners are clearing out the church and churchyard in order to decorate it for All Hallow's Eve. I am sure Vicar Herrington and Mr Harris would be glad of your help, if time is lying too heavy upon your hands."

The words were out before she knew what she had done,

the invitation spilling from her naturally, an instinctive desire to want to spend more time with him.

Did I not just promise Albert I would not encourage Edward? Why am I inviting him out now? And yet, it is a church event. It is hardly romantic. Nobody could see anything amiss about that, surely . . .

"Oh lord, can you think of anything worse?" Edward groaned, but he obediently followed her to the door. "You must promise to douse me if I set to flame stepping across the threshold of the church," he teased, offering her a cape and she could not help but laugh.

The world outside was overcast and heavy, the clouds dark and so low Charlotte almost thought she could stretch up to touch them if she tried. She limped down the front stairs and set off stoically down the driveway, a grimace upon her face.

"I could call for the carriage," Edward offered, his hand trapping hers gently against his arm.

"No, no. It is only at the bottom of the hill and across the field. It would be foolish to call the carriage for such a little way."

"Your stubbornness will be the death of you yet, Charlotte Mayweather."

"So I have been told." She grinned. "But I am sure a little exercise will do my ankle good, if we do but walk gently."

This was almost certainly not true. The wretched thing hurt like blazes with every step she took, and yet she would not stay home today. *We always help at the clearing day. I do so every year. I would not miss it now.* It was the duty of the lady of Drymote, and though she was not the mistress of the estate, as Albert only too often reminded her, she had undertaken that duty every year since Aunty Ursula had passed. Until Edward married a wife of his own, she would continue to undertake that duty, come hell, high-water, or even twisted ankles.

Still, I should not have gone to the ball. It was too much, too soon.

And yet, with the memory of Edward's arms around her, his teasing warmth, the way he had drunk her in as she wore her new ball-gown, she found she could not rue it as much as she should.

She glanced over at him as they meandered their way through the winding garden paths companionably. How strange it seemed that she should have first met Edward down here and stranger still that she should not have known him before that fateful day. It scarcely seemed possible that there was a time when she did not know him at all.

"Life in the country is too dull for you?" she asked aloud as they paraded together down amongst the once manicured, now woefully neglected, pathways. Edward grimaced.

"Birchton is hardly London, is it?"

"I like Birchton, though it might not have all the gay pursuits of the city. Tell me, Edward, how did you occupy yourself there?"

"Far too frivolously. Gambling and drinking, theatre trips and music halls, coffee houses and opium dens, all night parties with social pariahs, men of literature and science, scandalous atheists and polygamists and three-headed men from the Indies."

She rolled her eyes. "You get worse every time I speak to you. I do not think you even know how to give a serious answer about anything."

"Of course not, a serious answer is a fearful thing. I do not think I could bear for anyone to take me seriously. They might begin to actually expect things of me, and they would be so dreadfully disappointed when they found out how shallow and worthless I actually am." He laughed again, long and loud, but this time Charlotte did not join in. It occurred to her for the first time that perhaps Edward was not joking as much as he seemed to be.

"An occupation would be good for you, I think," she said

as they paraded slowly down to the large gates which hemmed in the Drymote Estate, arm in arm. "People were not made to be idle. We must all be about some work, paid or otherwise."

"Ah, it is to be a sermon, I see. Should you not wait until we have arrived at chapel, though?"

"Actually, that particular homily came from Uncle John and, indeed, from common sense. Boredom does not suit you, Edward. It provokes you to foolishness."

"And I am already foolish enough without it," muttered Edward beneath his breath. They slipped through the gates together, out onto the winding road which bordered Langhorne, Miss Bletchley's home, and led down to the village of Birchton.

And how handy it would be that their lands were bordered when they were wed, Charlotte thought. They could easily combine the two estates into one large one and be the wealthiest and most popular couple in the whole county. No doubt that was another reason Albert was so keen to secure the match. She glanced over at the trees hiding Langhorne from view and could not withhold a deep sigh.

Edward glanced over at her. "What is it that troubles you, Charlotte?"

"I was just considering which occupation to prescribe for you," she lied quickly. "You do not have a taste for politics, whatever your father desires, nor do I think you a man for the military, for I do not imagine you take orders well. You spout too many heresies to take to the church, and you love the outdoors too well to take to scholarship. I declare, Mr Cotterhugh, I do not know what to do with you. Perhaps you could try gentlemanly pursuits if you have nothing fitter to fill your time? Pheasant season has started now, has it not? I could well imagine you as a huntsman, for you have the air of a poacher about you, you know," she teased. He flinched a little, though he quickly hid it behind a tight smile.

"I fear I have an aversion to guns."

She raised an eyebrow. She would not have credited it, from the rumours swirling in his wake, but then again, perhaps she ought to have known better than to listen to such things.

"Perhaps I ought to fall in love with someone," he teased, raising an eyebrow at her. She could not shake the feeling that he was trying to change the subject. "I have heard that that is a good way to while away the hours, sighing romantically out of rain-bedecked windows, musing on the qualities of your fair Madonna and so forth. I could even try my hand at composing a sonnet or two. I have heard that it is the quantity and not the quality of odes and ballads which mark the earnestness of a lovelorn youth."

She ignored his flippant tone. She cast a look across at the borders of Langhorne as they walked beside it.

"I thought Miss Bletchley looked most becoming at the ball," she said guilelessly. He laughed—clearly she wasn't as subtle as she imagined.

"Oh yes, a paragon of beauty in every way."

"She will probably be down at the chapel today too. She often undertakes charity in the village I hear."

"And why, pray, are we fixating on Miss Bletchley today?" he asked.

Charlotte considered him, and then decided that the truth was her best form of attack. She sent a glance over her shoulder, but there were no eagerly listening ears following them. She dropped her voice anyway, so that it whispered over him low and confidential.

"Your father was hoping you would be fond of her. He is hoping you might grow attached to her in time."

"Ah! I see! She is the bookmaker's favourite for my bride-to-be, is she?" He chuckled darkly. Charlotte just shrugged.

"Well? And where do you lay your wager?"

"I am not the gambling type."

"Well, let me give you an inside tip, lest the urge to wagering come upon you. As comely as Miss Bletchley is, she is not to my taste."

"She is exceedingly beautiful, has impeccable manners, is very kind and her charitable works are known across the county."

"Are you trying to recommend her, or not?" He laughed. "What would I do with a saint? I like women with a sharper tongue and a slice of wickedness in them."

"You like women you think you can debauch," she retorted. And he thinks you are one of them, Charlotte, she added to herself. No doubt the reputation of her mother had preceded her, and the injustice of it all stung against her skin like ice. Was it not enough that she had never known her father? Must she also bear the crimes of her mother's foolishness too?

"I like women who are not too bound by the rules of courtesy to tell me what they truly think," he replied with a grin.

"Well, let me tell you this then, Miss Bletchley is a wonderful person, and she has the funds to save Drymote. I do not know of a single reason why you should not wed her."

His face contorted through various emotions so fast that she could not read them all. At last it settled upon arrogant boredom.

"Well, thankfully it is not your place to arrange my marriage. And what do you mean *the funds to save Drymote*? I was not aware that it needed saving."

Charlotte just shrugged angrily. It still stung that Uncle John had kept that from her. She did not think they had secrets from each other—well, not until those last few weeks when he had succumbed to paranoia and delirium. Again, Albert's taunting words echoed in her head, *perhaps you did not know him as well as you thought you did.*

Edward shrugged as well. "Perhaps the time for the great estates is passing anyway. This is the era of the self-made man, Charlotte, perhaps it is time to put the relics of the past to bed."

She could not help but stare in horror. "You cannot mean that?"

"You think I should live an idle life on the backs of the poor, just because I can?"

"I think, Edward, that the estates here are the lifeblood of this village. They provide work to scores of villagers and support the church and the parish. I think they provide an important political seat in the county and wield influence at parliament, influence which could be used to do great good."

He looked a little taken aback by her vehemence.

"Perhaps you should inherit Drymote instead. You are clearly more passionate about it than I am."

She pressed her lips tightly together to stop the torrent of torrid anger from overspilling, but they dropped open a fraction once again as a dark shadow flittered between the trees behind them. She stared out between the tree trunks of the native wood, but saw only moss and mist. Her fingers instinctively clutched at Edward's arm, seeking strength and reassurance from his solid presence, and he looked at her with alarm.

"Charlotte? What is it?"

He followed her wide-eyed gaze into the woods but saw nothing there.

Did I imagine it? Am I conjuring up shadows to haunt myself with now? That was almost as frightening as if they were being followed. At least if we were being hunted I would know that I was not going mad . . .

"Just a trick of the light," she assured him with a light laugh, far more carelessly than she felt. "Come, we are almost at the chapel, let us stop bickering and do some good."

Still, she could not stop the fear from prickling at the back of her neck as she hurried her footsteps down the path, practically towing Edward along in her wake. Nor could she stop the frightened glances behind her, horribly superstitious that she would see that shadow following her after all . . .

Miss Bletchley of Langhorne was already busy at the chapel when Charlotte and Edward arrived. Her cheeks were dimpling prettily as she laughed in the dim autumn light, and it was a mark of her good nature that she could pretend to be transfixed in whatever earnest homily Mr Harris was capturing her with so convincingly, Charlotte thought. A handful of old, dead flowers were bundled in Miss Bletchley's hands, but she seemed to have forgotten they were there. She startled as they approached, and blushed pinkly, bobbing into a small curtsey.

"How good of you both to come! Miss Mayweather, will you come with me? The women are cleaning the inside of the chapel, and the men are clearing the churchyard ready for the bonfire tonight."

"Bonfire?" Edward frowned. "Guy Fawkes night is not for many weeks yet."

"He is a city man, he cannot help it." Charlotte laughed, and the other two laughed as well. She smiled a fond goodbye to Edward, who scowled playfully at her, as if asking how she could leave him alone with the painfully earnest curate, and followed Miss Bletchley inside the church.

A group of old wives, widows and spinsters from the village were already scrubbing at the windows and darning up the delicately embroidered kneelers in the pews. A couple of men from the village were up ladders and crates, untying the sheaves which were looped in swathes across the ceiling, from arch to arch, from the Harvest festival a few weeks before.

The last harvest sheaf had not been taken down yet from

where it hung, like a condemned man in the large stained glass chapel window. The altar rail was still bedecked with a garland of woven wheat sheaves, now filling the air with a stale and musty scent, threaded through with autumn poppies, scabious and yarrow. The scent of it clawed at her throat as she picked up an old rag and began polishing the communion cups and offering plates.

It was good to be able to busy her mind and body, to chase away the grief, fear and pain that had been haunting her footsteps recently. When she had at last finished scrubbing, Charlotte looked around to find that the candles within the church had been lit and the world beyond the windows had darkened into gloom.

"It always gets so dark so early this time of year, does it not?" Miss Bletchley laughed, seeing Charlotte's expression. "It happens every year, I do not know how it still manages to surprise me every time. Still, without the darker nights it would be difficult to have the bonfires, would it not? And I have always loved a good bonfire. Shall we go and see if the menfolk have finished setting it up yet?"

Charlotte glanced at Miss Bletchley to see if this was condescension or kindness and found she could not tell. She followed the heiress out through the chapel and into the grounds beyond.

Edward had removed his fine waistcoat. He had draped it over a nearby headstone, and he had a faint sheen of sweat lingering on his forehead underneath his curls, but he was grinning. He held up a hand and she and Miss Bletchley both walked over to see him.

Charlotte dared not glance across to see how Miss Bletchley fared. With Edward's face ruddy from exertion, his shirt rolled up to his elbows and unbuttoned at the collar, and that gleam only earned by honest labour sparkling merrily in his eyes, Miss Bletchley must surely fall in love with him on the spot—if she had not already. Charlotte could not bear to watch it happen before her eyes though.

"Well now," Edward said, and it was a brighter sound than usual, far from the ironic, wry mirth he usually threw out. "Who knew that all this toil was so good for the soul, eh? I have been working like a farm-hand all day, clearing out the hedgerows and piling up leaves, dead branches and bracken from the churchyard, and I have never felt better in my life."

"You might not appreciate it so much if it was a daily necessity," Charlotte pointed out with a laugh. "I'm sure any of the village men would gladly swap lives with you if you wished it."

"Not tonight, they wouldn't. Look at them! Have you ever seen a merrier bunch?"

And, indeed, Edward seemed to be right. Now that the hard work of clearing the church yard and preparing it for the coming winter was done, the village seemed to come alight with life and joy. The bonfire was being lit, the farrier from the village trying his best to get the embers to catch, the landlord of the ale-house was rolling up some barrels of autumn cider and ale for the workers to enjoy, the children were swarming up the path towards the glow, giddy with the excitement of being allowed out after dark, and some fiddlers were setting up on a bench, ready to send their music out into the wild, waiting night.

"My father will be sore to miss this," Edward said, looking around at the festivities. "He always enjoys a good party."

Charlotte secretly doubted it. This wasn't the sophisticated balls of good society that Albert enjoyed. This was a night for the village folk. Uncle John had always attended, of course, and done his duty by providing half a pig to roast for the hungry workers and a couple of barrels of drink to keep them warm, but Albert only ever cultivated the good opinions of people he could use. He never bothered keeping traditions alive if they could not benefit him. *At least Edward enjoys it here. Perhaps he will be a better kind of lord than his father is . . .*

"Fletch always loved the bonfire as well," Charlotte murmured, more to herself than anyone else. *What a pity that he should miss it this year.* She did not even know where he had ended up. She rubbed her tingling hands, absent-mindedly trying to shake some life back into them. A horrible thought struck her — what if Fletch had ended up in workhouse? She clenched her fist, the thought sending tears springing to her eyes — and yet there was scarcely anything she could do about it, even if he were . . .

She looked over to see that Edward was watching her keenly.

"You miss him, don't you?" he murmured, his voice low enough to be hidden by the crackle of the catching fire. She blinked and nodded.

"It is strange, knowing he is out there somewhere and I cannot see him. I scarcely got to say goodbye to him . . . I wish I could see him just one last time."

She looked away as the tears swam up to meet her, but swallowed her sorrow by force. *There is a time and a place for grief and it is not in company . . .*

"Ah, Miss Bletchley, Miss Mayweather, Mr Cotterhugh! What do you think of our bonfire this year?" Mr Harris said excitedly, appearing at their elbow abruptly and looking more puppy-doggish than ever. "It is burning bright and good, is it not?"

"Yes, a real *bon* fire, as the French might say." Miss Bletchley laughed at her own joke, and Mr Harris did as well, a little too loudly.

"Ah yes, that is a common misconception, in fact. It does not come from the French, *bon,* it actually comes from middle-English, *bonefyre,* a fire of bones, from the saint days." Harris launched himself into a complex etymological lecture enthusiastically, and Charlotte could not help but laugh as she felt

Edward stiffen and groan beside her, his good humour evaporating.

"Come, Charlotte, the fiddlers are playing. Dance with me," he said abruptly.

"And leave Miss Bletchley unchaperoned?"

"I am sure I will be more than safe in Mr Harris' company," Miss Bletchley said, the fire-glow burning brightly in her eyes, the flames lending a lick of colour to her cheeks.

"Of course, Miss Bletchley, it would be my honour," said Mr Harris gallantly. "Miss Mayweather, before you go, I wondered if Drymote was still available to provide for the All Hallow's Eve parade this year? We begin the preparations soon," he added.

Charlotte bit her lip anxiously. Once she would have said yes without hesitation, but Albert had all but stripped the garden bare for his own ball, his community obligations forgotten.

I will find the flowers from somewhere. There must be some corner of the gardens Albert has not plundered.

"Of course, Mr Harris. It is always an honour to be asked. I will bring some down for you when I can. Drymote will not let you down."

"Oh, I am certain of it, Miss Mayweather. You never have yet."

Edward snatched at her hand, as if he thought someone else might steal it, and whirled her away into the glow of the bonfire. Charlotte felt herself blushing for Edward's rudeness, but Mr Harris scarcely seemed to notice, his attentions already drawn back to the lovely and long-suffering Miss Bletchley.

The music was simple and cheery, bouncing through the night air like the sparks and flames, tangling itself up in the smoke. Edward's hands slipped around her waist once more. He whirled her madly around the bonfire with the young village beaus, making her ankle scream at her, and yet she found she could not tell him to stop. The feeling of his warm hands around her were surely worth the pain. She did not know when she might get another chance to dance with him, after all. She looked up at his eyes shining brightly down into her and was reminded starkly of that night of the ball once more.

He dances with me in the dark, but he will never claim me in the light. He only dances with me where it doesn't matter. It is Miss Bletchley he dances with in the ball rooms before the eyes of the world.

How could she expect it to be any different? She was not a lady. She was just someone to while away his hours with before he made a good match.

She pulled herself out of his arms, and staggered over to a bench to sit down. He was beside her in moments.

"Charlotte? What's wrong? You're looking a little unwell."

"It has been a long day. I need a moment to collect myself."

Her head was spinning, the music and the flames making it seem giddy and dizzyingly unreal, and her ankle was throbbing. The shadows were flickering closer and she felt as if she had been drinking strong cider, though she had not touched a drop of it all evening.

Her fingers crept to her temples and she found them pulsing and pounding—she was not sure if the mysterious beat was lingering in her fingertips or her head though.

She whipped around suddenly, staring off into the dark.

"Charlotte?" Edward asked again, concern evident in his tone now.

"I thought I felt someone out there. I thought I felt someone watching us."

The village crowds were dancing and whooping before them and Miss Bletchley had even graciously conceded to give Mr Harris a dance and was being spun around stiltedly by the young curate, but the world behind them was dark and empty, whispering with the winds.

She was not sure why she was so convinced there was

someone there, lingering beyond the glow of the light, but she felt their malevolent presence out there, watching and waiting. She shivered closer to Edward, who was scanning the dark with a frown.

"Stay here," he said sharply, getting to his feet. "I will investigate."

She clutched at his arm in fear.

"No! Please, Edward, no, they might mean you harm."

He laughed, a low and bitter laugh, but shook her off and went striding out beyond the halo glow of the bonfire.

The night grew colder and wilder as she waited, her fingers at her lips, her heart in her throat. She strained her ears and eyes, but the blackness of the night mocked her. The moments grew longer, and then the crack of gunfire shot out across the night. Charlotte screamed.

Nobody else seemed to hear it, at first. The fiddlers carried on playing, the villagers carried on dancing and laughing and Charlotte screamed and screamed. She tried to stumble to her feet, out into the darkness, out to save him, but her limbs would not obey her.

Hands were shaking her, cool against her skin.

"Miss Mayweather? Whatever is the matter?"

Miss Bletchley's dark eyes were there watching, Mr Harris by her elbow.

"Gun-shot! Edward!" Charlotte gasped out the words, jabbing into the darkness madly, unable to string them into a sentence. She turned back to the darkness, and found her breath flooding back into her chest in gasps as Edward himself came striding back out of the dark towards her. She tore herself out of Miss Bletchley's hands and threw herself into Edward's instead, abandoning all thoughts of dignity or propriety.

"You're bleeding!"

Blood was trickling down from his temple, but it seemed

to be coming from a graze and nothing more.

"Is everything all right, Mr Cotterhugh? Miss Mayweather said she heard a gun-shot?" Mr Harris asked anxiously. "Should we send for the magistrate?"

"No, no, do not bother about that. It was just a poacher. He tripped on his gun when I startled him, and we had a round of fisticuffs before he took off into the night. Do not bother the law about it on a festival night like this," Edward said cheerily.

He's lying. Charlotte did not know how she knew, but the knowledge lingered like a stone inside her. *Whatever happened out there in the blackness, Edward is lying about it now.*

He looked down at her and gently prised her clutching grasp off his chest.

"I'm fine, Charlotte. Truly. See, just a graze, nothing more. Still, perhaps it is time to return you back to Drymote. There are some unsavoury types about here, after all."

"Ah, where else should they be but in God's house?" Mr Harris said with a solemn earnestness. "If they cannot be here, where else could they be?"

Edward gave the clergyman a long, hard look and then walked off without another word and Charlotte, still clinging desperately to him, followed after.

Chapter Six

Charlotte straightened with a grimace, rubbing her muddied hands against her apron. Autumn had settled in sternly since the ball as October slogged its way through. The winds were cold as they whipped about her, the skies hanging heavy overhead with rain which threatened but never fell, the leaves wrinkling and crumpling on the trees and on the ground, as she knelt amongst the fading flower beds, as she finally began her duty, desperately searching for enough blooms to fulfil her obligations to Mr Harris and the All Hallow's Eve parade. She had put it off for far too long, for she knew all too well what she would find — nothing. The main beds had already been ravaged, and the walled garden was all but empty too, the glass houses had stood abandoned since Fletch had left. Still, she had found some small measure of success in these little nooks by the lake. After a hard morning's foraging, her basket was slowly but surely filling up.

The Michaelmas daisies, battered by the heavy autumn rains, bowed their heads before her like courtiers. She ran her hands through the twiggy undergrowth, deadheading the bush just as tenderly as Uncle John once had.

"He is with Aunty Ursula now," she told herself sternly. "He is far happier there than he was here." And yet, selfishly, spitefully, childishly, she could not help but feel abandoned. First, by the father she had never known, who had forsaken her mother so cruelly, then by that self-same mother, who gratefully cast off her disgrace and the torturous charity of the asylum for the quiet pity and gentle forgiveness of the grave.

By Aunty Ursula, with the slow and lingering death of cancer which she bore with meek stoicism and resignation, and then by the thunderclap death of Uncle John, whom she had not expected to depart so soon, leaving her bereft and alone in this wide world, with so little to depend upon.

At least he had gone quickly, far more quickly than any of them had expected. He had seemed to be in perfect health one day, and then scarcely more than three weeks later he was dead. Whatever infection he had caught had plummeted him down into its depths with a ruthless haste, so speedily that she had scarcely had time to say goodbye to him.

She felt her eyes prickling with tears. Sometimes it did not feel real, even now. Sometimes she still could not believe that he had died, and that her whole life had been turned upside down so soon.

She flinched suddenly. She had thought she had seen a shadow move amongst the undergrowth, as though someone or something was lurking there, watching her. Her neck prickled and her heartbeat began to race as she fumbled for a twig on the ground.

"Who is there?" she asked, trying to make herself sound braver than she was. The garden did not answer her, and somehow that was worse.

You are growing paranoid, Charlotte Mayweather, she thought, but her hackles still did not settle. The wind set the plants dancing around her ankles as she staggered forwards towards the shadows of the undergrowth, determined to root out the trespasser, and she could not help but feel as if they were closing in on her malevolently. She cursed her over-fevered imagination and tried to get herself back under control once more, but her attention was drawn by a splash and a scream just through the hedges.

She leapt to attention at once. Stumbling over the basket at her feet, sending it sprawling, she limped as fast as her aching ankle could allow her through the hedgerow to the lake. It stretched out eerily empty before her, the water rippling, autumn mists hanging low over the water, the weeping willows kissing the surface with their sorrowful tendrils, the far side almost hidden by fog.

There was no one there.

She stood frozen for a moment, staring out at the glassy surface and then, even as she watched, a head broke through the surface by the water's edge, clawing and gasping for air. Charlotte surged forwards at once. The water clung to her dress, seeping through it, dragging her down. The water weeds tangled around her ankles like chains, the stones beneath slipping under her boots as the frigid water rushed in.

The head went down again, but Charlotte was there now. She grappled with the woman beneath the surface, hauling her up with a splash which sent stagnant water into her own mouth. She spat it out, trying to keep hold of the woman thrashing in panic, sending fresh waves across the waters in foamy white.

"Get off me! Help! Help!"

She all but went under again, and Charlotte, her hands still fixed firmly around the woman's waist, nearly went under as well with the force of trying to keep her upright.

"Charlotte!"

Charlotte turned with her struggling handful to see an alarmed Edward wading into the water, too.

"Help me with her!" she called urgently, and he was with her in but a moment. He hauled up the woman in his arms, carrying her like a child, and she went limp in his grip.

"You can walk, Charlotte?" he asked curtly, and Charlotte nodded, struggling back to shore weakly.

As he lay the limp woman down on the shore, her dark hair painted almost black by the water, her uniform clinging to her in wet folds, Charlotte saw to her surprise that it was Maud.

Her skin was pale and blotchy under the icy water, her eyes blood-shot and raw, stung by the lake water. Edward ripped open the front of her dress, placed his ear to her chest, and then tipping her onto her side instead. As the dress loosened, Maud spluttered up mouthfuls of water, taking in deep, panicked gasps, and he rubbed her back calmly.

"There now, it's Maud, isn't it? You're all right, Maud. You're all right."

"What happened?" Charlotte asked, kneeling down beside her, trying to chafe Maud's hands warm again.

Maud looked at her in horror, but did not say anything. She just pushed her benefactors away, stumbled to her feet and started to leave.

"You must see a doctor," Edward called after her, concern etched into his face. "You must take to your bed. You will be freezing."

Maud ignored him, all but fleeing the lakeside. Charlotte stared after her. *The poor thing has gone quite mad.*

"It's probably the shock," Edward told her, reading her expression. "I'll have Farringham or Mendle sent for. I'm sure with a hot tea and a quiet day in bed she will be fine."

"What on earth was she doing down here anyway?" Charlotte asked. Now that the moment of excitement had passed, she, too, felt cold and shivery. Edward's gaze scoured her, too.

"I could ask the same of you." He grinned. "Come on. None of us should be out and about this foggy autumn morning."

He offered her his arm and she accepted it weakly.

"This dress is destined to be ruined," she said bleakly. "First mud, now lake-water. It's doomed."

"I've never believed we should wear mourning for so long anyway. Life should be full of joy. I'd much rather see you in a summer blue, or an autumn red, or even a winter's evergreen. Life is for the living. We should not dedicate so much of it to those that have passed."

"Perhaps you would not think so, if you had ever cherished anyone who had fallen," she snapped.

He pulled away from her in horror, and she felt her temper mounting, the lingering aftertaste of fear making her sharp tongued and bitter, her moods swinging volubly around like a lantern caught in a gale. She could feel herself being cast adrift on them, and yet could do nothing to stop it. She tugged her hand free of his arm and tried to pull away, but her ankle twisted and she went down to the lakeside ground again.

Edward frowned and swept her up in his arms.

She tried to resist, but she was cold and tired and had not the strength to fight it anymore.

"I am sure that ankle should not still be paining you? It must have been a fortnight since you hurt it. Have you not been taking your vitamins?"

"Thrice daily as prescribed," she snapped. The taste of them had not improved with time and, unfortunately, it seemed to come with side effects, something Dr Farringham had assured Albert was common-place, apparently.

And what of it? Surely, I should be glad to exchange frequent headaches, fizzing fingers and changeable tempers for the freedom to walk and run as I please. I should not be so ungrateful.

Edward just hummed out a small noise, which could have meant anything. His gaze landed on the little boathouse on the water's edge. He strode up towards it and pushed it open with an elbow.

It was cold, damp and empty within, littered with the remnants of a life abandoned, as if its inhabitants had just stepped out of the room for a moment, and it made Charlotte's throat close up with pain.

"Nobody has been in here since Aunty Ursula died, I think," she whispered hoarsely. "We used to go out on the rowing boat across the lake in the summer, and picnic on the little island in the middle. It was her favourite thing to do."

She buried her face in Edward's chest and tried to bite back the tears which spilled over her cheeks. Edward strode over to the dusty chair by the empty fireplace and deposited her gently in it. A musty, damp smell clung to the chair fabric, only made worse by her own dripping dress. Edward unlaced her boots for her, tipping out the water collected within by the door, and then propped her foot up for her on an old stool. She could not deny that it was nice being taken care of, for once.

He threw a picnic blanket over her and then fetched the tinder box from atop the mantle-piece, making a small fire in the grate. The little hut burst into light and warmth, the smoke choking up thickly through the little chimney. The oars were still strapped to the wall, the boat in the corner thrown over with a tarpaulin, a crate full of old picnic things neatly stacked collecting dust beside it, and an old tin cup near the kettle on the shelf.

"We used to have cocoa in here, if the rains caught us suddenly," Charlotte remembered, looking into the flames. "Aunty Ursula used to sing silly sea-shanties to make me laugh or tell me tall-tales of pirates and mermaids."

The tears poured down unrestrained now, and she hiccoughed wetly, unable to stop them. The grief poured over her in waves, and she clutched the picnic blanket to her sodden chest, as if it could shield her from the pain expanding there between her ribs.

"I'm sorry," she panted. "I'm sorry, I'm being foolish." She tried to wipe her tears away, but they fell over her fingertips.

"Despite what you might think, Charlotte, I also know grief," he told her. She looked up at him, but he would not meet her glance, as he was fumbling through the old wardrobe in the corner. "It is all right to be sad sometimes. It is all right to be weak. Here. Put this on. You'll catch your death in that."

He threw a dress at her, and she caught it, holding it up to the firelight. She let out a choked little laugh.

"Aunty Ursula's garden dress," she said. "She used to keep it down here for mucking about in." She ran fingers over the rough fabric. It was brown and hardy, a little patched in places, but sturdily made. "I had forgotten all about this. She used to change into it whenever we went in the boat, because she didn't want to ruin her good dresses. I had forgotten," she said again softly. *How quickly my mind has abandoned those it once loved . . .*

"You should get changed. You cannot take a chill on top of everything else. I will wait outside whilst you do so."

She blushed, a horrible scalding burn. "I cannot," she muttered through her teeth. "This dress laces up at the back. Maud always helps me in and out of it."

To her surprise, Edward seemed a little uncomfortable at the thought. He coughed awkwardly.

"Ah. Right." There was a moment's pause and then he added all in a rush, "Well, you'll just have to trust to my honour, I suppose."

He held out a hand for her, and she got tremulously to her feet.

"Turn around."

She turned to face the fire and was suddenly very aware of her own body. Aware of the whisper of his fingers on her skin as the laces slackened behind her, aware of his stilted breath whispering upon her neck. She closed her eyes and the firelight danced through her eyelids pinkly, playing across her face.

Edward coughed. "There. Will that do? Can you manage now?"

"Yes, I think so." Her voice sounded faint and strange, as if it did not belong to her anymore.

"Right. Good. I'll be outside. Holler if you need me."

She did not open her eyes until she heard the creak and click of the door behind her, and then she slipped out of the black dress and small clothes. They pooled damply on the floor by her feet. Shivering, she stepped into Ursula's gardening dress quickly. It was a shapeless wraith of a thing, with the merest hint of pleating around the hips and a row of neat buttons running up the collar. It was an almost perfect fit.

I have grown a little. Aunty Ursula was always an inch taller than me when she was alive.

She wished she had a mirror. When she was growing up, Charlotte had always thought that Aunty Ursula was a fairy-tale princess, with her golden ringlets and kind smiles. The yellow hair and diminutive stature were all the traits Charlotte shared with her aunt, but she wondered whether if she could but peer in a looking glass now, she might see something of the woman she missed staring back at her.

She clenched her fizzing fingertips together. They were going numb in the cold autumn weather. *I must pull myself together. I cannot let myself lose control now, for if I fall, there will be no one to catch me.*

She picked up the handfuls of sodden fabric by her feet and draped them over the chairs to dry, then fetched the old gardener's blouse and trousers from the cupboard. She paused as the cupboard's contents stared back at her. Ursula's Indian Shawl was folded neatly on the topmost shelf, as if Ursula herself had placed it there for safekeeping. Charlotte frowned. She reached up wondering fingers for it, and as it slipped off the shelf, a small purple ribbon tumbled to the floor, too.

This must be where the gardeners put the lost things they find in the estate, Charlotte thought, clutching the ribbon in one hand and the shawl in the other.

"Charlotte, are you doing all right in there?" Edward called anxiously through the wood, and she realised she had been distracted for far too long. She closed the door to the cupboard, shutting out her wistfulness with the dusty contents, and opened the door to the hut instead, handing the gardener's clothes to Edward with a small smile as she ushered him back into the warmth within.

"I am not the only one wet through," she told him. "You should get changed, too, Mr Cotterhugh."

He held up the blouse and grinned. "I will look like I am attending a masquerade, or like I stepped straight out of a Coleridge poem."

"Now is the time for practicality, not vanity," she told him sternly. "However could I explain to Albert that his precious son got pneumonia trying to save the penniless ward from drowning?"

"I wish you wouldn't do that. You are more than just a penniless ward. I wish you wouldn't constantly reduce yourself to your past or your bank balance."

Charlotte did not reply. She could not, for as he had been talking, as if unaware of what he was doing, Edward had stripped off the waistcoat and shirt he always wore, discarding them carelessly before the fireplace, and stood barechested in the glow.

She could not help but stare. She had never seen a man's bare chest before. She found her fizzing fingers reaching for it without her knowledge, hovering half an inch from his skin, the air between their flesh crackling with invisible lightning. His breath hitched slightly, and she closed her hand into a fist with a Herculean force of will. She looked up, and they stared at each other for half a moment, speechless.

Edward broke the silence first. "Forgive me. That was . . . I should have . . ." He coughed. "I suppose I ought to have given you some warning. I fear I do not have the manners I ought."

He pulled the blouse on over his head, and she frowned suddenly. As his arms were raised over his head, a puckered slash was exposed across his ribs, lingering beneath his arm, level with his heart.

Her fingers had fled to the scar before she even knew what she was doing. "What is that?"

He shook his head, removing her fingers with gentle force. "Do not ask me. I dare not tell you." He pulled the top down over his chest, hiding the mark from view.

The fire crackled between them, whispering of secrets and the past.

"I should go," he said at last, hoarsely. "You stay here. I will go up to the main house and send someone for the doctor, for you and Maud."

"I really do not need any fuss."

"Perhaps I like fussing over you. You should not be so independent and prideful all the time, Charlotte."

"Pride is all I have. Besides, I cannot take to bed today. I must deliver the flowers to dry in time for the All Hallow's Eve parade and kindling for the torches. I don't suppose you sophisticated city folk celebrate it that way," she added upon seeing the expression on his face, "but out here we parade with lit torches and foliage-crowns from the church around the village borders and back again. Everyone who can donates flowers and branches for the occasion, and the church has volunteers make up the necessary equipment." She had left the basket in the garden, she remembered abruptly. She had surely scattered its contents everywhere and trampled them all underfoot when she darted forwards to help Maud. She restrained a sigh. *I will probably have to start all over again now.* She did not know if there would be enough flowers left in Drymote to begin anew, and the thought left her feeling hopeless and weary. *There were always flowers enough in Uncle John's time . . .*

"It sounds a bit pagan for a holy occasion."

"The Queen celebrates it thusly," Charlotte said stiffly. "There's nothing wrong with a parade of light to drive the shadows away."

"No," he agreed. "We could all do with a bit of light in these dark times."

"Well then, you will see why I must deliver my basket down to the chapel for Mr Harris."

"I'm sure the *inestimable* Mr Harris will understand."

"What precisely is your problem with him, Edward? He is a good man."

"Oh yes, I'm sure he is. Much better than the rest of us poor sinners, as I'm sure he never misses an opportunity to remind everyone," he spat, striding about before the fire, leaving damp footprints in his wake.

"Come now, Edward, that is not fair. You do not know Mr Harris at all, if you truly think so. He lives out the doctrine *judge not lest ye be judged,* and his charity is earnest. He is not a man who holds religion skin deep, whatever else you think of him."

"Would you marry him then, if he asked? If Harris asked you to be his wife, would you accept him?" he asked abruptly.

She drew back a little, her face burning. "Edward! It is scarcely your place to ask me such a thing!"

"Ah, so you *will* accept if he proposes?"

"He has not proposed, so the point is irrelevant. Besides, I'd have thought you'd have been glad of the chance to be rid of the old maid cluttering up your estate."

He snorted. "If you are an old maid at twenty-one, I must have one foot in the grave at twenty-five." His look was shrewd as it raked over her. "You still have not answered."

"Honestly, Edward, why do I need to decide such hypotheticals now? It might be difficult to imagine, what with my exceedingly fair face, vast fortune and placid temper, but I have not had suitors lining out the door quarrelling for my hand. I cannot say what I would do if I was ever asked. In truth, I don't know what other options I have. I have no prospects, very little education, no way to earn my living. I have no great desire to marry Mr Harris, but I think him a good man, and if it was a choice between him or the work-house . . ."

"You cannot think I would ever let it come to that, Charlotte?" he asked, clearly appalled.

She did not say anything. She was sure he would never intentionally send her away, but if he married, she would have to leave. And, though the young bachelor liked to deny it now, the truth was he would eventually have to wed — and wed well — if Drymote was to be saved.

"He has not asked me," she said instead. "And I doubt he ever will, so let us not argue over it now. We have more than enough other things to squabble over, I am sure."

"The parade is not until All Hallow's Eve. The flowers can wait until tomorrow. I am sure not even the beloved Mr Harris would begrudge you one day to rest after your near drowning."

She sighed, but accepted the compromise stoically. "One day then, but tomorrow I will be back on my feet. I cannot rest forever. After all, Maud will not be granted any more respite than that. Why should I be?"

And what was Maud doing by the lake in the first place, she could not help but think to herself as Edward strode out of the door once more to go and fetch help.

CHAPTER SEVEN

Aunty Ursula visited Charlotte in her dreams that night, walking across the surface of the lake like a spectre in her old garden dress and Indian Lace shawl. When Charlotte reached out to touch her, she found it was nothing but her own reflection—and yet she was the one trapped beneath the glassy ripples, unable to break free. The moonlight streamed down like dancing rain, painting her silver and white, and Ursula—her own reflection, whomever it was—kept trying to say something, but Charlotte could not tell what. It was only as the word at last echoed distantly through the fog-shrouded trees, *Emily, Emily, Emily,* that Charlotte woke up panting and painted in sweat in her own bed.

The word lingered on her lips in the daylight now too. *Emily.* Her mother's name. She hardly dared wonder why the name of the disgraced, mad woman should find its way into her dreams now.

The dawn had begun to slip through the curtains and she found she could not be chained to her own bed any longer. She rose and washed hurriedly in the ewer, trying to shake the last of the nightmare away.

She choked down her morning's bitter pill and looked at her own reflection in the mirror. It stared back at her, haunting and weary, like a stranger's.

Is this what happened to my mother? Is this the first slippery slope? Does it begin with not recognising yourself, and end with not recognising anyone else about you either?

She could not answer. She did not know. She touched the

85

cold kiss of the glass with numb fingers, as if she might fall through it completely. The stranger stared back at her and kept her secrets.

Secrets, secrets . . . there are too many secrets at Drymote these days.

"And you are not the only one who keeps them, Charlotte," she murmured to herself aloud, recalling that scar nestled underneath Edward's arm. *Why will he not tell me how he got it? He has been lying to me. He lied to me the night of the bonfire, too. He lied to me the very first time we met.*

"Perhaps he does not want to remember the truth," she said aloud. "Perhaps he is trying to escape it." Did she not know well enough how that felt? Would she not run away from the painful truth of her circumstances if she only could?

"Who are you talking to, Miss Mayweather?"

Charlotte flinched with a little yelp and saw Maud lingering behind her in the reflection. Her eyes and hair were darker than usual, it seemed, as if she were still wet from her near drowning. Charlotte almost expected to see a puddle appearing by the maid's feet, the lake-weeds clinging like spectral chains to her ankles — but no, Maud was standing prim and proper as ever, a look of quiet, bemused scorn hiding beneath the dignified expectancy. Charlotte had not seen her come in.

"I — no-one — that is — only myself."

"First sign of madness, so they say."

"Uncle John used to say it was the only way to get any sense," Charlotte said with a forced laugh. It sounded shrill and unnatural in the morning light.

Maud stepped forwards and took the hairbrush from the dresser. Charlotte snatched it off her and held it up to the light. There, amongst the strands of gold was a tangle of whisper thin black hairs — as if Edward's presence in her thoughts had somehow seeped out of her mind and tangled itself on her hairbrush bristles instead.

Maud took it off her, apparently not noticing the smoke-smudge of black there—was it even real? Another residue from Charlotte's nightmares?—and pulled it through the night-tangles of Charlotte's hair instead, curling them up in place upon her head and weaving them through with a ribbon. She looked as grim and tired as Charlotte felt, and perhaps it was not surprising.

"How are you feeling this morning, Maud?" she asked as kindly as she could. "If you would prefer time to recover, I can finish preparing myself for the day."

Maud regarded her darkly, as if trying to discover whether she was being mocked or not.

"I know my place, Miss Mayweather," she said stiffly.

"I was not trying to insinuate anything to the contrary, but everyone needs a little kindness now and again, do they not?" She tried to force her warmest smile on her face, but it was an effort when it was so coldly received.

Maud ignored these overtures of cordiality and finished pinning the ribbon in place. She gestured Charlotte to stand, so that she could help her into her mourning dress and tie the laces properly.

Charlotte burned at the memory of Edward's hands there, unlacing them just yesterday, far more tenderly and hesitantly than Maud did. *Am I a fallen woman now? Is it really a sin?*

Charlotte shuddered, her eyes closed. She knew all too well what Ursula would have said. *Do not end up like Emily, child. Do not end up like your mother. First disgrace, then the madhouse, then death. It is a bitter path for you, Charlotte, do not make me watch you tread it.*

Well, Charlotte consoled herself silently, whatever else happened now, Aunty Ursula would not have to watch her disgrace. She had fled where infamy and pain could grieve her no longer, and Charlotte was left out here alone, with nothing but a tattered old mourning dress for comfort.

She stroked the pleats of her skirts silently as she thought about such things. It had been a fine dress once. Fitted and pleated, neat fabric buttons at the wrists. It was a shame it was so shabby now. The mirror she stared into agreed with her solemnly.

Charlotte had been eighteen when Aunty Ursula had died. She had cried for an hour straight when she had first tried the mourning dress on, just because she could not shake the thought that it was exactly the sort of dress Aunty Ursula would have chosen. She always did have a tasteful eye that Uncle John sadly lacked.

She would be ashamed to see how far I have fallen now, and how disgraceful my attire is. My shabby appearance surely brings shame upon the whole of Drymote.

"How ever did you end up in the lake in the first place?" Charlotte said loudly, trying to drown out the fickle thoughts stalking through her mind.

Maud hesitated at the abrupt question and then shrugged.

"I was walking by the shore when I slipped on the pebbles and fell in. It was an accident, nothing more."

"Well, I have had enough of those in my time. I twisted my ankle so badly last time I fell that I had to *crawl* upon my hands and knees to find shelter, which was especially humiliating, as Mr Cotterhugh caught me at it," Charlotte confided with a smile. Maud did not smile back. She did not even seem to notice this small attempt at friendship. She just bobbed a silent curtsey and swept away.

Why can I not make her like me? Charlotte sighed long and deep. *Perhaps the better question would be why am I so desperate that she should?*

Besides, she had enough things to do without constantly worrying about Maud's regard. For one thing, she had to go and find a whole new basket of flowers before she could take it down to the church this afternoon.

But when she made her way down to the front door, she found Edward already waiting for her, flush-cheeked from the cold, her basket swinging idly from his hand. His face lit up as he saw her.

"There you are! I did not like to rouse you this morning. I thought perhaps you needed the sleep after your misadventures yesterday, but I confess, patience has never been one of my strongest suits. Here." He handed her the basket, and to her surprise, she found it full of blooms. She stared at him and he shrugged. "I knew that you would go traipsing all over the garden doing yourself no end of mischief if I did not do it first." He grinned. "Shall I accompany you to deliver them, or would you prefer to see your beau alone?"

"Mr Harris is not my beau," she retorted automatically. "Thank you, Edward, this was very kind indeed. You must have been up at dawn to have picked them all by now."

"Ah well, I have my uses. I fear I have never really been one for lazy lie-ins anyway, only do not tell anyone. It quite ruins my reputation as an idle layabout."

She could not help but laugh.

"May I?"

He offered her his arm and she gladly accepted it.

The hillside was steep and slippery with the last vestiges of dew, and Charlotte had to cling to Edward tightly so as not to lose her footing once more. She could not deny the little thrill that shot through her as her hand rested nestled on his arm, a claiming she did not want to shake.

Would this not be perfect? Spending all the rest of my days walking arm in arm with Edward around the estate?

She shook the thought off hard before it could take root. She knew it would only wound her later if she let it settle there in her mind. You cannot worry about the future, Charlotte, she reminded herself. Edward will not always be yours. You must just enjoy him whilst you can.

She looked up at him, taking in the loose curls of his dark hair, shining like ink in the sunlight, the way his eyes crinkled as he laughed, that little arrogant toss of the head he did whenever he was getting too defensive, hiding underneath his lightning fast, sardonic wit.

I must memorise him and fold these moments away in lavender for when I am an old, lonely maid.

Edward froze suddenly, as if he had heard her thoughts. His body stiffened underneath her hand, his head turning to glance through the hedges and bushes they slowly paraded past as if he were a deer out on the fields. He dropped his arm, releasing her hand, his body slipping into a wary, defensive pose, and she felt a jolt of alarm spiking through her.

"Stay here." His voice was a curt command, and it sent a thrill of fear down her spine.

"What is it, Edward?"

"Nothing that need concern you, Charlotte. I will deal with it. Stay here for a moment more and rest your ankle a while."

He threw her a lightning-fast grin, but it sat falsely on his mouth.

He is anxious, she thought.

He darted off beyond the hedge, hunting some prey she could not see.

The world grew quiet around her. Birds sang their choruses in the leaf-emptied branches, seeking desperately for bugs and berries in the chilly autumn days. The basket tapped idly against her leg and she waited impatiently.

Footsteps sounded behind her.

"At last," she said, turning around, but it was not Edward standing there. It was a stranger.

She took a step back, afraid, though she could not say why. "I'm sorry, sir, but this is private property."

The stranger lunged forwards, gripping her hard, his hands digging into her skin, glaring wildly around.

"He did it on purpose, you know. I know he told you it was an accident, but it was a lie. Do not let him fool you. He will turn on you, too." He had a thick Italian accent, and she frowned at him, trying to place where she had heard it before, and then the memory came flooding back in. This was the same intruder from the night of the ball . . .

"I don't know what you're talking about," she said, her voice unusually shrill. "Take your hands off me. You're hurting me!" She tried to wrestle her way free, but the man would not release her.

"You cannot stay with him. You are condoning his actions. If you pretend they do not matter, then you are every bit as bad as he is."

Edward appeared out of nowhere, charging in from the left and grasping the stranger's arm hard.

"Don't touch her!" Edward roared, pulling him off her by force. The men wrestled angrily, neither able to grab the upper hand, and Charlotte heard herself shrieking.

"Or what?" The man swore. "You'll do to me what you did to Giuliani?"

Edward's fist connected with the stranger's face in a sickening thud, sending him sprawling to the ground.

"Edward!" Charlotte yelled, holding him back before he could lay another blow on the impudent stranger. Edward whirled around in panic, his eyes wide.

"Please, Charlotte, I need you to go. I need one person upon this whole wretched earth to still think me good." His fingers clutched hard into her arms, leaving marks even through the fabric of her dress.

"What about what Giuliani needed?" The man was rubbing his face, where a bruise was already beginning to blossom. "Tell her, Cotterhugh. Tell her the truth. Tell her what you *are*."

"Why must you plague me, Marcello? You know you cannot kill me. You tried the night of the bonfire, and found you could not steel your nerve to do it."

The man—Marcello—was back on his feet, shaking with

rage.

"There must be revenge. There must be atonement — payment for your sins, and whilst there is still breath in my body, I will dedicate my life to ruining yours, and only when you have lost everything and are desolate and alone, will I be satisfied. Why should you be the great and beloved heir of Drymote, when you are nothing but a murderer?"

The word resounded through the silence, and Edward shuddered under the weight of it. When his eyes shone into Charlotte's, they were wild with pain and panic, burning with all the fire of hell itself. His words were whispers, desperate and pleading, as his hands once more clutched hers.

"Edward?"

"All that Marcello says is true, Charlotte. I shot my dearest, my oldest and truest friend. I have killed a man. I am a murderer."

Charlotte could only stare at him, her mind racing. She pulled herself out of his arms, and Marcello laughed triumphantly.

"There, you have taken your revenge, now leave," Edward snapped at him.

"Oh, my revenge is only just starting," Marcello promised darkly. "Every time you find a glimmer of happiness in your life, I will be there to snuff it out once more. I will never rest until my brother's murder is avenged," he added bitterly, almost to himself. Edward swore at him, but Charlotte scarcely heard.

The world seemed to swim around her, hazy and unreal. A thousand possibilities threw themselves up before her mind, and she tried to picture Edward shooting someone in cold-blood, the pistol smoking in his hand, but the image would not fit. It was not Edward. Even now, the confession fresh from his own lips, she could not believe it.

She turned to see him standing there alone in the clearing,

staring at her hopelessly.

"Tell me what happened," she said quietly. "Was it an accident? A crime of passion? Self-defence? There must be some reason. Tell me the whole of it."

"It was a duel." His voice was leaden and dull. "Such things are illegal now, I know, but they are always winked at by gentlemen of a certain disposition, and the law rarely pursues them. The challenge was not mine, but I had too much pride not to accept it. I was outraged at the time, for I thought I was the one who had been ill-treated. Now, I see how wrong I had been. He was right to be hurt so cruelly. I owed him an apology, and instead I gave him death."

She stared at him. He ran a hand through his hair and continued, the words jolting free from him in fits and bursts, stiff and uncertain after their long constraint.

"I was young, foolish, still in college, hot-headed but invincible, so I thought." He struggled to pin the words together. They came out halting and stilted, every one of them gilded in the oily sheen of self-loathing. He sighed long and deep. "Her name was Theodora," he said. "Our little Dora. And she was . . ." He sighed again. His lip twitched upwards in a derisive smile, scorning himself for his own naivety, the past self he could not hope to save. "She was beautiful. Hair of fire and a temper to match. Pale and lustrous skin, freckled in the sun, eyes more emerald than any I'd ever seen. I had never wanted anyone more than I wanted her, perhaps because she showed little inclination to me at all. Without too much arrogance, that was something I was little accustomed to, even in my youth."

Charlotte did not hesitate to believe him. She was sure that even five or six years ago, fresh from his plump-faced teen-aged years, his handsome looks had been beginning to bloom, and his confident swagger would be coming into its own. She had no doubt at all that he had always been used to the attention of the world, particularly the feminine half of it.

Edward ran his hand through his hair, dishevelling it. "Giuliani, my dearest friend, also fell under her spell. It was hardly surprising that he should do so. There was something . . . captivating about her. We studied together at Cambridge, Giuliani and I, though, in truth, there was very little studying about it. We far preferred drinking, wagering, society balls, hunting—all the entertainments fit for brash young gentleman such as we, more inclined to pleasure than profitable pursuits." His voice was dark and bitter. He rubbed a hand over his face as if he could wipe away all traces of the past.

"We spent our summer taking a tour of Giuliani's homeland, that is where I met his younger brother, Marcello." He gestured vaguely to the direction the man had disappeared into once more. "My father warned me not to make any entanglements whilst we were away. he feared I would fall for some enchanting Italian seductress and be whisked away in a whirlwind elopement, but it was here, in the quiet greens of England, that I found my doom.

"I had agreed to pay a visit to Uncle John before term restarted, and I was bringing Giuliani with me, but on our journey, we found Dora. I fear I did not make it here that summer, or, indeed, any summer after. Only a few villages out, we met our fate."

He sighed again, long and deep, and Charlotte felt her heart yearning intensely for him. She held out a helpless hand to him, and he took it gratefully.

"I cannot recall how long we lingered there," he said. "We missed the start of term, I remember that. My father was growing anxious about me. The college fees were large, he said, but necessary for my advancement, and I was squandering my opportunities. He was right. I squandered all my opportunities, then and now. I could not pry myself away, though, and neither could Giuliani. We walked and talked and laughed and drank, the three of us together, every day, it seemed. The world was a little less bright when she was not in it—duller, grimmer, weighed down with boredom heavy in my hands."

He stared down at those hands now, as if he could still see the blood staining them.

"I tried to kiss her one autumn night. It was not so different from now, changeable weather, the nights drawing in. She rejected my advances. Told me her heart was already given to someone else—that she, she and Giuliani—" He choked off the end of that sentence. He shook his head grimly. "I was hurt. Angry. I thought I loved her well, but perhaps it was just my pride talking. I took myself back off to college alone. I grew bitter and took to drinking far too much. They threatened to have me sent down if I did not make amends, so I left. My father was in a fury, but there was little he could do. When Giuliani heard of my depression, he came to find me. He wished to make friends, he said. He could not help loving her, he said." Edward closed his eyes, bitter self-loathing on his face.

"I was spiteful," he whispered. "I was in pain and I wished to hurt him as I was hurting. So I—heaven forgive me, I told him that Theodora came willingly and often to my bed. I told him that she had played him false, that she had played us both false, and that it was because I had discovered it that I left. It was a lie, of course, but he believed it." Edward laughed bitterly. "He said he knew that she was too good for him, he had never truly believed she could have loved someone like him, he had always wondered why she had not preferred me. He challenged me to a duel, and I was so reckless and self-destructive that I gladly accepted. I thought it no longer mattered whether I killed him or he killed me, just so long as the pain ended one way or the other. I was wrong."

He could not meet Charlotte's gaze. She could not look

away. The silence spanned between them painful and close.

"He was an expert duellist," he said at last, the words all too loud in the silence, though he barely more than whispered them. "He was famed for such things in college." He gave a wry smile, tilting up at the lips. "They had a lot to say about the hot temper of Italians and the passions of the continent. It gave him quite a reputation, and I used to admire him for it at the time."

Distantly, Charlotte recalled those rumours which swirled around Edward irresistibly. *The famous duellist. The famous lover.* They were all true then—she had not really credited them before now.

Edward shrugged bitterly. "Giuliani used to boast that he was undefeated. He had come out victorious in seven duels before now, but it only takes one time, does it not? His shot hit me here, beside my heart, but it was off to the side and only grazed me, drawing blood but not enough to kill. I can never decide in the long watches of the night whether he missed on purpose, or whether he was aiming to kill. It does not matter either way. He died, and I did not.

"I did not mean to kill him" he added hoarsely. "Even in my anger, even as I cocked my pistol and took aim, I did not mean to kill him, I swear it. I only aimed for his leg, a shot I thought he could survive. I think I knew, even then, that I was the one in the wrong."

"Your shot hit too high?"

"No," he said bitterly, "No, it hit true. But I was a poor student of anatomy in my youth. I did not realise there was such a large artery in the thigh. I thought if I avoided the torso or the head, it would not be a fatal shot, but I was wrong. He bled out there in the park at dawn as I tried in vain to stop the bleeding, wearing his blood upon me like Cain's mark as our seconds ran for a doctor. He was dead before the doctor arrived. They told me to go—to flee—but I could not. I stayed until the law arrived and I went with them willingly. My father was furious at it, he said that I had irrevocably ruined the reputation of our name." He laughed bitterly. "I did not, Charlotte, for no one cared. Giuliani was only a foreigner in our midst, and it was an *honourable* fight. I confessed it all, but they acquitted me. I was fined — as if money could make up for such a crime – for causing an affray in a public place, but on the charges of manslaughter I was acquitted. If Giuliani had been an Englishman, it would not have gone so," he added bitterly. "Do you know the funny thing? It is an open secret, and no one seems to think less of me for it, save Marcello and myself. It is the mark of a man to defend one's honour, it seems, even if it means taking another's life. They expect me to boast of it, to wear it with pride, and I cannot Charlotte, I cannot. It haunts me still. *He* haunts me still."

Charlotte felt her blood run cold, and she could no longer deny it, however much she wished to. There was the chill of truth about his words, stark and honest. *He has killed a man. A man is dead because of him.*

"Marcello is right to swear revenge upon me, but he does not know how to take it, and it burns him up inside. He came to the ball that night to denounce me publicly, to try to stop me from gaining a position in parliament, but little does he know I have no desire to go to parliament at all. Then, the night of the bonfire, he followed us down to the churchyard and challenged me to a duel, but I would not take aim. I will never shoot a pistol again. He pointed it in my face, but found he could not kill me in cold blood, for he is a better man than I, it seems. We grappled a little and the gun went off, and then he was gone into the night and I thought, I hoped, perhaps his honour might be satisfied now — but now he has come back and he is threatening you instead. I do not know what I can do, Charlotte. I cannot call the law on him, for he has a right to be angry, a right to want justice, and yet I cannot let him threaten and hurt all the people I care about, either. I have brought this ruination down upon us by my own hand, and I cannot escape it now."

He grabbed her, swinging wildly from desperation to desperation, and before she knew what had happened, his mouth was upon hers, desperate and urgent, a wound more than kiss.

"Absolve me," he pleaded huskily against her lips, his breath sweet against her own. "Give me absolution, and I will be free at last. Kiss me, tell me that you can love me, that you see something in me worthy of your love, and teach me to believe it. Please, Charlotte, please."

She tore herself out of his arms, and he did not try to restrain her. He only watched as she grabbed at the basket and stumbled back down the path alone.

It was just a mistake, she told herself desperately. An accident. A duel—a fair fight. Both men knew what they were getting in to. His honour was at stake. But he had blood on his hands, there was no denying that. He knew it, too, that was clear enough.

She fled, though she scarcely knew where she was fleeing to, the knowledge haunting her footsteps, prowling like a lion, snarling at her heels. The world seemed to crowd in around her, as if the gnarled twigs were fingers clutching for her, as if the shadows lurking amongst the undergrowth were watching her, as if the world was full of eyes—all seeing her thoughts, all seeing her sins, chasing and ready to devour her, for daring to love him—for still loving him—for wanting to exonerate him even now.

CHAPTER EIGHT

She scarcely realised her feet had taken her down to the little stone chapel until she reached there. The world was silent around her, and every footstep she took seemed to echo with Edward's confession. It was unaccountably warm for an autumn day, the fog of yesterday burnt away in the bright sunlight which painted the underside of the leaves golden and ruby and glinted off the tops of the marble gravestones sprouting through the long grass of the graveyard. Somewhere here was a fresh gravestone, newly engraved, sitting next to his wife's, but she had not had the heart to visit it since the day of the burial. She found her uncle's memory more keenly within the over-spilling acres of his estate than she did in a lump of cold granite.

"Did you know?" she whispered to her uncle. "You must have done. It would have been in the papers. Why did you not tell me? Why did you keep it a secret?"

The silent world did not reply.

How could I have been so naïve? How could I have been so innocent?

She did not have an answer for herself either.

She pushed the unlocked church doors open and took herself inside.

Her footsteps echoed down the main aisle, up towards the stained-glass windows at the back of the church, sending little patches of jewel-light across the floor.

Miss Bletchley, who had been sitting quietly in her family pew talking to Mr Harris, leapt up, her skin scalding as

Charlotte approached.

"Miss Mayweather! I did not hear you come in! We were just talking about the parade preparations."

"Yes, excuse me, I must go and update Vicar Herrington. Forgive me, Miss Mayweather. Farewell, Miss Bletchley." Mr Harris cast a lingering look in Miss Bletchley's direction, bowed to both of them and then fled.

"I did not mean to oust the good curate from the chapel. The door was open," Charlotte said distantly, putting her basket down upon the floor. "Forgive me if I interrupted your discussion. I suppose a chapel is not really the place for privacy. People are always wandering in and out, are they not?"

Miss Bletchley let out an unusually bitter laugh. "There is nowhere for privacy these days, it seems. Langhorne is always overrun with servants and visitors, the woods are full of wanderers, and even here, in church, one cannot get a moment of peace."

"My uncle always went to Ursula's Abbey for peace," Charlotte said in that same distant, foggy voice. "It was the only reason he built that folly, I think, so that he could have somewhere to be alone with his thoughts. He always said there was nowhere like it for keeping the secrets of your heart. Even now, hardly anyone goes down there. It reminds me too painfully of him . . ." To her horror, she found her cheeks were wet. As she raised fizzing fingertips up towards them, she found that tears were running unchecked from her eyes. She swallowed and wiped them fiercely away, trying to pull herself back from the chasm which threatened to swallow her. "Forgive me. I still miss him."

Miss Bletchley breathed out a smile.

"That is natural. Lord John Cotterhugh was as a father to you, and he has passed so recently. It would be strange of you not to feel grieved."

"I feel so alone without him. He never left me feeling

unwanted. He never made me feel like the future was shifting and uncertain beneath my feet. Everything is so foggy and frightening without him, I have no one left to provide for me. No one left who would wish to," she whispered, and then pressed her lips hard together, to stop anything else escaping. Her fingers were tingling with pins and needles, and she shook them back to life. She forced an unconvincing laugh. "I did not mean to say so," she said. "Forgive me, Miss Bletchley, I did not want to push my burdens on to you."

Miss Bletchley's hands were soft and kind as they lingered upon Charlotte's forearm.

"You are not alone. You are not unwanted. You will not be abandoned, friendless, left to the helplessness of the fates. We are in a holy place, are we not? Trust in providence, if nothing else. You have people who love you yet, Miss Mayweather."

"Charlotte, please," whispered Charlotte, still wiping away the streaming tears. She desperately needed to hear her Christian name upon some friendly lips right now.

"Georgiana," confided Miss Bletchley, leaning in towards Charlotte with a small smile.

"I am not usually so emotional, I promise."

"I well believe it." Georgiana grinned. "That is not the reputation you have garnered in Birchton."

Charlotte smiled ruefully back, remembering what Edward had said the night of the ball. It had never occurred to her before that the world might see her as aloof and standoffish. She had thought they had walked away from her. It never once occurred to her that she might have wrought her own isolation . . .

Georgiana is a good woman, she thought. A beautiful, rich, kind, good woman. The sort of woman Drymote needs. The sort of woman Edward needs.

"I hope you do not think I am impugning Edward's reputation," she said. "I was not meaning to imply that he would act wrongly by me. Both he and Albert have been more than dutiful in their treatment of me. He is a good man."

Georgiana just laughed, her voice bright, almost holy, as it blessed the air. "Put your mind at ease, my dear. I had no intention of spreading slander about Mr Cotterhugh."

Charlotte felt herself blushing, "I was not implying that. Truly, I never believed you to be the gossiping type. Only I did not want there to be any lingering impediments in your mind, if there were any questions, any stumbling blocks hovering over a marriage with Edward . . ."

"Oh!" Georgiana declared with genuine impatience, her anger blossoming up out of nowhere with all the force of an erupting geyser, driving that compassionate smile away.

Charlotte could only stare at her. She had never seen the amiable Miss Bletchley lose her temper before.

She all but stamped her foot beneath the voluminous pleats of her skirts. "I am so wearied of our names being coupled together like this. I had thought that you of all people might spare me the match-making, Charlotte."

Charlotte felt the blush burn deeper. *You of all people?* What was that supposed to mean? Georgiana seemed scarcely to notice or care about the effect she was having on Charlotte.

"Whenever a new man comes into the neighbourhood, it is always the same—here is someone we can couple up with Miss Bletchley, here is someone Georgiana might like to wed. Well, perhaps Miss Bletchley would like to decide for herself! Perhaps Georgiana looks for more than a pleasing countenance and a bulging pocketbook!"

"I meant no offence, Georgiana," murmured Charlotte meekly and Georgiana sniffed.

"No. Well. Apology accepted, I suppose, but you will do me the good turn never to mention such things again. If you think him such a good catch, Charlotte, you may do me the favour of marrying him yourself and taking him off the market. Then I will no longer be tormented by these constant, inane insinuations!"

Charlotte stared at her and could not help but laugh. She had been so torn trying to persuade Edward into marrying Georgiana, it had never once occurred to her that Georgiana might not wish to marry Edward either . . .

"Forgive me," she said again. "No one ever couples my name with anybody else's. I can only imagine how wearisome that must be."

Georgiana sniffed, but seemed a little mollified. "Of course I will forgive you. How could I do anything less in a place like this?"

Charlotte looked around at the empty chapel, too. The pews stared dustily back at her, tinged by the stained glass above them, the arches on the ceilings clinging onto their cobwebs.

"Do you believe there can be forgiveness for all sins?" she asked those echoing, vaulted ceilings. Blood on his hands, and yet those hands were full-burdened by the weight of it. Surely that should count for something? "If someone truly regrets the pain they cause, there must be forgiveness, must there not?"

She looked over at Georgiana, desperate to be assured, desperate to be comforted. Georgiana opened her mouth, hesitated, and then shut it again.

"I am no theologian," she said. "You would have to ask Mr Harris." She glanced over at the altar before them and she sighed long and deep. "The better question is what happens if you cannot regret it," she murmured, and Charlotte was not entirely sure the words were meant for her at all.

The world still smelt like ash and smoke, though it must have been a week or more since the night of the bonfire. She walked back up to Drymote alone, the distant roofs of the great estate peeking up at her from the hillside.

Edward was not waiting for her in the gardens, nor could she find him about the house. Perhaps it was as well, for she did not know what she could say to him if she did find him.

He was late to dine that evening, and it was only as he came stumbling in, shrouded in the heavy stench of ale, that Charlotte realised how he had been entertaining his long and lonely hours that day. She shot a glance over at the irritable Albert, presiding over the head of the table dourly.

"You are late, Edward. *Again.*"

Edward took in the table, the dinner cooling rapidly upon their plates, the abandoned napkins scrunched upon the table like fallen roses.

"Well, now, is this not a sight? Are you not waiting for me to dine today? You, who are always lecturing me upon my social graces? Is that not an irony?"

He leant against the doorframe, laughing heavily. Charlotte looked away. She could barely stand to see him like this, his clothes loose and dishevelled, his hair messy, his eyes blood-shot and blurry. The scent of strong cider clung to him and she could only wonder how many pints of it he had downed in the public house down at Birchton.

"Perhaps we would have waited for you if we had known you were coming. Is it too much to require a little notice from you? You could have died, and we would not have known of it. How will you manage such things when you are the head of Drymote? You cannot come and go as you please without giving your servants notice. You must learn a little more reliability if you are to become a gentleman of honour."

Edward laughed again, wild and manic.

"A gentleman of honour — yes, yes. We all know that it is punctuality to the dinner table which defines honour in a man. Well, if it pleases you, I will do better with my time-keeping. Tardiness is the only unforgivable sin, is it not, Miss

Mayweather?" He laughed again.

Charlotte could not help shrinking back from him, a little frightened by his bitter tone and reckless self-loathing.

"At least I have always been *reliably* unreliable."

Albert just pursed his lips. "We have port, whisky and wine enough in the cellars here at Drymote. The next time you wish to make a fool of yourself, at least do it in the privacy of your own home and try not to let the world abroad know how disreputable you are."

"Maybe they should know. Maybe everybody should know."

"Go to bed, Edward, and do not bother coming down until you are in your right mind once more."

Edward held his hands out wide, laughing up to the ceilings.

"Am I child to be sent to bed so? Tell me, will you take away my supper next? Set me to writing lines in the schoolroom?"

Albert slammed his hands down upon the dining room table, sending cutlery clattering.

Charlotte stared at him in horror. It was very unlike him to lose his temper towards his only son and heir. Albert had gone very red about the face, and Charlotte feared a physical fight might break lose there in the dining hall. She hurried up, her hands resting lightly upon Edward's chest, standing between the two men. She looked at Edward earnestly, trying to secure his gaze upon her instead. He was having trouble meeting her gaze, and she could not tell how much of it was the liquor and how much of it was the shame.

"No one is ordering you to do anything," she said quietly. "Only we care deeply for your well-being. You will feel better for finding your bed, and that is all we want for you, to be well and happy and safe."

Edward reached up and curled a loose strand of

Charlotte's hair around his forefinger. It twined around the digit like a ring, and she felt her eyes shuddering closed at the surprisingly gentle and intimate touch.

"Are you my conscience, woman?" he whispered.

"No, but I hope to be your common sense. Do as you have been bidden. Please, Edward."

He stared at her for a moment longer, then sighed deeply. "As you wish, mademoiselle," he said sarcastically, detaching himself from her grip and bowing low. He almost stumbled and fell as he overbalanced himself, but he held tightly on to her instead, resting his weight upon her, his arm upon her shoulders, her hands lingering upon his chest. She thought for one breathless moment he might kiss her again, as her face was upturned from his, mere inches away — and she could not tell if she wished for it or not — but he merely righted himself and pushed himself out of the room once more. She watched him stumble away helplessly and turned to see Albert facing her with a furious expression on his face.

"So you are the only one he listens to now, are you?" Albert spat out. His hand was shaking, and Charlotte could not tell if it was his anger or his sickness making it convulse.

Tread lightly with him, she advised herself, even as she felt her temper flare. He is sick, and he has been worried for his son. Besides, if you push him too far, he will oust you from his house entirely, and you will be penniless, desolate and homeless.

She clasped her hands tightly before her, as if she could squeeze her temper out that way, trying to ensure she kept her calm.

"I hope he will always listen to sense," she said, keeping her voice as flat and emotionless as possible, "no matter whose mouth it comes from."

Albert wobbled upon his feet, his balance unsteady, and she took a few steps forwards to help him, too, but he warded her off with a scabby, sore-covered hand. His ailments were growing worse — it would not be long before he fell into the last stages completely. No wonder he was bitter, and no wonder he worried so bitterly for Edward.

"Do not forget our bargain, Miss Mayweather," he growled at her, his eyes narrowing as he glared in her direction. "My munificence supplies the vitamins which keep you standing upon your own two feet, and my justice can withhold them just as easily."

She felt herself flushing, and every good intention she had been schooling herself in fled her mind.

"My ankle feels much better now," she said stiffly. "Perhaps I no longer need your charity after all."

He threw his hands up with a scornful exhalation. "You and Edward are one of a pair. Neither of you see long term consequences for your folly." The words *I am not the one with syphilis* were just arranging themselves upon her tongue, but she bit them back hastily as Albert continued his rant. "Fine! You wish to discontinue the vitamins, which are the only thing which stands between you perpetual lameness, I will not stand in your way. If you are so stubborn and hot-headed that you would throw my charity back into my face for spite because you feel better upon the very medications that are saving you, I cannot force you to do otherwise, but when you have tasted the bitterness of this decision, do not cry to me." He barged past her, stumbling almost as much as his son, though he had not taken a drop of drink.

She sat herself back down at the table alone, for she did not know what else to do. The food was tasteless in her mouth and she chewed it on compunction. The silence beat against her eardrums, like a wall closing in within her own brain. When she could bear it no longer, she rose and fled the empty room, which was echoing spitefully at her.

She made a quick detour to the kitchens to fetch a tonic and some bread. The staff all stopped talking when she walked in, getting to their feet and bobbing in respectful curtseys. They fetched what she required with a quick and respectful efficiency, but she almost thought she saw Maud exchanging a meaningful look with her neighbour, and the thought plagued her all the way up the long, winding stairs to the upper floors. *Heaven alone knows what they had been whispering when I went in. Heaven alone knows what they will be whispering now I have left.* She shook her head, trying to clear it of such nebulous fears and lingering discontentment, Edward's words echoing in her ears. *You always care too much for other people's opinions . . .*

She took a deep breath, steeling her nerve as she lingered outside his door. *Is my reputation not already shredded enough?* And yet, he was not as unfeeling as he made himself out to be, she knew that now for certain. He was desperately unhappy, and he needed someone to care for him. She had to be that person, even if she would gain no reward for it. Even if he did not love her and could not marry her, she must tend to him if she could.

She knocked and waited. He did not answer. Perhaps he was asleep? It would be best for him if he were. A rest could only do him good right now.

She slipped the door open silently and crept her way inside. She stopped dead in the threshold as she saw Edward sitting up in bed, propped up upon a nest of plumped pillows, covered by an intricately embroidered coverlet. He looked the very image of decadence and utterly, utterly miserable.

She felt herself blushing.

"Oh, I—forgive me. I thought you were asleep."

He smiled sardonically at her, his grey, wan face wearing a bitter expression. "Tell me, Miss Mayweather, do you often make a habit of slipping into men's bedchambers whilst they sleep?"

His words were less slurred now, though they were still

weighed down with weariness, and she suspected the worst of the drink was starting to make its way out of his system.

She flushed, but held her swelling temper. *He is only trying to chase me away.*

"I have brought you a drink and some bread," she said quietly, holding up the cup and plate in her hand. "I thought to leave it by your bedside table."

She closed the door behind her and took a few steps forwards. He did not say anything more, just watched her approach. She did not know why she felt so nervous, but she was suddenly keenly aware of her own body, lingering there in the confines of his bedchambers, alone and un-chaperoned. Those few steps between the door and the bed seemed many miles, and he watched her walk all of them silently. He did not ask her to leave.

She sank herself down into the rickety wooden chair beside the bed and pushed the cup into his hand, placing the plate upon the side-table.

"Drink it," she said quietly. "It will make you feel less nauseous."

"A hair of the dog that bit me would make me even better," he said, but he accepted the cup.

"You cannot run away from things all the time, and you cannot drown the truth."

"The truth? That you hate me? That you deserve to. That everyone deserves to."

"That sounds more like self-pity than genuine sorrow," she told him sternly. "You made a horrible mistake with terrible consequences. You can try to run from it for the rest of your life, or you can try to atone for it."

"A life for a life," he slurred contemptuously. "Only who would want my life in payment? I am worth nothing." He took a deep swig from the cup and grimaced. He slumped against the pillows once more, grey-faced and wan, and Charlotte darted forwards to catch the cup before it slipped, and their fingers brushed together. He threaded his fingers through hers, catching at her hand and trapping it against his chest. She could feel his heartbeat pounding beneath her fingertips, or perhaps that was merely her own pulse betraying her. She licked her lips and retracted her hand softly from his.

"This is not seemly, Edward. I must go."

His eyes flickered unsteadily in the candlelight. "Must you?" His voice was bitter. "Or is it that you wish to, now you know what sort of man I am."

"I do not think you a worse man than I did yesterday, but neither do I think that you try hard to be a good man. You make your choices anew every day. Let this be the day that you live to the potential you have, and not the past you had. Or tomorrow rather," she added smiling. "I will confess the hour is late today."

His hand snatched at hers again and held it tight. "Stay," he whispered. "I will not debauch you. I will not degrade or dishonour you, I swear it upon my eternal soul if I can still claim to have such a thing. Only stay. I would not be alone tonight."

Is this how my mother fell? Not in a flurry of lust and passion, but in a moment of pity? Charlotte stared at Edward hopelessly. His gaze, desperate, miserable, pleading, did not flinch from hers.

"The servants will talk," she whispered. They were already talking, whispering together down in the kitchens, full of idle speculations and wrong assumptions.

He did not argue. He did not even try to persuade her. He just looked at her with those dark, midnight blue eyes, and she felt her resolve slipping.

She sighed. "I will stay a little longer," she whispered, feeling as if she were damning her own soul, the whisper of the executioner's blade cold against the back of her neck. "I will stay until you fall asleep."

She settled herself upon the covers beside him and stared

up at the underside of the canopy.

"He was my friend," Edward muttered abruptly into the darkness. "I wronged him, and then I killed him for it, and he was my friend."

She did not know what to say to this. There were no words out there to absolve his guilty conscience. She lay down beside him, and he wrapped an arm around her shoulders. She stiffened slightly for a moment at the quiet, intimate touch, but it felt good.

Can this truly be wrong? Is it really a sin to find peace and to give it, to taste comfort in the only man who offers it to me freely and expects so little in return?

She found no answer, for she did not know. All she knew for certain was that the world quieted a little when she was with him, and she craved that now. She nestled into his side, even knowing that she was buying herself disgrace. Her head rested upon his chest, the steady *thunk* of his heartbeat echoing beneath her ear, lulling her into sleep with its metronomic melody.

No. I must not sleep here. I would be ruined if they found me in his arms in the morning. And yet, she was finding it hard to care. She could do some good to him, just by her presence here. Was that not worth something? There was so little good that a penniless dependent could do, should she not do what she could?

Her fingers traced hesitant patterns across his chest, and he did not bid her stop, as if they had a right to be there.

"You should not disappear like that again, Edward," she chided softly. "Your father was worried about you."

"My father worries a grand deal too much."

"I was worried, too."

He glanced down at her and she looked steadfastly back up. His eyes were so dark that she could see her own expression reflected in them. His hand wiped a stray hair from her face.

"Tell me, Charlotte, was it my body or my soul you feared for the most?"

"Both, for you do not take care of either."

He laughed a bitter laugh and slumped back again against the pillows.

"Do not leave me, Charlotte, promise me you will not."

How can I promise that? I have no right to him, no right to claim him as my own, no right even to be here, offering him the comfort of companionship and warmth. How could he ask it of me? And, more to the point, why does my foolish heart want to give in to it anyway, even knowing the truth?

"They should have hanged me. I wish they had."

"And how could you atone beyond the grave? What would Albert do without you?" *What would I?*

Edward snorted out a bitter laugh. "Perhaps he would be relieved. I never do anything but disappoint him."

"He loves you, Edward."

"A little too much, perhaps, or, at least, he loves what I represent — the continuation of the Cotterhugh name. The legacy of his line. That is all anybody sees when they look at me. Edward Cotterhugh. The next Lord Cotterhugh. The heir of Drymote. You are lucky, Charlotte. You have been loved dearly for who you are, not what you ought to be. That is a gift indeed."

She looked over him, as his words lengthened and slurred, as he plunged beneath the warm waters of sleep, his eyes fluttering shut. She did not reply, did not want to wake him, he needed the rest, but she could not drag her gaze away from him. She did not know how long she lay there, staring up into his slumbering face by the dancing flickers of candlelight.

His breathing had slowed into deep and regular hushes. She stroked a strand of hair away from his face. *He looks so peaceful in his sleep.* She could not help herself, she reached forwards and pressed her lips against his, a soft benediction, a breath for a breath lingering there gently for a moment more, and then she rose, blew out the candle, and left without looking back.

He is not mine. The words seemed to sink in deeper with every silent footfall which took her farther and farther from his gently dreaming form. *He is not mine to keep or mine to lose. He is not mine.* And yet it did not stop her heart from yearning.

Maud was lingering in the hall as Charlotte slipped out and closed the door behind her. Maud's eyes filled with bitter, acrimonious judgement as she watched Charlotte leave, but she did not say anything, and Charlotte did not bother to defend herself either. *Let the world watch and scorn. Perhaps Edward is right. Perhaps I should care less for other people's judgements after all.*

CHAPTER NINE

Perhaps it was her imagination, but Charlotte could not help but think that Maud treated her to a thin lipped disapproval as she helped her dress the next morning. *I should not let her opinion sway me so much, I promised myself just last night that I would not.* And yet it was hard not to feel panicked and overwhelmed by the sheer weight of Maud's silent judgement.

At last Charlotte could bear it no longer.

"If you have something to say, Maud, say it now."

"It is not my place to talk against the house, Miss. I know my place, if nothing else," she added bitterly.

"Just say it," Charlotte commanded again, wearily. Maud met her gaze in the mirror's reflection and she shrugged a bitter, sharp jerk of the shoulders, fierce and angry.

"You are not the only one Mr Cotterhugh has been seeking comfort with of a night, Miss Mayweather."

Charlotte stiffened at once.

"We have not—You should not spread rumours like that, Maud. You will ruin a good man's reputation for a lie." And mine, too, she added internally.

"I am not lying, I am trying to warn you before you end up like your mother," Maud spat. "They still tell tales of her wantonness here, you know. They whisper that you will end up just like her."

"That is enough, Maud."

"You bade me tell you the truth, and I will. No one will judge Mr Cotterhugh for bedding as many maids as he can take, but they will hold it against you forever. Did he whisper to you in the night that you were the only one? Did he make you believe he loved you? He is his father's son, right enough. None of the Cotterhugh men scruple about the chastity of maids. Ask him, if you think he will give you the truth. He will not besmirch Miss Bletchley or her ilk, but he will not think twice about taking you to bed. And if you let yourself fall, it will be upon your own head, I wash my hands of it. Now, go on. It is the Lord's day, you ought to be off to church to play the saint amongst the good folk. What would they say if they knew where you had been last night, though?" She spat out as a last bitter jibe. She strode from the room, and Charlotte found she could not even find the voice to refute it.

Charlotte stared after the closed door. *She is right. The old matrons of the congregation would chase me from the chapel as a pariah if they knew I had willingly laid myself down beside Edward in his bedchamber last night. They, like Maud, would never believe I had kept my virtue . . . Perhaps I should not go. Perhaps it is mere hypocrisy . . .*

But Mr Harris' words came back to her. Where else should the wretched and unsavoury be?

Albert was not deigning to join her at chapel today, which was not like him. He liked to be seen there, practising his piety. He said he was unwell today, and she found she believed it. His skin looked an unhealthy grey and his eyes were bloodshot and raw. *He is falling into the last stages of his illness. It will start to go downhill soon.* She did not voice such thoughts aloud — they would not help anybody — but she set off down to the chapel alone, her prayer book clutched between her old and neatly darned gloves.

The Vicar was preaching over at Heddlingcote today, so it was Mr Harris upon the pulpit this morning. Charlotte settled herself on the lonely Cotterhugh family pew to listen to the long service commence alone. The tangles of coloured light from the stained-glass window caught in Mr Harris' bouncing brown hair as he gesticulated enthusiastically through his exposition, but Charlotte found she could not keep her mind upon him. It kept darting back up the hill to Albert and Edward, waiting up there for her. One who cared far too much for his reputation, and the other who cared not enough.

If only Edward would deign to speak to Mr Harris . . . Charlotte herself always found comfort in Mr Harris' earnest homilies, even if they were a little dull. He would know the right words to say to help Edward's fraught and turbulent mind, would know how to reach him, how to make him see that even for the worst of men, there was a road back home . . .

She realised she had once again let her mind drift and pulled herself firmly back to attention as Mr Harris at last announced the final hymn. She rose to her feet with the rest of the congregation, and they mumbled their way through the last song, the ancient organ wheezing through the melody, struggling almost as much as the equally ancient organist. Mr Harris gave them a benediction, and then the service spat them out into the sunlight. Charlotte tilted her face up towards the sunlight and drank it in, savouring the moment of peace it brought.

"Lady Cotterhugh always said you were part flower, Miss Mayweather," Mr Harris said beside her. Charlotte blushed a little, but smiled.

"Thank you. And thank you for your sermon today, too, Mr Harris. I've never heard someone expounding on the differences between *agape* love and *philia* love in St. Paul's letters with so much thoroughness before."

Mr Harris blushed, too. "It was a little dry for the lay-person perhaps," he admitted. "I find such differences fascinating, and I forget that the parish at large does not share my enthusiasm."

She instantly regretted her words. He was not Edward, she should not tease him like this. It occurred to her, not for the first time, that a marital life with Mr Harris would be a very earnest one. If she ever married anyone, a prospect that looked increasingly unlikely, she would marry someone who made her laugh.

"Not at all," she said. "Should we not make a study of love?"

Georgiana walked past them both. She looked particularly fine today in a new plaid dress, her curls tied demurely back in a matching ribbon, her prayer book clutched meekly in neatly gloved hands. *That outfit probably cost more than the entirety of my wardrobe.* Charlotte tried not to begrudge her it — after all, did she not have a beautiful violet dress, courtesy of Edward? She should not be greedy.

Georgiana's gaze lingered upon the two of them for a moment as she passed, but though her footsteps faltered, she did not stop. She nodded at both of them, sparing a warm smile which lit up her whole face, threaded her arm through her guardian's, and began to wander down the winding path, out to the country lanes beyond, chatting decorously. Mr Harris watched her go.

"I ought to be getting home," Charlotte said delicately, and Mr Harris flinched, as though he had forgotten she had been standing there. She offered him her hand and he shook it, though he still glanced down the path towards Georgiana's retreating back. She gathered her skirts about her, lifting the black fabric out of the last vestiges of the early morning dew, sparkling like tears upon the grasses, and set off once more alone for home.

"What was Harris talking to you about?"

Charlotte let out a yelp, all but jumping out of her skin, drawing the stares of several scandalised old matrons in their Sunday best.

"Edward! I did not know you came to church this morning. You did not sit at the family pew with me."

He grinned unrepentantly at her, as he fell into step beside her.

"No, I came in late and did not want to cause a disturbance. Besides, I did not want word to reach my father that I actually came to church upon a Sunday. He might think I am turning respectable, and I cannot have that now, can I?" He caught her hand and threaded it through the crook of his arm, accompanying her down the uneven gravel path, through the churchyard and out to the village roads beyond.

"Perish the thought," she said dryly. "And yet even the most scandalous of us need comfort and guidance sometimes." She looked up at him from beneath her lashes. "Did you find any today, Edward?"

Edward looked at her, and she thought he was going to say something earnest for once, but then he changed his mind.

"Are you trying to force me into a compliment for your beloved Harris? You know how much that pains me, Charlotte. Besides, he did manage to make a half an hour sermon last fifty minutes. Is he always that long winded, or was he especially distracted today?"

Charlotte just shrugged. She had thought it seemed like things were weighing heavily on the curate's mind as well, but she liked Mr Harris. She did not intend to indulge in petty gossip about him. She let herself out of the little churchyard gate.

The hedges, bursting with bindweed flowers, all bobbing their heads at her in the drizzly autumnal breezes, grew higher and more unruly with every winding bend. They rounded another corner, and the trees edging the Drymote Estate came creeping into view along the horizon. Down the road, turning towards the valley, Miss Bletchley was making her way back to her own estate, talking blithely with her guardian. Edward, noticing her gaze, also looked down at the small figure traipsing delicately through the puddle-strewn roads. Charlotte could have sighed. *There is no danger of Georgiana becoming an old maid, at least.*

They climbed a stile over the fields, Charlotte holding her skirts up inelegantly as she clambered, wincing slightly as she placed all her weight on her still weakened ankle. Edward offered her his hand again, but she ignored it. He leapt the fence with far too much aplomb, effortlessly athletic. Mud squelched up his boots as he strode along beside her, and a few bored sheep watched them passing.

He gallantly opened the gate of the estate for her, gesturing her up the wide and sweeping driveway. The small carriage was waiting at the front door. Charlotte frowned at it as they approached.

"Why is the carriage out? It is not usual to go visiting on a Sunday."

"No, and we all know how much you care for propriety, Charlotte. Nonetheless, I intend to steal you away."

He opened the carriage door for her and bowed low, gesturing her sardonically within. She just stared at him in astonishment.

"Steal me? Wherever to?"

He leant in towards her, the corner of his mouth twitching up once more in that smirking, roguish grin. "You have forbidden me from giving you flowers from the garden, Charlotte, but you never forbade me from gifting you gardeners." He held out a hand to her and all but bundled her within, climbing up eagerly behind her. She was still staring in astonishment as the carriage jostled down the driveway and out into the afternoon.

The house they pulled up outside was almost dismally small, one of a long terrace of stone cottages a village or two over, edged in shoulder to shoulder, their small windows staring blackly at the intruders with mistrust.

"Fletch lives here?" Charlotte whispered to Edward,

horrified, as she alighted. There was scarcely any garden at all, just a small yard to the fore. He would be miserable, she thought.

"Yes, with his widowed sister and his niece and nephews."

"Nephews, plural?" Charlotte asked, aghast. She eyed the little stone house once more.

"Three, apparently."

"Six of them living in that house?"

"It's better than the workhouse." Edward shrugged pragmatically.

Charlotte had thought herself hard done by to live under Albert's snide remarks and chiding tongue, whilst Fletch was here, crammed into a dark and airless shack, with no security and no pension to support his failing years. A flush of anger and reprobation swam over her. She clutched at Edward's sleeve abruptly and he turned frowning towards her.

"I should not have brought you here," he muttered, his glance raking over her agonised face in concern. "I only thought you missed him so much . . . but of course you did not want to see him like this. Forgive me, it was a foolish idea."

"I know Drymote is failing," she whispered, ignoring him, "but promise me that when you come into your inheritance, you will provide something for Fletch. Promise me you will never see him in the workhouse. Please."

He stared at her, and she could not blame him for it. She usually kept her emotions in far better check. He nodded, leaning his forehead down so that it kissed her own.

"I will swear it, Charlotte. Even if I end up in the poorhouse myself to see it done." The words washed over her in a low and husky growl, and she shivered, clutching on to him still, though they were standing on a public byway for any to see.

"Mam! Mam! There's a proper carriage in the street!"

Charlotte tore herself out of Edward's arms immediately,

staring at the child in the open doorway. He was stick-thin, but clean scrubbed and bouncing with energy, his eyes as round as saucers. He could only have been four or five years old. She could not help but smile.

"Tell me, good sir, do you know anyone of the name Fletcher about these parts?" she asked with all the solemnity she could muster.

The child giggled brightly. "I'm no sir," he said. "I'm only four, miss."

"Well! And there was I thinking I was talking to the man of the house!" she exclaimed to Edward, who grinned back.

"An easy mistake to make," he assured her gravely. "I was all but sure I saw beard bristles growing underneath that chin, the lad is so tall."

The boy's grin split even wider, as he went bouncing about on the balls of his feet.

"*Does* Mister Fletcher live here with you?"

"Aye, Uncle Fletch lives here, sir. Shall I be fetching him for you?"

Charlotte could not help but smile. Even Fletch's nephews called him that. She suspected he himself must have forgotten his Christian name by now.

"What a helpful young man! Thank you. Tell him Mr Cotterhugh and Miss Mayweather have come to pay a visit, if he has a mind to receive us."

The boy darted back inside, the door bouncing on its hinges as he went.

"That child puts a steam-train to shame," Edward muttered at her with a wicked grin. "I've never seen a body with so much energy."

"No? What were you like at his age, Edward?"

"I was an angelic child who sat meekly memorising and reciting poetry for pleasure, seldom forgot my please and thank yous, and never ever scrumped apples."

"I am impressed you managed to say that with a straight face. Did you not know lying on a Sunday is a mortal sin?"

Before Edward could retort, Fletch appeared in the doorway suddenly. He leant against the lintel, his thick thatch of grey hair mussed underneath his cap, his tanned and weathered face a welcome sight.

"Well now, as I live and breathe! What are you doing here, Miss Charlotte? I scarcely believed the boy when he said you'd come a'visiting."

"If you are too busy to entertain us, we would not like to intrude, Fletch," said Charlotte meekly, but Fletch had waved the words away before they were halfway out of her mouth.

"We've not got a grand parlour to be greeting you in, lass, but what's ours is yours and welcome to it. In, come in!" He stepped back to gesture them inside, and Charlotte could not help but smile. He had not changed a jot and she told him so. He blushed a little and grunted something, but she thought he was pleased all the same.

The house seemed even smaller inside than it had done from the outside. A large stone fireplace dominated the room, with kettles and pots hanging from metal arms over the grate, and dripping washing steaming merrily nearby. A thin, ladder-like staircase ran along the wall to the upper room where, presumably, they all slept bundled in together, and yet more clothing hung to dry from nails wedged into the edge of each step. A dryer, rosemary and lavender bunches mixed amongst the heavy fabrics, hung from the ceiling, and baskets of neatly pressed clothes stood by the window. There was a large table with two benches pushed up close to it, and two large chairs by the fire, and a collection of children peeked out from behind them warily. Charlotte smiled at them. The little girl blushed and giggled, hiding her face in her elder brother's side.

A woman bobbed a curtsey, looking flurried. She wrung

her hands in her apron, looking between the two of them and her brother in a rather flustered way.

"Forgive us for the mess," she said, her hands fluttering to the nearest bundle of washing, tidying it away awkwardly, though she had nowhere to put it once she had picked it up. "I've been taking in washing since my Harry died, especially now the children ain't allowed to work anymore. Matthew, my eldest, he was helping some, but now it's just up to me and Fletch and — oh I'm sorry, it's just such a mess."

She looked like she was about to cry. Fletch took the bundle from her hands with a gentle force and gave it to the eldest boy instead, with a gruff injunction to *run that upstairs, lad, before your mam has a fit*. He pushed the two chairs together towards the fire and waved Charlotte and Edward down towards them, settling himself on a frayed footstool, which was spitting out tufts of horsehair between its patched and worn embroidery.

"Settle yourself, Martha," he said. "They've seen washing before, I'm sure, and no folks should be ashamed of hard working now."

Charlotte smiled at Martha and Martha blushed, bobbing into another curtsey.

"This is my sister, Martha Holloway," Fletch added to Charlotte, as if belatedly aware that he hadn't fulfilled the correct customs of courtesy. "And these are the brats," he said affectionately looking around at them. "That's the eldest, Matthew." He jerked a thumb at the large, shy boy of around ten who was coming back down the stairs now empty-handed. The lad settled himself over on the staircase, his big eyes watchful and wary. "Luke's the red head, the lass is Sarah and the baby is Tommy."

"I'm no baby!" he said in great indignation, and Fletch ruffled his hair. "Go on now with you," he told them all sternly. "Leave your elders to the talking."

The children obediently retreated into the corner, but they did not stop gazing at their illustrious guests.

"They're very well behaved." Charlotte smiled, and Mrs Holloway beamed with reflected pride.

"Aye, well, that's because you're here. You should see them normally, little terrors, all of them." But Fletch's eyes were crinkled in a smile.

"You're settled here?" Charlotte asked him. "Happy?" She desperately needed to hear him say so, and it occurred to her that it was only selfishness in her seeking it, something to assuage her own guilty conscience. She swallowed. "Fletch, I— I'm so sorry about—"

"Now then, it was none of your doing, was it? Nor yours neither, Mr Cotterhugh," he added with a respectful nod towards Edward, who was inspecting his hands uncomfortably. "It's just life, lass. Things come and things go and the world keeps turning, hmm?"

"But you'd worked the gardens for so long." She could not keep the tears from prickling in her eyes.

"Aye, and I'll not say as I don't miss it, for you should not be lying on the Lord's day, but I've got Martha here, and the children, and we've bread enough on the table and plenty of folks have worse."

She was again reminded how petty and ungrateful she had been to be squabbling over Drymote with Albert. Her throat felt thick and she tried valiantly to hide the tears welling up within her eyes. Edward appeared to notice, and he stepped in to take over the conversation whilst Charlotte discretely regained her composure.

"You have found work, Mr Fletcher?"

"Aye. I keep the churchyard trimmed nowadays," he grunted. "It's not so much gardening as I'm used to, just hedges and lawns mostly, a tree or two around the verge, but it's something. Keeps your fingers in the soil, and it's pretty enough in bloom, though it be small."

"I would love to see it," said Charlotte. "Do you think we could visit sometime?"

"No better time to visit a church than a Sunday." Fletch heaved himself up to his feet with a groan and offered her his hand. "Shall we take the kids, too, Martha? It's good for them to get some air when they can, hmm?"

The children, who had clearly been listening in, bounded forwards eagerly, yelling over their mother's polite protests.

"Let's all go," Charlotte said, smiling at Mrs Holloway, who blushed and dimpled as she smiled back, bobbing a pleased curtsey, holding her apron out like the pleats of a grand ball gown.

Edward offered Martha his arm just as gallantly as if she had been a fashionable heiress, and Martha blushed bright red, giggling a little. Charlotte could not help but smile. *At least I am not the only one that Edward affects like that.* It was nice to see other women falling infallibly for his charms. Fletch did not offer Charlotte his arm. He was never one for fine manners and frippery in his own words, but he did stroll companionably alongside Charlotte as they slipped out of the tiny yard and out into the country lane beyond. The gate clattered shut behind them as the four children ran ahead, laughing and calling for one another, pushing each other into the bushes whenever they got too close and screaming as they tumbled roughly. Martha was calling after them, a little harassed and embarrassed by their behaviour before *the good folks*, as she insisted on calling them, but Edward was just laughing. Fletch smiled indulgently down at his niece and nephews.

"You *are* happy here, aren't you, Fletch? You aren't just saying that?" she said anxiously.

Fletch laughed. "I'm with my family, lass. Folks cannot ask for more than that."

Charlotte looked down at her mud-besmirched boots. *I do not have any family left.* Uncle John had been more of a father to her than the rascal who had impregnated her mother and left poor Emily Mayweather in infamy and disgrace. Now Uncle John, too, was dead, and she once again had no one to care for her.

That's not quite true, is it? Edward takes care of me. He brought me here to find Fletch just because he knew I missed him. But Edward was not hers, not truly, not in any legal, binding way and, despite the secret wishes of her heart or the wild, illogical fancies of her daydreams, she doubted he ever would be.

"He's a good'un, that young Mr Cotterhugh," Fletch said, as if reading her mind, or perhaps just her expression as she stared wistfully down the road towards Edward. Fletch had always been keen-sighted and quick to understand. His weathered hand patted Charlotte's arm with a familiarity she had missed. "He always was. I remember when he used to come down to Drymote Estate when he was just a sprout. You'd be too young to remember him then, I reckon, but he was a good kid. Always into mischief, of course, but kind at the core. It don't do to judge folks by their blossoms sometimes, pet, you need to look down to the stalk and root to see if a tree is growing right. He likes to play the worldly young fool, but I reckon as he has a good heart."

"I know he does," she said quietly. "I think it is Edward himself who needs convincing of it."

Fletch laughed. "Some folks is like that," he agreed. "He reminds me a lot of your uncle, you know."

"Uncle *John*?" She could not help but be incredulous, and Fletch laughed again, a great rumbling sound that made her heart ache sorely.

"Aye, well, not in all things perhaps, but your uncle was a man who took the weight of the world on his shoulders and never let folks see that he had. John hid it in his bulbs and blossoms, and young Mr Cotterhugh hides it in his fancy manners, but they both do it all the same. They both take responsibility for more than they ought to, perhaps."

She looked over at him sharply. "Do you mean me, Fletch?"

Fletch just laughed. "I don't know much, lass, but I know as John loved you dear as any daughter of his own blood. He did not begrudge taking responsibility for you, not even after Ursula died. I reckon as after his wife went, you and those plants of his were the only things keeping him tethered to this mortal coil. He went too soon, even as it was. Never thought it of him. He didn't seem like the sickening type, did he?" he added reflectively. "Still, maybe he had some sort of premonition on it, for he was awful set on getting that will made."

Charlotte stopped dead in the road and stared at him. He turned too, obviously confused at her abrupt halt. Far ahead, up the road, little Tommy was calling for them all to watch him as he scampered up a tree as quickly and heedlessly as a squirrel might. They all ignored him, bound up in their own breathless affairs.

"Uncle John never made a will," she said.

"Aye, certain sure as he did. I signed as witness to it myself."

She stared at him still.

"It was not with his lawyers," she said. "It was not in his study."

"He made one," Fletch said stubbornly. "Don't know what was in it, not being a reading man myself, but I know full well that he made one."

"Well, maybe he changed his mind and had it destroyed."

Fletch took hold of her hands and held them tightly. "He'd not do that to you," he said seriously. "He left the will so you would have something to be provided with after his death."

She felt the world reeling around her and rebuked herself for her greed, and yet, if it was true, if it was really true . . .

The estate would still go to Albert, of course, and through Albert to Edward, but if Uncle John had really left her a stipend, or a small inheritance, just a little money, just a little nest egg so that she could be independent . . . she knew how to scrimp and save, if there was just a little money she could take a small cottage, perhaps a maid of all work from the foundling house, grow lettuces and cabbages in the garden to make ends meet . . . already her mind was racing with new possibilities and the prospect even of leaving Drymote did not seem so dire, if she could do it upon her own terms.

I'd still have to leave Edward behind, he's not the sort to scrape a life on a pittance and a prayer. And Albert will fight me for every last coin. Drymote probably needs all the money it can get. Was it selfishness? Was it greed? She could hardly tell anymore.

"Are you sure?" she asked again, hardly able to contain the quiver in her voice.

"I'm sure."

"But where is it? Where would he have put it?"

Fletch just shrugged. "He'll have hidden the will somewhere safe. You find it, child. You make good and sure to find it before anyone else does."

Charlotte opened her mouth, but she was not really sure what reply she was hoping to find. Before she had the chance to summon the words to her mouth however, a piercing shriek shattered the still, Sunday afternoon air.

CHAPTER TEN

Charlotte's heart leapt into her throat as she whirled around to see the cause of the commotion. Martha, still screaming, was cradling Tommy as he lay upon the ground. Fletch swore darkly and pounded down the road, waving at the other children to clear the way. Charlotte followed him, her skirts in her hands as she fled. Edward was kneeling down, looking over the child that was held suffocatingly close to his mother's breast.

"Let him breathe, Mrs Holloway," he said, gently prising her hands off the boy and laying him down on the ground. The boy did not stir, his eyes remaining steadfastly shut.

"He's dead! He's dead!"

"Hush yourself, Martha," Fletch said crossly, "Any fool can see he's breathing."

He always got cross when he was anxious, Charlotte recalled, and she could see the fear crackling like lightning in those shrewd, dark eyes now. Fletch pulled his sister away, holding her tightly, whilst Edward ran his hands over the boy.

Edward shook his head. "Broken arm," he muttered, "And probably concussion, too, though we won't be able to tell for sure until he wakes." He looked up at the others. "We need to get this child to a doctor as fast as possible. Where is the closest?"

"There's the free hospital at Highpass, but that's a half-hour walk from here," Fletch said grimly.

"Matthew, run back to your house and fetch the carriage to

us," Edward commanded. "Tell them Mr Cotterhugh is in need of it desperately and tell them not to spare the horses. Go!" he added fiercely when the child looked uncertainly at his mother. Martha nodded, and Matthew fled back down the road they had just come down.

"What happened?" Charlotte whispered.

"He fell from the tree. Landed upon his arm and hit his head."

Martha sobbed again.

"Well now, Martha, don't take on so. He'll be grand in a moment," Fletch said roughly, but Charlotte could not help but notice that his face was grim.

"Come here with me, you two," Charlotte said to the other children, clasping them tightly in her arms and pulling them away from the scene. "You don't need to look."

And yet she herself could scarcely pull her gaze away. Edward seemed to shift into an entirely different person, professional and efficient, his hands running over the child with a gentle detachment, so far from his usual lounging arrogance.

It suits him. It does him good to be able to help in some practical way. She snorted out a hollow little laugh, though there was very little funny about this situation at all. Albert would be horrified at the notion that his son and heir might be happier as a working man than as a gentleman of leisure and propriety.

The minutes seemed to drag past, the cheerful chirp of the birds in the trees above incongruous with the scene unfolding before them. Charlotte felt so helpless as she held on tightly to the trembling children, watching the others work. It was with a great sense of relief that she heard the familiar clatter of wheels and hooves approaching, and she pulled Sarah and Luke out of the road.

The carriage came rattling down the road, the wheels practically leaping off the uneven path as the coachman sped them along, the horses' hooves spitting pebbles in their wake. Matthew was clinging onto the buckboard beside the driver desperately, pointing them out. The Growler earned its nickname, the carriage wheels rumbling over the earth with a low persistent roar. It drew up short just before them, and the driver leapt off at once to open the doors.

"We're going to Highpass," Edward said curtly, sweeping the boy up in his arms. Tommy's head lolled unconsciously about, and Martha wept as she tried to hold it steady. "There's a free hospital there. Matthew, you know the way? You can direct the driver?"

"Yes sir," said the lad eagerly.

"Good. Hurry, then."

They all piled into the carriage together. Even though Albert had splashed out for a Clarence carriage, it was a tight squeeze with four adults and two children wedged within. Matthew stayed outside with the driver, and Luke clambered hastily up beside him. It was a pity that the excitement of getting to ride on a real gentleman's carriage should be marred for them by the pain of their brother, Charlotte thought distantly. They were unlikely to get to ride a Clarence or even a Brougham again.

Edward was still carrying the unconscious Tommy, and Charlotte pulled little Sarah up onto her own lap. Mrs Holloway was sobbing quietly in her brother's arms. The seats were plush and well-stuffed, but they still made for an uncomfortable ride as the driver drove them onwards with reckless haste. They went careering around corners, practically leaping from the seats with every bump, and Charlotte could not help but feel a little nauseous as the carriage fled down the road. Pedestrians leapt out of the way before them, yelling after the driver, but he did not stop until they had pulled up sharply before the large brick building in the middle of Highpass.

Charlotte stared at it as they disembarked on somewhat wobbly legs. It was an impressively tall building, with dozens of windows staring down at them, and a steady queue of invalids waiting to limp through its doors.

"All built on subscriptions," Edward whispered to her, catching sight of her expression. "But don't be too impressed. It's the kind of charity that boasts but doesn't get its hands dirty when the bills for wages keep coming through."

He barged forwards past the coughing, wheezing, groaning queue still carrying the prone boy, but was stopped at the door by a porter.

"May I see your letter of recommendation, sir?"

"My what?"

"All admittances must be made under a letter of recommendation by the board of trustees, sir. We can't have unsavoury types trying to play the system. You get all sorts, folks faking being ill just to avoid the workhouse, just to get food and a place to sleep." He preened smarmily, obviously pleased with this petty power, but Edward was not in the mood to play games.

"And do I look like that type to you?" he snapped. "I am my own letter of recommendation—Mr Edward Cotterhugh of Drymote Estate. If you do not let us pass immediately, I will take it up with your board of trustees personally. If the child should die because of your delay, I will do more than see you fired, man, I will have you prosecuted for manslaughter. Move."

Taken aback, the porter stepped smartly out of the way, his pomposity suddenly deflated, and all of them hurried inside.

It was even busier within than it had been outside, and Charlotte held tightly onto Luke's and Sarah's hands lest they should be separated in the melee. Edward strode forwards in the lead, the child lolled across his arms, a dead weight, his head swaying to and fro with every hurried footstep, and the others were all swept along in his wake. Edward barked a question at a nurse hurrying past, and Charlotte could not help but think he looked unaccountably Albert-like in his pompous manner, but Albert only used his power to aggrandise himself. Edward was at least using his blustering, arrogant privilege for good, she thought charitably. The nurse in her fresh-pressed whites ushered him hastily to a free bed and told them all that she would find a doctor for him just as soon as she could. Edward laid the boy down gently on the mattress, and the other children bundled onto the bed beside him.

The ward they had been shown to was long and crowded, filled with an indiscriminate mix of old and young, men and women, but this bed was well placed, at least. It was fairly close to the large stove striving to heat the tall airy room, but also beneath a window letting clean bright light fall upon the bed, and a hint of a fresh breeze wafted beneath the gap in the lintel. A wilting, drying posy had been hung there to mitigate against the worst of the miasmas that carried infection on the air, and its scent whispered up to them as they crowded round.

"He's waking up!" Sarah said, peering down into her little brother's face.

Indeed, he did seem to be, for he thrashed from side to side for a moment, and then began to cry.

"It hurts, Mam, it really hurts."

"Oh, my baby, oh Tommy love." Martha was there in moments, pulling him up into her arms and weeping copiously into his hair.

"Leave him be, Martha, you'll only do him more mischief," Fletch said, but there was unmistakable relief written there on his gruff and weathered old face, too.

"We should go," Charlotte murmured to Edward. "We should leave them to it. They will not want us intruding on them at a time like this."

Edward nodded to her silently.

"We are going to make our adieus, I'm afraid," he said to Fletch, grasping him warmly by the hand in a firm handshake as he might to a business partner or a friend. "We'll see if we can't rustle up a doctor for you on the way out, though. And here," he added in an undertone, and Charlotte saw him slipping some coins into Fletch's hand, too. Fletch tried to protest, but Edward refused to hear it.

"It's a costly business being ill, even at a Free Hospital. Buy the lad some treat to cheer him up if you don't want to put it to better use." He clapped Fletch on the shoulder and moved aside to say goodbye to the Holloways as well, where he managed to produce some shillings which he withdrew by magic from the children's ears, one apiece, much to their delight.

Charlotte clasped onto Fletch's hands tightly.

"Let me know how he fares," she said. "Let me know if there is anything you need, anything I can do." There was so little she could do. She knew she could barely support herself, let alone anyone else, but if there was anything, she would do it for Fletch. He just patted her hands.

"Remember what I said, Miss Charlotte, that's all. And take care of yourself, if you possibly can. You're not looking well." He squinted at her with suspicion and she laughed.

"It's just a slight headache," she said. "Over-excitement, I fear. And I dare not complain, for I suspect it is a grand deal less painful than poor Tommy's head."

She squeezed his hands tightly, then threaded her hand through Edward's waiting arm. She could not resist a last look over her shoulder as they made their way through the crowded hall. Now that they had walked away from the anxious family, Edward's over-confident demeanour started to slip a little. He stepped out of the way, flattening himself against the wall, as a porter brought a wheeled chair whizzing through the gaps in the crowd with undue haste, but he did not straighten up again even as the porter passed. Charlotte looked at him. He seemed suddenly exhausted, as if the effort of pretence had cost him.

"He's going to be all right, Edward." Charlotte said softly, taking a step towards him. Edward looked up as if he had only suddenly become aware of her presence and forced a grin to his face.

"Of course he is. Children that age are irrepressible. Bouncier than Indian Rubber." He rubbed a hand over his face, his skin was still grey. She was not fooled.

"It must have been quite a fright to see him tumble like that."

"I have seen worse things in my time," Edward laughed. He flexed his fingers, and she longed to lace hers through them and squeeze them tightly. She folded them meekly before her instead, nestled amongst the heavy pleats of her skirts. She took her place next to him at the wall, and they watched the busy corridor bustling past.

"You don't have to play the careless unfeeling aristocrat for me, Edward Cotterhugh. I know there is a heart in there somewhere."

He laughed once more, but this time it rang true, the bitterness lingering there slipping away into the air.

"Oh no, Miss Mayweather. I fear I lost my heart long, long ago." He straightened up once more with a sigh and offered her his hand. "Come, my father will be wondering where we are by now. He will think I have absconded with you."

"The other way around, rather. He is always on the watch for penniless women ensnaring your heart, Edward. He has far grander plans for you than that."

Edward grinned at her wickedly. "My father can plan all he wishes. I make my own path. You surely know that by now." He threaded her hand through the crook of his arm and guided her surely down the bustling corridors of the free hospital. Even on a Sunday afternoon, the halls were over-crowded and packed. The smell lingered thickly in the air as the nurses, looking harassed and stressed, bustled about at the doctors' behests. Patients groaned in beds, unheeded, and their loved ones saw to them the best they could, awaiting the infrequent care of the staff.

They tried ineffectually to corner a nurse, but they were all busy, hurrying past with pitchers and bed pans, clean sheets or bandages, a rattling trolley of medicines, all preoccupied with their own endless chores. Eventually, Edward flagged one down by standing directly in front of her and refusing to move.

"There is a boy in ward five who needs a doctor," he said firmly. "He has broken his arm and possibly his head, too. When will a doctor be free to see him?"

"As soon as possible."

"Would you be able to find one and hurry that process along? It is quite urgent."

"Everything is urgent here," she snapped. "It is also *urgent* that I change the bandages on Mr Collins, bathe Mr Greening and take Mrs Antinori her medication."

"We're sorry to have disturbed you," Charlotte began meekly, but Edward cut across her.

"Mrs Antinori?" he said sharply, his face pale. "I know her. I am a . . . friend. Where is she?"

The nurse blinked at him in surprise, and she was not the only one. Charlotte could not help but stare at the abrupt change in Edward's voice and demeanour. He did not look at her though, his gaze still fixed upon the nurse.

"Ward three, bed eight," the nurse said, gesturing down the corridor, and Edward was already off at a run before any more could be said, forgetting all about summoning a doctor for Tommy, apparently. Charlotte hurried after him, calling his name, but she doubted he even heard. He barged nurses and patients out of the way with equal disdain and they called after him, cursing, as he skidded to a halt outside ward three. She had not thought it possible, but he went even paler as he stared within the sunlit room, frozen to the spot like a trapped and frightened hare.

A woman's voice came from within the ward, a voice that sounded as shocked and horrified as the expression cast upon Edward's face.

"Edward?" it gasped.

"Dora," Edward replied.

CHAPTER ELEVEN

Edward could scarcely move. He seemed frozen there, amidst the bustling corridor of the free hospital and Charlotte found herself rooted to the spot, as well. The look upon his face made her ache, a physical pain, and she longed to go and wipe it away from him forever, but still she could not move.

After an aeon, Edward forced his stiff limbs to stumble forwards. His hands groped blindly for the door frame, desperately trying to steady himself.

She suspected it was only sheer willpower keeping him on his feet, for his skin was grey and he was swaying, as if he were drunk once more.

Charlotte hesitated. This felt like a moment too personal to intrude upon, and yet she could scarcely keep away. She hovered in his wake like a shadow, timid, half-visible, perhaps even half-incorporeal, as if she had already begun to melt out of his existence.

Is that all I am? Do I only exist when he looks at me? And yet she could hardly hear the chiding voice reprimanding her. Everything seemed to halo out of sight apart from his ghastly, agonised expression. The noises of the hospital dispersed, the hurry and the pain, the nurses and the patients and the visitors. She stepped forwards into the light once more and followed his gaze to the woman sitting up on the bed.

She was dying. There was no doubt about that. She was gaunt and wan, her eyes were already losing their lustre, her once flame-bright hair now lying lank and dim, like the last smouldering embers of a fire. Her hand, as she reached disbelievingly for him, was barely more than bone.

"Is it really you, Edward?" she croaked, her voice scarcely more than a whisper.

Charlotte could barely look at her, and apparently Edward could not, either. He stood beside her bed stiffly like a recalcitrant schoolboy, his head bowed, his gaze fixed upon his shuffling hands clasped before him. She had never seen him like this before, so uncertain, so vulnerable — so *young*. Though he had four years on her, and a wealth of world-experience she could not begin to imagine, suddenly Charlotte felt like the older of the two. She longed to reach out and comfort him, but she could not make her hands obey her. She was not sure the gesture would be welcome, even if she did. *This moment is for the two of them. I do not belong here.* And yet she could not force herself to leave, an unwilling witness to their reunion and their pain.

As if hearing her thoughts, Theodora turned to Charlotte. There was something startlingly shrewd about her expression even now, encased in pain and weariness as it was. She smiled weakly at Charlotte, but Charlotte could not force herself to smile back.

"You are failing in your manners, Mr Cotterhugh. You have not introduced me to your acquaintance."

Edward startled, his head whiplashing upwards. He turned to see Charlotte, his eyes wide, his face pale, as if she were an apparition there beside him, as if he had forgotten that she even existed. A faint tinge of colour ran high across his cheekbones.

"Miss Renley — forgive me — that is — Mrs Antinori, may I introduce you to Miss Mayweather. Miss Mayweather, Mrs Antinori. Miss Mayweather is my late uncle's ward, Theodora. And Mrs Antinori is . . ." He trailed off, clearly not knowing how to finish that sentence.

Theodora laughed with an acrid weariness. "*Mrs Antinori* is not Mrs Antinori at all, as I suspect you know. It is nothing but a lie to save my reputation. In the eyes of the law, at least, I never wed Giuliani, though I claim his name for myself and for his daughter. I know that we were married in our hearts, and that is enough." She laughed again at Edward's horrified expression. "Ah, you did not know I was a fallen woman, Edward? You did not know I was bearing his precious gift within me when he fell? Come, do not reproach me. Am I not tasting my just rewards?" she asked bitterly, gesturing around at the hospital bed. A tear trickled down her face, but she wiped it brusquely away.

Edward took a staggering step forwards. "Giuliani had a daughter." The words came out in a soft breath. "There was a child."

"Julia," Theodora said reverently, the name a prayer on her lips. The tears began to fall again, thicker and faster now. "Oh, Edward. They have taken her from me, and I do not know where." She buried her face in her skeletal hands and began to weep with abandon. Charlotte felt tears pricking to her own eyes in sympathy.

"You!" Theodora said suddenly, wiping away the tears that still streamed freely down her gaunt face. "You, Edward! You have been sent to me from heaven to find her!"

Edward reared back, his hands held up as if protesting his innocence. "Dora, I would not know where to start."

"You must find her, Edward, you must. You owe me that much at least. She is losing her mother, and you took her father from her, you owe her! You must repay your debts!" She was speaking wildly, urgently, desperately, but Edward did not protest it.

"Please, she is so young to be alone in the workhouse or the poorhouse, or wherever they have taken her. What hope will she have then? Abandoned in the world, alone, oh, what will become of her? What will become of my baby? How much more can one heart take?" She burst out into fresh tears, weeping freely, despite the crowded room. None of the other patients paid her the least bit of mind, Charlotte noted. They were all too busy groaning and crying out with their own agonies in their own, last lingering moments of pain.

"You wish for me to bring her to you?"

Theodora laughed hollowly. "No. I do not want her to see me like this, though my heart is breaking to see her one more time, to hold her one more time—oh, Julia, oh my Julia." She clutched herself desperately as she whispered the name, as if it were the phantom of her child she was holding. Her eyes were bloodshot but determined as they met Edward's. "I will be gone long before you can find her—I doubt I will see the end of the week, my strength is failing so fast. But I still want you to find her nonetheless. My widowed mother still lives in Priestborne village. I was too afraid to return to her, too ashamed of what I had become, but she will not refuse to take my child, I know she will not."

Those skeletal hands fumbled for a scrap of paper and she wrote down an address with weakened fingers. "Find Julia and return her to my mother. Please, Edward, you can *save* her, I know you can, you can save her from the cold cruelty of the world and all the hardships she will taste within it. Promise me! Give your sacred word to a dying woman and bring me some peace in my final hours. Save her—oh, please, please, by heaven, save her."

Edward reached forwards and gripped her hand tightly, snatching the address so hard that the precious shard of paper crumpled. As Charlotte watched them, lingering awkwardly by the edge of the bed, an interloper on this private moment, she could not help but think how the dying woman, spurred on, perhaps, with her last few moments of anguish and adrenaline, a mother's borrowed strength, seemed somehow more alive than the man sitting beside her.

Edward did not seem able to speak, but he nodded once, tersely.

That seemed to be enough for Theodora. She slumped against the pillows in exhausted relief, her hand falling free from his. Edward stood and left without bidding either of them goodbye, striding from the room as if he could not bear to be in it one moment longer. He seemed to have forgotten that Charlotte was still there, but Theodora had not. She glanced at Charlotte, who blushed, aware again how much she must seem like an intruder on this private, last moment.

"You must think me cruel, Miss Mayweather, to burden him with such a task, and to remind him of his sins to do so."

"I think a mother's love will pay any price to see her child safe, and I think there are few that would chide you for it."

"Perhaps you think a daughter of disgrace does not deserve such compassion? Ill deeds have their own rewards, and fallen women make fallen daughters, that is what the clergyman at the workhouse told me. Some people just do not deserve charity and the kindness of those more respectable, who have not fallen to the shameful sin of love."

"I do not believe that at all," Charlotte told her firmly, she leant forwards, dipping her voice low, though none of the other patients or visitors cared enough to listen. "I, too, am a daughter of disgrace. My mother also fell when she was scarcely out of her childhood years, younger, indeed, than I am now, wooed by a cad who abandoned her and me when she told him she was with child and left her to her shame. If it had not been for the kindness of my aunt and uncle, I would be in this very spot with you now, or in the workhouse with poor Julia. I will never judge you for that, Mrs Antinori. I know how easy it is to fall, even for those who claim to be above such things. All people are worthy of compassion, charity, kindness and love."

Tears once again prickled in Theodora's eyes, though surely they should have been drained dry by now. She held out a hand, and Charlotte hesitantly placed one of her own within it. Theodora's hands were icy cold, as if the granite grip of death had already taken hold of them, but they clung to her own with a tenacious strength Charlotte had not expected.

"I loved Edward, too, in my own way," she croaked unexpectedly. Charlotte flinched at the abrupt non-sequitur, but Theodora did not seem to notice. "Not as I loved Giuliani, not as a lover or a wife, but I was fond of him. I had all the affection of a sister for a brother. I do not like to see him hurting like this."

Charlotte did not know what to say to such a stark admission, so she held her tongue. Theodora laughed a little bitterly.

"It is not the thing to say in polite society, is it? But I am dying, such impropriety can scarcely hurt me any longer and it is far from the worst thing I have ever done."

"Do you blame him for Mr Antinori's death?" The words came out abruptly, tumbling over one another in their haste to be free.

Theodora sighed out long and low. "I blamed myself," she said. "And I blamed Giuliani, and yes, for a while I have blamed Edward, too. Now I blame no one but the fates. Such things are meant to be, I think. I am going to join him soon enough, and we will be reunited once more. Only, take care of my Julia, promise me that, if nothing else. Promise me my Julia will be taken care of. I know my mother will not turn her away."

"Yes," croaked Charlotte, squeezing Theodora's hand. She did not know how she could uphold such a promise, but she could not withhold it either, not from a dying woman, not if it could yet bring her peace.

"And look after Edward, too," Theodora added with a small and feeble smile, laying back against the pillows softly, her whole body relaxing now that the promise had been extracted. "I know he does not let people look after him easily, but it is good for him to have you. If my blessing is worth anything at all, Miss Mayweather, be assured that you have it in abundance."

Charlotte was blushing and stammering, but Theodora scarcely seemed to hear. Her hand was falling out of Charlotte's grip, slumping against the crisp white sheets, her eyes fluttering closed.

"I did love him, in my way," she murmured once more as exhaustion crept over her and she gave way to sleep.

Charlotte stared at her for a moment longer, the laboured rise and fall of her chest, the wheezing breaths escaping past her bloodless lips, the eyelids fluttering in a restless dream and then rose and silently took her leave once more.

The carriage ride home was much quieter than the ride out. The air hung thickly between them, Edward lost in his own mired thoughts, and Charlotte did not know how to reach him. A headache was growing upon her once more, making her feel heavy and sluggish, and her fingers were tingling again.

I should have seen a doctor about it whilst we were at the free hospital. At least that was a price I could afford. And yet it seemed arrogant and entitled to demand a doctor's precious time for such a small ailment as fizzing fingertips and toes and an aching head, when they were so over-stretched with true illnesses. She rubbed her hands together, trying to get some life back into them.

Edward seemed to notice the action, for his gaze followed the movement in the grim evening light seeping through the carriage window. He reached forwards and chafed her hands between his own, trying to warm them.

"You are cold, Charlotte. I should not have kept you out so long. Forgive me."

"There is nothing to forgive. We could hardly have done anything else, could we?"

"It was not the afternoon I had planned for you. Nothing ever works out as planned," he added, bitterness lying thick and unwieldy in his voice. She feared for a moment that he might seek out the reckless refuge of drunkenness again — or flee out into the darkness as swiftly as he had come bursting into her life. She clutched at his fingers desperately, as though she could make him stay. He looked up at her, frowning, misinterpreting the action.

"Do not fear for the boy, Charlotte. He will be fine, I promise, even left in such ungentle care as the free hospital affords."

"Ungentle, perhaps, and certainly over-worked, but capable nonetheless. Your quick work with Tommy stood him in good stead. I confess I was impressed, Edward. You ought to take to medicine."

"What for?" he muttered. "People die anyway. You saw the hospital. You saw what little they could do. It is all pointless."

"It is not all pointless, it makes some small difference in this world and that is all we can do."

"It is not enough!" he growled, snatching his hands from hers and thumping them down on the faded upholstery beside him. "They cannot stop those people from dying in their hundreds. Did you not hear their screams haunting those corridors? Did you not feel the miasma of infection lingering in the air? They are scarcely places of healing at all, Charlotte, they are merely somewhere for the poor to die. They cannot heal *her*." He bit his lips down hard upon that final word as it escaped from him treacherously, but Charlotte heard it anyway. Her chest constricted hard, as if she were bearing the weight of grief with him, and she leant forwards in the jostling carriage.

"I'm sorry, Edward," she said softly, her hand lingering on his forearm. "It must have been hard to see her like that."

"Yes," he said shortly. He turned to look out of the window, and for a while, she thought that was all he was going to say. As they bumped and clattered along, he kept to his own thoughts until, breaking out with a deep and heart-felt sigh, he ran his hand through his hair, that old, familiar gesture, his gaze turning back to hers, agonised and brimming with tears he would not let fall.

"The heart is a fickle thing, Charlotte. I thought I would die of love of her, and yet now when I see her, all I have is the memory of love. I do not feel it burning, painful and hot in my chest any longer. Her sickness pains me to the heart, but it is not the pain of loss which burns there, it is only guilt. Giuliani is gone, and for what? For a fleeting passion? Everything I once felt has wisped away into the wind. Can time truly do so much, or is it just the heart which deceives itself? What is it that Shakespeare says? *Love is not love, which alters when it alteration finds*, hmmm? Is it not *an ever-fixed mark*? If it is real, if it is worth anything at all . . ." He trailed off, his eyes red and bloodshot.

It was a sonnet that even Charlotte, in her pocked and blotchy education, had heard. It had been one of Uncle John's favourites. He had often murmured it to himself as he practised his isolation down by Ursula's Abbey, seeking solace in his memories there amongst the empty stones. Edward did not find the same comfort in those words that John had. As Edward stared imploring at her, she found him haunted and hurt.

"What if I never loved her at all?" he whispered.

Her heart constricted within her, pain and pity bound together in a knot none could untangle.

"I never liked the Bard, though perhaps it is sacrilege to say so. Does he have the monopoly on knowing love? Is his truth the only truth to know?" Her hand, still lingering upon his arm, slipped down to tangle amongst his fingers instead. His hand squeezed hers tightly, clinging on as a lifeline in the tossing tempest. "You loved her as a youth loves, hot and fierce and fast. The fact that you outgrew it does not mean it was not real. Now you have a man's heart, and you will find a man's love."

"I already have," he vowed, his voice little more than a hoarse croak. His gaze met hers, and she saw that he had seen all too much. Though she had tried to hide it from her own heart, she could not hide it from him.

"Do not mock me, Edward," she said, scalding. "You think the world is all a game, but people have feelings, and though those feelings might belong to someone poor and plain and stubborn, they do not deserve to be held up to ridicule."

He grabbed at her hands but she snatched them away. He caught at them once more and held them all the tighter.

"I am not mocking you, Charlotte. Since that day you crawled in to my life, sodden and bedraggled, berating me for stealing my own rabbits, I have been enchanted by you."

One hand reached up to her face, his thumb brushing against her lip, whispering it open. She felt her breath shuddering, bursting forth in uneven bounds, and she tried to find some words to save herself, to stop herself from falling, but then his lips were on hers and nothing else mattered at all. The world fell into twilight, grey and hazy, lingeringly unreal beyond the two of them, and her eyes fluttered closed.

His lips were soft, softer than she had been expecting, a strange contrast to the scratchy hush of stubble surrounding them, and his breath whispered against her own, sweet and melancholy, like a promise, or a memory.

His tongue flickered against her lips, then deeper, deeper

against her own, and abruptly all of that lingering gentleness was ablaze, burnt up in a tidal wave of desire.

She let out a low and guttural moan, her own tongue flicking against his, and suddenly his hands were in her hair, her own hands reaching up to frame his face, his mouth moving hard and persistently upon her own, drawing out her passions, as to yet untasted.

She was all too inexperienced in such matters, but it did not seem to matter. Her body seemed to know what it was doing all on its own—it sought with a hungry desperation, craving passion, craving comfort—craving *him*. He breathed her name out against her lips and she cried out again, a wordless, animal cry. His hands slipped lower, and she felt the loss of them there, tangling in her fair hair. She slipped her own hands around the back of his neck, pulling him ever closer, not letting him escape. She had thought he would laugh, he was always laughing, glorying perhaps in her wanton need of him, the ease with which he had toppled her icy reserves and propriety, but he did not. He was too consumed with her even to savour his victory, and the knowledge flared up within her, spurring her on.

He spoke her name again, a growl in the back of the throat, claiming her as his, and she let herself be claimed. I *am his. I am* his. A truth that would wound her deeply later, a fatal wound, a killing stroke, but for now she let it flame and burn through her veins. He pulled her hard against him, tugging her up upon his lap so that their bodies were pressed together in a frantic, fumbling tangle.

His hands were hungrier even than his mouth. They hitched at her skirts, pulling them up to her waist and seeking hastily for entrance within with experienced efficiency. *This is not the first time he had done this.* A cold bite of reality began to seep in, dulling the heated frenzy within her and Maud's warning echoed at the back of her mind. He would take her, all of her, body and soul, and she would be nothing more than a frolic for him. She would be just one of many, interchangeable, disposable, meaningless, and when he had conquered the prize, when he had beaten the challenge — when he had *won* – she would bore him, as the rest of the world bored him. She pushed him away.

He pulled back a little all too reluctantly. Though his lips no longer rested against hers, his forehead did, pressing brow to brow as if he could find a haven there. His voice was low and pleading as it whispered against her skin.

"Do not, Charlotte, please. I cannot believe it is a crime to love one another, not when one feels as we do."

But he did not love her. He lusted for her, perhaps, though heaven alone knew why when he could have any woman he pleased, but she was not fool enough to believe he actually loved her.

It is because he believes he can have you, a nasty little voice at the back of her head whispered. He believes that you, like your mother, are weak and wanton and easily persuadable. A woman of no reputation and no virtue. Someone he can have with no consequence. And isn't he right? Look at yourself — would you really have denied him? A moment more, and you would have been lost irrevocably . . .

For half a moment she wondered what Edward's daughter would look like if, like her mother, she, too, bore an illegitimate child. Would it have his dark hair and deep eyes? Would it have his roguish half-smile and disregard for rules? She did not fool herself even in her maddest dreams into believing he would claim it, no matter how much of his likeness it bore. She would be left to raise the child alone. *Not even Mr Harris would have me then.* She would be nothing more than a woman of disgrace, as her mother was before her.

"The world does not agree," she said as firmly as she was able, hating the breathless urgency and need still lingering in her tones as she climbed out of his lap and settled herself beside him once more.

"Hang the world!" he spat out. His hands were still about her cheeks, his callused thumbs stroking there with a surprising gentleness, given the fury in his voice. "What have we to do with the world? What world is there beyond these four walls? What is there in the wide plains of the heartless and unfeeling earth that can change the way we feel? Let it disapprove and approbate, let it chide and scorn. Charlotte, *Charlotte,* you are mine. I feel it, more deeply than I have ever felt anything else. Do not deny it. That would be the only true crime."

She wanted to believe him. She wanted to believe the urgency pulsing in his eyes, the fearsome intensity burning in his gaze, the pulse pounding in his fingertips against her cheeks, fast and erratic and desperate. But she could not quiet that nasty little voice once more, asking how many other women he had proclaimed these words to, for them to fall so smoothly from his tongue. She placed her own hands gently over his and withdrew them from her face. He closed his eyes, sighing long and low, shaking his head as he drew it back from hers at last.

"I cannot be your absolution." She looked over to him and drew the only shaft she knew would find its mark. "Do I not deserve to be loved in my own right, poor and plain-faced and disagreeable though I am? Not as a salvation or a comfort, but as a woman of flesh and blood, for my own sake and no one else's?"

"I—" he began to protest, but then closed his mouth, the words left unfallen. He turned back to the window. His hair looked so deliciously disarrayed that Charlotte longed to reach out and stroke it, either to lay it flat once more or to tangle it up further, she did not know. She tightened her hands upon her waist instead, urging that longing within them to quiet once more.

"Forgive me," he grunted at last.

"There is nothing to forgive," she said once more. She would say it a thousand times if she had to, a hundred thousand times if he could only learn to believe it but once.

He just grunted again and lapsed into silence. She wished she knew what he was thinking, there amidst his turmoiled thoughts, but for once she did not dare ask. The journey lapsed into silence as the world darkened outside the carriage windows, jolting along into the burgeoning night. The carriage seemed to become closer, tighter, warmer, almost, just the two of them bound together within it, and yet Edward was still so far and unreachable.

As they turned up the final hill towards Drymote, something of his usual insouciant arrogance slipped over his features, that haunted, hunted look in his eyes falling behind a curtain of self-assurance as he raised his chin and affected an easy lounging complacency upon the faded velvet carriage cushions.

It is a façade. The realisation hit her hard. She could only stare at him as he transformed before her eyes, hiding all his wounds from view. She wondered that she had never seen it before.

The carriage drew to a stop outside the front of the house and before they had even finished descending, Albert had thrown the front door open and was staggering down the front steps uneasily. He was still in his bed-clothes, an old dressing gown wrapped around him as he came fumbling forwards.

"You cannot keep doing this to me, boy," he was roaring, and she could not tell whether the blotches on his face were sickness or fury. "You cannot keep disappearing upon me like this."

"Forgive me, Father," Edward said wearily. "We were

detained at the free hospital at Highpass."

Albert faltered, his face paling instantly. He looked between Edward and Charlotte with something akin to uncertainty.

"The hospital? Something is amiss."

"Certainly, it always is, but not with us this time. We saw a child fall from a tree and accompanied him to seek treatment, that is all."

Albert began to breathe again.

Whatever his faults, and no doubt they are myriad, he loves his son deeply and truly. She had missed being loved like that. It felt like a long time since she had been.

"Well, I suppose I can hardly begrudge you charity," Albert grumbled. "I wish I had known you were practising good works, Edward. I could have told the good vicar when he came to call this afternoon."

Edward laughed bitterly. "Let not your right hand know what your left hand does, Father, is that not what the good book says?"

"Well, no one in the good book was standing for parliament."

Edward just patted his father's shoulder companionably. "And neither am I," he assured Albert. "At the moment I intend to stand for nothing save a large drink and a long sleep. Goodnight, Father. Goodnight, Charlotte." He nodded vaguely in her direction, but he would not look at her. It is because you saw him at his most vulnerable, that insidious voice whispered at the back of her mind. He does not know how to be known like that. She sighed long and deep as she stared after his retreating back and watched him ascend the stairs without saying anything.

You cannot save him, Charlotte, she told herself firmly. You cannot fix him. No one ever found happiness that way. He needs to find his own peace first. And yet her heart was aching for him, and it seemed that the more she knew him, the more it ached. At first, she'd only seen what the world saw, the insouciant smirk, the wicked repartee, the irreverent flirting, and yet it was all but whitewash on a broken wall. It covered, but it would not mend.

Be careful, Charlotte. You are half in love with him already. It will not take much to tip you irreversibly into the ravine.

She could have laughed at the cold and quiet voice whispering its warnings at the back of her mind. Surely they both knew they had come far too late for that?

CHAPTER TWELVE

The library was quiet in the still morning light. The hush of ancient silences calcified between the shelves, lingering in the leather, paper and ink. It had been a lifetime since she had been in here.

There were some gaps in the shelves now, she noticed. Some of the older folios were missing. Sold, probably, to pay for Albert's carriage, parties and fine clothes. She could almost hear his sneering voice. *Appearances must be maintained. Cotterhugh is a fine old name. It must not be disgraced now.*

The shelves were emptying, the servants' quarters, too . . . how much longer would it be before Drymote was hollowed out entirely?

She ran her fingers over the old atlas open on the centre table. It seemed smaller now than it had when she was a child. Back then, the world had seemed so large and exciting.

She sighed and drew herself back out of her wistful dreams. If that will was anywhere, it would surely be in Oldridge's Garden Compendium. Charlotte staggered up the ladder to the topmost shelves, her ankle complaining within her battered leather boot with each step. She felt tears prickling at her eyes as her hand closed over the embossed cover. Her emotions had been uncharacteristically fragile lately. She was not one given to crying, and yet now she constantly felt on the edge of a breakdown.

It was just weariness, she lied to herself, for an aching exhaustion had been creeping into her bones these last few weeks, dragged in with the longer nights and darker days, perhaps.

"Charlotte?"

She yelped, astonished at the sudden sound, and slipped from the ladder, the book flying from her hand. Edward's arms were around her waist in a moment, guiding her gently down to the library floor. She blushed.

"Forgive me. I am not usually so clumsy."

He just grinned and fetched the book from the floor. He had fallen back into his over-bright and teasing ways now, as if he could wipe away the memory of yesterday's vulnerabilities if only he could smile wide enough or laugh loud enough. He looked weary as well, though, she noticed. His eyes were dark, his skin pale. He clearly had not slept last night. A surge of sympathy swept over her, but she did not voice it. He does not like being seen, she reminded herself.

He just raised an eyebrow as he placed the book into her hands and helped her to the window seat, where the autumn sunlight blessed them both.

"What are you doing here? I did not think I would see the day when you were indoors whilst the sun was out."

She hesitated and then shrugged, her fingers stroking the cover of the book idly. "It is a long story."

"I have little else to occupy the weary hours. You would oblige me by filling them with even the longest of tales."

"Truthfully, I do not know whether to credit it myself, only Fletch seemed so sure, and he's not one to invent mysteries for pleasure . . ." She trailed off and shrugged again. It sounded so foolish to say it aloud. "Fletch told me yesterday that Uncle John left a will, and a bequest for me within it. He thinks if I can find it, I can have an independent income. He thinks I will be *free*."

Edward stared at her for a moment, and she could not read his expression.

"That's wonderful news," he said hoarsely at last. "Truly,

it is fantastic, Charlotte. I confess, I thought it strange that John did not leave any provision for you. I always assumed he would have, and then when there was no will to be found, I thought it was only because his last illness came on so suddenly and left no time for such things. So what is the problem?"

"Fletch says he hid it. Uncle John's mind was loosened near the end. This was his favourite book. I thought it might be in here . . ." She looked down at the well-worn book within her hands. Now that it came to it, she found she could hardly dare check. If it was not there after all . . . and perhaps worse, what if it was? *Things will change then. Am I really ready for that?*

"Well, look!" Edward said impatiently. "Do you wish me to do it?" he added when she did not move. She placed the book silently into his hands and he flicked through it fast. Nothing was hidden between the leaves. He held it by its covers and shook it vigorously, but nothing came out. He ran his hands through the illustration plates with far too much roughness, and she could not help but wince as his fingers scratching over the delicate ink-drawings. She lay a hand upon his arm.

"Stop, Edward. It is not there."

He frowned in frustration, looking around at the rest of the library. "Well, come on. We have plenty more books to check." But Charlotte shook her head.

"No. This was the only book he ever read. If it is not here, I doubt it will be in the library at all." The words choked her, but she forced them out. She tried to sound bright and cheery, though the world blurred before her. "Perhaps it is as well. I should not try to steal your inheritance out from under your feet. I know Drymote needs the money —"

"It need it no more than you yourself do," he argued. "I am a man, am I not? Capable of earning my own bread by the sweat of my brow, whatever my father thinks of it." He grinned his best libertine smile, and Charlotte could not help but smile back, too. His hand lingered over hers, there upon his arm, and she felt herself burning under his touch. "I do not begrudge you a single farthing of it, Charlotte, however much it might be. Come! Rack those brains of yours, you must have some idea where the old coot would have kept it!"

"I honestly do not. If it were not with his lawyer and not in his papers, I do not know where it would be. Fletch thinks he hid it for safety, though I cannot think why he should imagine that necessary."

Edward grimaced, and blushed slightly. "You are an optimist at heart, I think. You like to think the best of people. My father can be a little . . . single-minded when it comes to the good of the Cotterhugh name. He is not a bad man, Charlotte, but I do not think him above *accidentally* burning a will if it contained a codicil he did not approve of." He turned horror-struck to Charlotte as an unpleasant thought occurred to him. "You do not think he has found it already? You do not think he has already destroyed it?"

Charlotte felt her heart plummeting, her stomach knotting with disappointment. How strange. She had not even known she was harbouring hope, so why did the dashing of those dreams taste so bitterly in her mouth?

"We will keep looking, I swear it," he promised her hoarsely. "And if we find it, we will not tell my father at all. We will take it straight to the lawyers in London and make them implement it before my father can object."

A laugh burst from her lips before she could stop it. "I think, Mr Cotterhugh, that however hard you try to hide it, there is a good man lurking within you. Not many people would work so vehemently against their own interests."

"Oh yes, they are sainting me any day now," Edward agreed sardonically. He smacked his hand against his head suddenly. "That's it, of course! The abbey! John spent all his time in the abbey, did he not?" He stood at once in a flurry, his hands clutching at her excitedly. "It will be in the abbey, Charlotte. It must be. Come! We must search at once!"

"What is going on here?" Albert croaked from the doorway. He was still in his bedclothes, despite the hour. Clearly, he was not feeling any better. Charlotte flinched again. She had not seen him sneaking up upon them. She looked over to Edward and found him looking warily back at her. How much had he heard?

"We were just going for a walk, Father," Edward said breezily. "I was just saying that Charlotte looked a little under the weather this morning. I thought some fresh air would do her good."

"She would be feeling better if she took her vitamins like she ought."

"I have been taking them!"

"Well, perhaps we ought to up the dosage. I will write to Dr Farringham and get him to prescribe you some more."

Perhaps Albert should get Dr Farringham to prescribe some for him as well, Charlotte thought. That sickly grey tinge still clung to his skin, he flinched repeatedly at the morning shadows, and he kept glancing wildly around the room.

"I'm sure a little walk is all the tonic she needs. Come, Charlotte," Edward said with a bright forcefulness, grabbing her arm and guiding her past the protesting Albert, who was still watching them with a flickering suspicion, glaring at the two of them as if he had caught them plotting his demise.

"Do not venture farther than the estate," Albert called out after them. "It will only cause talk."

Charlotte went to fetch her cape and pulled it about her firmly, hiding her tingling fingers in her gloves and scrunching her fizzing toes up within her boots. The cold seemed to make them worse than ever. She was sure she had not been feeling the numbness in them so often as all this.

Perhaps she ought to take a stronger dose of vitamins to counteract the damage, as Albert suggested, and yet she hated to be indebted further to him.

If it gets worse, I will return to the free hospital. The worst they can do is send me away unseen and chide me for wasting their time. I can stand a little rebuking, I have done so before.

She threaded her hand through Edward's arm and he led her down towards the folly with an excitable haste.

"Slow down, I cannot walk as fast as you. Are you really in that much of a hurry to be rid of me?"

"Never, but I want you to be free, Charlotte. I want you to be able to choose your path without restraint and not because you have no other options available."

She did not know what to say to such a proclamation, so she said nothing.

Edward took a deep breath and then plunged onwards. "I think that I acted ill towards you in the carriage. I have been considering it deeply through the long, dark hours last night, and I think you are right. I have been seeking comfort in you, trying to escape myself in you, and you deserve more than that. I want to give you more than that. I want to give you everything."

She turned away, pulling her hand from his grasp, but he caught at her face.

"Charlotte? What is it? What is wrong?"

"I have told you before not to mock me."

"Why can you not believe I am sincere?"

"You would marry me?" she asked sceptically.

He growled out a breath of frustration. "Why not? There is no law forbidding it. We are both single and of no close blood to one another. There is no legal impediment that would take you from me. I could have you as my wife, and there would be none who could foreswear it. Tell me, Charlotte, if I summoned the courage to ask, would I receive a kindly answer or hopeless one?" His eyes were burning brightly, lost somewhere between hope and desperation, and Charlotte scarcely knew what to say to that. Her heart was screaming at her to say yes, but her mind knew it must say no for, even if all her wildest, most romantic, most improbable daydreams came true, and in a fit of recklessness and passion Edward actually married her, what then? They would still lose Drymote, the home she had cherished since her childhood, the heart of Uncle John and Aunty Ursula, the place where she had first tasted love. She would still have to see it sold off in parcels or given into the unfeeling hand of a stranger. And Edward would find the first fires of his passion and lust cooled by deprivation, poverty and the hard grind of reality. He would grow to despise her for marrying him, for stealing him away from everything he had once been promised and she would look into his eyes and find nothing but coldness lingering there beneath the sardonic remarks.

She thought for a moment he was going to kiss her again, for there was the same yearning hunger flaring through his face, that need to be with her, to be lost and found within her, but he held himself apart with a rigid self-control she did not know he possessed. She took a step back, even as she longed to step forward.

"I'm not sure what Albert would have to say about such a thing."

Edward laughed, a bitter, mirthless laugh as dark as the sky at midnight. "I know all too well what my father would have to say about such a thing, but as he is not the one asking, I do not think it matters much."

But Edward was not the one asking either, not really. He was dealing in hypotheticals, eager to be assured that she could be his, not that she truly was. She took another step back, trying to gain some space between them, trying to find air to breathe that was not alight with his presence and his scent.

"Have you not made enough promises in the last few days? Why, only yesterday you swore upon your honour to find a missing child and return her to her grandmother. That is no small task."

He stared at her for a long moment and then sighed. He clasped his hands before him, as though he could hold himself under control, and that ever-ready façade came back up, shuttering all that vulnerability from view once more. She rued its absence, her heart aching with the thought that he would trust her with his weakness, and yet, what else could she do? He deserved a life she could not give him.

"No small task indeed. And do I not know it? It was another thing plaguing me through the long hours of the night." He smiled ruefully at her, and she smiled back, glad that frantic desperation had been brought back under control once more.

"I do not even know where to begin." He sighed, running a hand through his hair, making it stand askew in the morning light. "Where does one go to find that which has been lost?"

"I only wish I knew," she muttered.

The path to Ursula's Abbey was overgrown with moss-covered trees, and on a day like today, mist hung between their gnarled and curved branches. She walked beneath the alley of their outstretched arms, feeling unaccountably as if she was being watched. The abbey loomed up ahead out of the autumnal mists, and she could not help but shudder.

It had always been a place of peace, but now it was beginning to feel like a haunted space, as if Ursula and John still resided here. She shivered, the hairs upon her skin prickling. She knew she was being paranoid, but she could not help it.

The door to the abbey was open when they arrived and she felt panic spiking in her pulse at the ominously open doorway. She clutched at Edward's sleeve and he looked down at her in surprise.

"Charlotte?"

She could not answer his unspoken question, for she scarcely knew what was wrong herself, only that it felt like a conspiracy and a warning. Sweat prickled against her skin as hurried footsteps echoed from within it.

"Hello? There's someone in there," Edward muttered, frowning.

At least he could hear the footsteps, too, at least she was not utterly mad.

Edward darted forwards and she followed, clinging to him. The vestry door was open, and Edward ran full pelt towards it, throwing it back on his hinges and found . . .

"Harris?"

Charlotte, peering around Edward's shoulder, saw Mr Harris half out of the glassless window, flustered and fumbling, red-faced and awkward. She could not help but laugh, more at her own relief than at the ridiculous sight before her.

Poor Mr Harris was a deep and burning shade of burgundy now.

He extricated his leg with difficulty, bowing a fumbling bow at both of them.

"Forgive me, Mr Cotterhugh, I did not mean to intrude. Your father was telling me of the follies your uncle built, the Hermit's retreat, the Bell Tower, and Ursula's Abbey. He said I ought to come and see them, so I availed myself of his kind invitation this morning, but then I heard voices outside and I thought perhaps I was getting in the way, so I . . ." He blushed even deeper as he gestured towards the hole behind him.

"Is that *all* you came to see?" muttered Edward under his breath, but Charlotte spoke over him loudly.

"And you are more than welcome, Mr Harris. You did not need to flee. We are always happy to see you. Tell me, how do you find the abbey?"

Mr Harris coughed, still burning, shuffling from foot to foot, casting another eye out of the window behind him, as if to see if anybody else was sneaking up upon them.

"Very well. It is very pretty. In truth, it reminded me of the first book of Samuel, chapter sixteen verse seven, *for the LORD seeth not as man seeth, for man looketh on the outward appearance, but the LORD looketh on the heart.* It is a stark reminder that God does not judge as man does, by outward appearances. To an untrained eye, the abbey seems like a true house of worship and yet, once within it, it becomes obvious that it is the mere illusion of honest religion — "

Charlotte felt Edward stiffening tightly beside her as Mr Harris prattled obliviously on, and it was all she could do to bite back a laugh at his agonised expression.

At least if I did become a lady of independent means, I would not have to entertain the merest thought of a marriage proposal from dear Mr Harris. He was a good man, what her uncle deemed dull but worthy, but the thought of fifty more years sitting across the dining table from him, listening to him prattle on about ecclesiastical matters, was a unique and sublime form of torture.

" — the outward vestiges rather than the inward heart," he finished, his puppy-dog eyes shining earnestly.

"And does it therefore have no value?" Edward asked darkly. "Because it is no true abbey, is it therefore worthless?" Charlotte suspected he was only asking the question to be provoking. She rather suspected he was inclined to take the opposite view to Mr Harris on any matter at all, just to be contrary. He had never shown any particular philosophical fondness for follies before now.

"Oh no, not at all! Why, beauty is its own reward, is it not? It all points us to the maker of beautiful things. It is almost a duty, I have often thought, to revel in the beautiful things of this world. To appreciate them truly is its own form of worship."

"Uncle John always thought so, too." Charlotte smiled, and Edward scowled harder.

"In physical forms as well as natural?" he asked sourly. Mr Harris blushed, glancing out of the window again, as if he might still make his escape that way even now.

"I . . . I do not . . . I fear I do not quite follow you, Mr Cotterhugh."

"There is nothing quite as beautiful as a woman now, is there? Or does the rigid training of ecclesiastical colleges blind you to such things? Is it a sin then to appreciate the beauty of the fairer sex? Is that not just mere lust?"

Mr Harris blushed even deeper and muttered something scarcely audible about such conversations hardly being fit in the presence of a lady.

"Forgive him, Mr Harris. He is not himself today. He has been burdened by a heavy weight of good deeds, and it tells upon his temper," said Charlotte in her most placating manner. "Perhaps you may yet be able to help him with it?" she said suddenly, the thought coming upon her abruptly. Again, Mr Harris mumbled some appropriate response.

"There is a poor woman's child," continued Charlotte. "The mother is friendless and alone, dying in the free hospital at Highpass, and the child has been thrown on the mercy of the parish. Perhaps, as a clergyman, you might know where she has been sent. The name is Julia Antinori and she must be five years old now."

"So young to be alone!" Mr Harris declared with a kind and manly sympathy, which quite inclined Charlotte's spirit to him. *He is a good man. If only I could learn to love him.*

"Why don't you take Mr Harris up to the house and discuss the details with him, whilst I *finish up here,*" she said significantly at Edward, who scowled at her once more, as if asking how she could leave him alone with such a man. Mr

Harris did not look any happier about the prospect either, she noted. She did not think she would ever persuade them to be friends, a disappointing notion as she loved both of them so dearly — in entirely different ways, of course, but dearly nonetheless.

Still, Edward reluctantly agreed, and Mr Harris had no choice but to fall in step beside him.

She looked around the now empty folly. Edward had been so convinced it would be here, and she had let herself be persuaded, but now that he was gone it seemed like nothing more than a cruel prank.

Perhaps he is part of it? Perhaps he is trying to lead me astray so that Albert can find and destroy it himself?

That thought was cruel and unlikely, she knew, but it crept upon her prickling at the back of her neck, making her pulse pound. She licked her suddenly dry mouth.

"You must think better of him than that, Charlotte," she chided. "You know who he is."

Yes, a libertine, who tried to seduce you. A good man who saved a child's life. A man who took his friend's life in a duel. Someone who regretted that mistake bitterly. A rake who knows nothing but the shallow pleasures of the world — someone who hid behind that façade because it was too painful to let the world see the truth.

"Stop arguing within yourself, Charlotte Mayweather. You will end up like your mother. Concentrate on finding that will."

She looked around at the empty shadows, the only thing lingering in the little room with her.

There didn't seem to be anywhere to hide the will here, even if John wanted to.

She turned to go, but was aware of eyes watching her out there amongst the undergrowth. She whirled around, but could not see anything.

"Hello? Edward? Mr Harris?" A pause, a heartbeat of fear

and then, more hesitantly . . ."Marcello?"

No answer, just the whisper of the wind bringing back the ghostly footsteps from the distance, echoing like gossamer threads across the morning and a faint whisper of silk on fallen, crunching leaves.

Her heartbeat was thundering in her throat as she crept across the room, her pulse pounding loud enough to echo. She was very aware of her own body as it made its way across the high and desolate vestry, dappled with sunlight from the windows and shadows watching in the corners. Hairs prickled and tingled at the back of her neck, and her headache began to intensify, a thick and thunderous pressure growing in her temples, like the way the air became charged before a storm. Her hands tightened on the glass-less window frame and she peered out into the overgrown shrubbery beyond. It was empty, and she was not sure if she was glad or not. The emptiness stared at her mockingly, almost a presence in and of itself.

Tangles of vines crept through the window hole like insidious, ghostly fingers clawing their way in, and they danced in the breeze as if beckoning her. She looked down and saw footprints lingering in the soft churned mud beneath the window — someone had fled this way . . . Her hands tightened on the windowsill, a bramble catching at the hem of her sleeve. As she wrenched herself free, she found a snag of fabric caught beside her own, a thin thread torn, she fancifully imagined, from an old abbess' dress. She shivered, feeling fear rake its claws over her skin once more and she felt a raw and powerful desire to flee overtake her, as if she could not physically bear to be in here any longer. She darted for the door, but even as it thumped closed behind her she could not shake that haunted feeling. She pushed herself harder — faster — her feet slipping in the mud, her ankle screaming at her as she over-exerted it after its long convalescence. She whipped around the corner of the winding path and collided headfirst into Edward and Mr Harris still walking slowly up towards the house.

"Miss Mayweather?" Mr Harris asked in concern, but she scarcely heard him. She buried her head in Edward's chest, her breath, still ripped out of her jagged and fearful, shuddering slightly as she clung to him — her hand lingering upon his chest as she regained her balance. It was reassuringly solid under her fingertips, his heartbeat pounding slow and steady as a river tide. She rested her forehead against his chest and told herself she was only being foolish.

"Charlotte? Whatever is the matter? You look as if you've seen a ghost!" There was amusement in his voice, and through his eyes she could learn to see such things as ludicrous, too, perhaps, but even as she threaded her fingers through his, she felt the eyeless windows of the abbey watching her malevolently. Frantic footsteps echoed through the quiet morning, and they tasted like fear on her tongue. She clutched at Edward and saw to his relief that he was frowning out through the undergrowth. Clearly, she was not the only one who could hear those ghostly steps, which made her feel better somewhat.

Maud came hurtling down the path towards them, her uniform askew, looking more distraught than Charlotte had ever seen her. Charlotte could not help but stare. She did not think anything could upset the icy reserves of Maud's propriety. The world had gone mad today, it seemed. Something was in the air, lingering like an infectious miasma and they breathed in lunacy on the winds.

She skidded to a halt before all three of them, red-faced and panting, sweat making her hair stick to her face, but she only had eyes for Edward.

"Please, Mr Cotterhugh," she gasped, doubled over and clutching her side, tears and panic swirled in equal parts in her hooded eyes. "I've been looking for you everywhere. You must come at once. It's your father."

Chapter Thirteen

Edward paced up and down the corridor like a wounded beast, and Charlotte could do little more than watch him helplessly.

"Farringham has been in there with him half an hour or more. Why will he not tell me what has been going on?"

"You know Dr Farringham only discusses ailments with the man who pays him," Charlotte reminded him gently. "Why, he would not even discuss my own diagnosis with me, and I was the patient! Give it some time, Edward. Your father will tell you all when he can."

Edward's eyes were haunted as they turned to her own, his face grey and slack. "I thought he was dead," he croaked. "When I saw him there, I thought—" He choked on the words, and Charlotte felt her heart fly up to her throat. Instinctively, she reached out for him and he tumbled gratefully into her arms. It did not feel improper, and even if it was, she scarcely cared anymore. She would never care if she could offer him but some little comfort, do him but some little good. She reached up and stroked his hair as he buried his head in her neck, trying to get his breathing back under control, hushing him as if he were a small child.

In truth, she had thought Albert dead, too, when they found him lying upon his study floor. He had been so still, had looked so very small.

Convulsions, the servants had said. He had been taken by an abnormally strong fit abruptly, and it had caught him unawares. He had hit his head upon the desk and collapsed to the floor. They could not rouse him, and, portly as he was, they could scarcely lift him. Someone had already been sent scurrying for Dr Farringham.

They had managed between them to manhandle Albert up the stairs and into his own bed at last, and then had come the long, agonising wait whilst Dr Farringham did all he could.

Perhaps it would be better for him to go quickly. Was that a callous thought? Charlotte could no longer tell, only she had heard that syphilis was a lingering, painful way to go . . . perhaps a quick accident catching him unawares was the kinder option.

Not kinder for Edward though, she thought as he clasped to her gratefully. His fingernails dug through her mourning dress, leaving tell-tale marks of anguish in her skin, but she did not tell him so. He could scratch her all to pieces if it would relieve him but a little.

Perhaps Drymote was cursed. It had had more than its fair share of death lately, as though the Grim Reaper was haunting its halls, lurking in the candle-lit shadows in each empty room, waiting just behind each door for them to enter. Was that just paranoia? Surely it was hopelessly morbid to entertain such thoughts?

Edward tore himself out of her grasp as the door opened, whirling around in an instant to face the stern-faced doctor.

"Well? Will he live?"

Dr Farringham did not seem the least bit perturbed by Edward's grasping grief. His voice was curt and professional as ever, as if any flicker of human warmth had been sucked out of it by monotonous years of service.

"For a little while longer, at least. He wishes to speak to you."

"Yes, yes, of course—" But it was not Edward Dr Farringham was looking at. His steely glare was fixed upon . . .

"Me?" Charlotte asked in disbelief. Edward turned to look

at her, too, outraged indignation echoing across his face.

"I am his only son! I have a right to see him!"

"The patient decides whom he will see," Dr Farringham said sententiously. "He wishes to see Miss Mayweather first and you after, Mr Cotterhugh. He made that very clear to me. I will return tomorrow. Good day."

Charlotte could scarcely do more than murmur *good day* herself in stunned disbelief as the doctor swept away down the corridor without waiting to be shown to the door.

She pushed open the door in trepidation and found Albert sitting up in his bed, clad in a night-shirt, grey-faced but alert. He had a large bump forming on his head already, shot with watercolour bruises seeping over the left-side of his face, his eye almost swollen shut. His right eye was blood-shot but sharp, fixing her with its penetrating gaze. He beckoned her forwards impatiently and she crept up to his bedside.

"I am dying, Miss Mayweather," he said shortly. Charlotte did not say anything, and Albert let out a bitter laugh which reminded her sharply for a moment of Edward himself. "This comes as no surprise to you, I see. I suppose Edward informed you of my position, and the — er — ailment which creates it."

"Yes," she said softly. She reached out across the coverlet and squeezed Albert's arm gently. He stared at her in surprise, as if he had expected judgement and not compassion from her. He sat for half a moment, and then, with a cough, extracted himself from her grasp.

"Well, you will understand why the situation has become so urgent. Dr Farringham has told me I am fast approaching the third and final stage of my ailment." He shuddered for a moment at the dreadful prospect looming up before him, his eyes flickering closed, before carrying resolutely on, his voice filled with nothing but steely determination. "I must see Edward well wed before that happens. I must see him settled before I die, so that I can go in peace, knowing his future is safe."

"I cannot make him marry Miss Bletchley," she said quietly. "Nor can I make him go into parliament as you desire. He is firmly set against both."

"He values your advice. Persuade him earnestly, Charlotte. His future happiness and the security of Drymote all depend upon it."

"Does his happiness truly depend on marrying someone he has little inclination for?"

Albert sighed deeply, and for a moment she could not help but think that he looked so old. His normal pompous bluster had fled away and he stared at her hard with his one good eye.

"I know it will not seem so to someone so young," he said quietly and there was something so earnest in his voice that she could not help but stare. "I know at your age it seems like affairs of the heart are all that matters, that romance is the only true course to fulfilment. I was there myself once, though I learnt to pay the price for such folly. But if you marry Edward, no, do not protest, any fool could see the two of you are inclined to one another, hear me through — *if you marry Edward,* both of you would learn to rue it in time. He is a hunter at heart, he thrills for the chase. He would revel in his victory over you for some little time, and then he would turn away to some new novelty that caught his attention."

She stared down at her hands, clasped tightly in her lap, her cheeks scalding. Her heart whispered to her that it was not true, that Albert had too poor an opinion of Edward, that Edward sought novelty only to escape his past and not for novelty's sake, and yet was Edward himself not saying that his heart was fickle only yesterday in the carriage ride home? Was he not ruing his affair with Theodora for that very reason?

"Even were that true, sir, it would not be any different with any other woman. If he had the type of heart to search after new loves every year, it would not be any more constant to Miss Bletchley than it would be to me. If it were true, she would not be able to entrance and keep him any more than I could."

"No," he agreed. "He has not the character to love deeply or constantly for anyone." This felt like a bitter slander, Edward knew how to love, she had seen it in him, she had seen the burning flame there, but Albert said it so calmly that it raised doubts like itching sores in her own mind. Edward was a man of passion, but was that passion truly love, or was it merely lust as the world knew it? She could scarcely tell. She looked up at Albert and saw pity staring back at her, pity for her, though he was the one dying. *How pathetic am I, to earn compassion in such a time as this?*

"His happiness would not be secured in Miss Bletchley any more than it would be with me," she whispered again, stubbornly defying the insurmountable odds rising above her.

"He will never love Miss Bletchley, that is true, but he would learn to hate you."

She gasped, the words striking at the core of her like a knife. "That is not true."

"I know you do not wish to hear so, Charlotte, but it is. He would grow bored of you once his inclinations passed, and, not having any other inducements to sweeten your marriage, he would resent being bound to you. At least with Miss Bletchley, he would be able to live a life of comfort, perhaps even luxury, as he has been accustomed to. He would never know want, could indulge in a few harmless pastimes and hobbies, would find contentment. He would respect Miss Bletchley, and they will live a quiet and harmless life, devoid of the furious passion of love, true, but also devoid of bitterness and acrimony. If he marries you, his love will quickly turn to boredom, and boredom to resentment, and resentment to hatred. The love that tasted so sweet to your youthful tongues would bitter into ash and limestone, and you will face the hard grind of poverty together with little to alleviate it. I love my son dearly, but I know his faults. His is not the character to face hardship. He has spent his life running from it and he will run from it still. As soon as he faces the first storm, he will abandon ship, fleeing for port alone and leave you, perhaps even with a child to care for, alone and unloved. It is a desolate world for a woman abandoned, Charlotte. My brother would not want to see that life for you, and neither do I. It is in your best interests, Edward's best interests and Drymote's best interests that this . . . youthful passion . . . does not develop into anything more."

"And if Miss Bletchley does not wish to marry him?"

"I hardly think that likely." Neither had Charlotte, but Georgiana had seemed quite insistent about the matter. "Well, and if she does not, there will be other heiresses with the funds to save Drymote and secure Edward's future. But he cannot marry you." He sighed when she did not speak. She could not speak. Her throat felt as though it had swollen to twice its thickness.

"I know you think I speak harshly to you, but my time is running out. I do not have the luxury of being less direct."

Still she did not speak.

Albert sighed once more, slumping back against the pillows and wincing. "Think on these things, at least. Not because I have bought your loyalty with my generosity — I see now that I should have offered you your medicines with an open hand, for yours is not the type of character to be blackmailed, I think — but because I know that you love him. And I know that you love him enough to work for his best interests, even if they go against the yearnings of your own heart."

She rose, sensing the dismissal, but Albert held out a shaking hand for her.

"I meant it," he said quietly. "I should not have tried to

blackmail you before. I was desperate, but it was wrong of me. From now on, I will see you provided with your tablets no matter what you decide to do, for you must continue to take them. Just promise me you will consider my words earnestly."

"Yes," she croaked, the words scarcely more than a whisper in her throat. "Yes, I will."

"Thank you, Miss Mayweather. Please, send my son in to me, I would see him now."

She scarcely knew what she did that afternoon. Edward spent many hours with his father that day, and several times she heard his voice ringing out through the dull, deadened corridors with rage and passion. She did not go to find him. She did not know how to, for Albert's words still echoed with a dreadful perseverance through her brain, and she could not help but wonder if he was right.

She had grown up immersed in Ursula and John's gentle love story — the way they complimented and completed each other, John's gruff quietness to Ursula's loving warmth, John's stoicism to Ursula's passion. The silent declarations of love in each crinkle-eyed smile they shared, the fleeting touches of a hand upon a shoulder as John passed Ursula sewing by the fire, or a hand resting in the small of the back as he helped her up the stairs, the smallest touches that spoke of deep rooted love, old and yet new and still ever growing. She had thought that was normal.

She had grown with the girlish expectation of finding a love like that of her own one day — a flourish of bonfire passion which turned into the steady glow of the hearth, warming the whole house through. Perhaps that was foolish, and yet she found she would rather not wed at all, than marry for anything less than what her aunt and uncle had shared. How could she persuade Edward to do any different? Would that not be the worst kind of hypocrisy? And yet, perhaps not all people were made alike, perhaps a more business-like marriage would be better suited to some people's temperaments. Could she trust Albert, of all people, to judge which marriage was best suited for his son? Was it not ultimately up to Edward to make his own decisions?

The thoughts chased themselves miserably around her mind, and she had still not settled upon a decision when dinner time came at last. She sat herself down in the dining hall, not expecting anything more than a long and silent meal, when Edward came in and threw himself down in a chair beside her.

"I did not think you would come," she said, throwing him a sympathetic smile. "I'm glad you did though, you must keep your strength up."

He grunted and rubbed his face. He ate without talking for a few moments and Charlotte thought perhaps it would be kindest to leave him to his silence.

"What did my father speak to you of?" he asked abruptly. Charlotte flushed a little, looking up from the peas she was chasing around her plate.

"I think he would not like me to talk of it with you," she said. "Sorry."

"Did he tell you that he has come off his medications? That is why he had such a fierce attack."

She stared at him in shock. "No! Why would he do that? They are the only things slowing his disease." A horrible thought occurred to her and she felt her cheeks burning burgundy. "You do not think he has ceased taking his tablets to pay for my own?"

Her stomach squirmed guiltily. If that were true, would she not ultimately be responsible for his death? Should she not refuse to take the tablets from him, so that he could afford his own medicines? And yet, if she did, she would be lame.

She was young and had her whole life ahead of her, and he was dying anyway — and yet, was that not complete selfishness?

Edward shook his head. "No, I am sure that is not why. Despite my father's miserliness, I am sure we have money enough for two sets of tablets. I think he grows weary of fighting it, to be honest. I think he wishes for it all to be over now and looks to hasten his own end."

"Oh Edward, no, I am sure that is not true either. He did not say as much, surely?"

"No, he did not, but my father is a liar." Edward laughed darkly and rubbed his face again. "He says he needs a respite from the side-effects of the mercury and then he will resume his tablets when he has recovered his strength, but he will never recover his strength without the tablets. He will just chase himself down to a quick, dismal end."

He ran his hand through his hair, setting it on end, and Charlotte was out of her chair and over by his side before she knew what she was doing. She wrapped her arms around his shoulders and he pulled her down onto his lap, burying his face in her neck. She stroked his hair flat again gently.

"I know what it is like to watch someone you love die," she murmured into his hair. "I understand how hard it can be, how it feels like you do not have the strength to carry on any longer, how you long for it to be over, and yet fear for him to pass at the same time."

"I do not know how much longer I can do this, Charlotte. I know that makes me a terrible son."

"Of course it doesn't, it just makes you human."

"I'm not sure I can stay and watch." The words were muffled in her neck, and she felt a flare of panic crashing through her. She tried to keep her body still, not allowing it to betray her response. He needed her to be calm right now. He didn't need her to add to his burden with the weight of her own needs.

"You can't run from everything," she whispered as calmly as possible. "If you leave now, you will regret it later. Say you will stay."

She desperately needed to hear him say it, even if it were just a whisper, but she would be denied even that small comfort by the door behind them opening.

"Oh, sorry Miss," the servant said in confusion, hardly knowing where to look. Charlotte leapt to her feet, abandoning Edward's lap hurriedly, but it was too late. No doubt the servant would be drawing his own conclusions now, and no doubt those conclusions would be spread abroad throughout the servants' quarters. She did not protest her innocence—it would not be believed anyway, and her scalding skin proclaimed her guilt all too easily.

I should have been more chary of my reputation. They will all think I am like my mother, a woman of loose morals and easy virtue.

Edward did not seem to care. He did not even glance at the servant as the man hurriedly backed out again. His gaze was still fixed on Charlotte's face, as if he had not even noticed the disruption.

"Tell me how to do it. How did you cope with John's death? I know you loved him as a father."

Charlotte hesitated and went back to her own chair. She felt the distance between them all too keenly, and yet she dared not resume her place in his arms.

Why not? The damage has already been done.

No, it had not. Not to her conscience, at least. They might spread all manner of rumours about her chastity below stairs, but if she stayed there in his arms, those rumours might yet become true, and she could not risk that.

She stared down at her half-finished dinner, cold and congealing on her plate. She pushed it around a little with a fork as she tried to summon her words.

"It was different with Uncle John," she said. "His death

was so sudden. He had hardly been ill at all, and then he came down violently with a virus no one knew how to cure. It was so abrupt that nobody had prepared for it. I hardly had to watch him die. I tended him in his illness, and then as soon as it had begun it was over." She felt the tears prickling in her eyes, her throat clogging with the memory of it, still so recent, still so raw. "It sometimes doesn't feel real, even now. It feels like perhaps he has just left the room for a while, and he will come in through the door at any moment."

Edward reached across the table and took her hand in his. She clasped onto it tightly with one hand and wiped her tears away with her other.

"There now, I'm supposed to be comforting you, not the other way around." She sniffed with a smile. "I think Uncle John would have preferred it this way if he could have chosen. He never did cope well with being ill. A short, sharp sickness and a hasty exit, that is the way to go. He is with Ursula now, and at least I got a chance to say goodbye to him. It was very providential your father had come to visit with us at the time, or Albert would have missed his chance to make a last adieu, too. I don't suppose either of them thought Albert would outlive John, given . . ." She waved her hand delicately, not wanting to voice aloud Albert's condition. She looked over at Edward and forced herself to smile. "There is no right way to grieve, just as there is no right way to love," she told him firmly. "I know right now that it feels like you cannot continue, that you cannot be strong enough to withstand this storm, but I am with you, Edward, and I will be with you through it all."

"Is that a promise?"

"For as long as you need me," she vowed. *And when he no longer needs me? When he finds someone else to fill that void within him instead? Someone else to offer him comfort and succour? Well, I will just have to learn to bear that burden alone, too.*

CHAPTER FOURTEEN

Aunty Ursula had always loved All Hallow's Eve. She loved the parade from the church. She loved the turnip-faces Bridget, her Irish-born lady's maid, insisted on carving. She loved gathering Charlotte up onto her lap to tell her stories of saints and loved ones past by the flickering fire-light.

The dead are always with us, Charlotte, as long as we hold them in our memories, but on some nights, like tonight, they are closer than you might believe... And Charlotte had laughed, too young, too naïve to really understand what Ursula had meant.

Perhaps she understood it a little better now.

She sat before the mirror, hand half-raised before her eyes, as if she had forgotten what it was doing there.

"Are you all right, Miss Mayweather?" Maud asked, a muted look of quiet concern on her face.

"Hmmm? Oh, yes, sorry. Just thinking."

"About ghost stories?" Maud asked, still brushing her hair and setting the dried flower crown in place amongst the golden strands. Dried poppy heads nestled like bulbous jewels there amongst the pressed cornflowers and sand-dried roses, woven round with evergreen leaves. "Do not tell me you are scared by spooks and saints?"

"Well, it is the night for it, is it not?" Charlotte joked weakly. She looked out across the fields. The night was settling in fast, her fingers were cold in the late afternoon light. Night would be upon them soon. Already, the lanterns were being lit down at the bottom of the hill, waymarking the parade's path through the woods and out across the fields. In the village, children would be gathering their little lamps, the adults their heavier kindling and brush torches, ready to hold them aloft as they walked, ready to drive the darkness back for just a little longer.

"It's a shame about the fog, is it not?" Charlotte said. "They might have to cancel the parade all together. We do not want people getting lost tonight."

Maud's face was a strange expression, but she merely bobbed a curtsey and made for the door.

"Oh," the maid added, turning at the threshold. "I have just remembered, I was supposed to tell you that Mr Cotterhugh will not be going to the All Hallow's Eve parade tonight. He does not feel up to task of facing so many people when his father is still such a cause of concern."

"Does he want me to stay, too?" Charlotte asked with a frown.

"No, Miss Mayweather."

"Perhaps I had better stay anyway," she mused, staring at her reflection with its dried flower crown nestled there amongst her artificial curls. "I have no one to chaperone me around the parade without Edward."

Maud let out a strangled laugh.

"Only ladies need chaperones, Miss Mayweather," she choked out. "Nobody bothers chaperoning maids or working women after dark. Tell me, which one are you closer to—a lady or a working woman?"

Charlotte felt a sharp retort coming to her throat, but Maud had swept out of the room haughtily before Charlotte could summon the right words. She really would have to say something about Maud one of these days, only the maid was Albert's, not her own, so she had no say in whether Maud was employed at Drymote or not.

Besides, it only stings because it is true. She wrapped her shawl around her shoulders and fled the house, her head held defiantly high. The night was falling heavily around her. The burning reds of the sunset over the horizon were all but obscured by the thick fog creeping over the hillside. She held her little lantern higher, but the circle of light it threw out was pitifully small.

Perhaps I should stay home, too . . . The parade would not be the same without Uncle John or Fletch anyway.

The wind whispered her name. She frowned, holding her light higher, as the darkness closed in.

"Hello?" No reply. "Edward?" *I am just growing paranoid. The ghost stories of All Hallow's Eve are over exciting me, that is all.*

Rolls of fog and mist started creeping up the hillside as she approached the lake, hovering over the glassy surface softly, but as she breathed it in, she found it was not fog at all. It was smoke.

She let out a sharp, frightened yelp, her stumbling feet hurrying forwards, trying to find the fire, trying to trace the coming destruction back to its source before it annihilated John's legacy forever.

Figures darted through the mist and smoke like nebulous dancers and she called out to them fearfully, but her voice was batted back to her, echoing mutedly on the smoke.

"Fire! Help! Fire!"

They did not reply. It was as if she had been abandoned entirely at Drymote, as if she were the only one left here alone. The world had taken on a nightmarish quality, and it was itching at her mind now, as if she could only wake up if she tried hard enough.

Another movement danced before her, the smoke growing thicker and blacker, and she followed it. There! The flames were taking root on a pile of dried leaves there by the base of the great oak. She darted forwards to stamp them out even as they licked up the tree trunk, but strong arms wound their way out of the smoke and held her back.

"Let go of me! I must put out the flames!"

She looked up to rebuke the gardener who held her firm, but found instead it was Marcello. His face was alight with grim retribution, the flames dancing wildly in his dark eyes.

"You! You have done this?"

"Why should he get Drymote?" Marcello spat, still holding her firmly in his arms. "His reputation will not be defeated, heaven knows I have tried. Even now, when you know the truth, you still stand by him. Why? Why does everyone always defend him? He cannot have it. He *will* not have it."

"He scarcely cares for Drymote at all, burning it down will not hurt him as you wish it to," she cried out in frustration. Nobody loved Drymote as she did. Why were they all so desperate to steal it from her?

She tried to dart forwards to stamp out the flames again, but Marcello pulled her away by force.

"Let it all burn down."

"No! Release me!"

The great oak had gone up, roaring like a bonfire, sending great pillars of smoke up into the air as though it were a torch for the parade. She fell to her knees, weeping into the soil for everything she had lost and everything she had still to lose and the smoke curled above her like her own funeral pyre. The great oak creaked, crumbled, fell — crumpling onto the Hermit's Retreat in a shatter of shells and pebbles.

"He does not love it," she wept.

"No, you are right, Cotterhugh neither cares for nor deserves this house. But you do — and he cares about you."

She looked up through streaming eyes. She could not tell if it was the smoke or the bitter sting of loss making them weep.

Marcello laughed manically in the flame-light. "I have seen where he has hidden his heart. I know now how to make him pay."

Marcello lunged forwards suddenly, grabbing her. His hands were hard and sharp, digging into her skin. She thrashed and screamed, but the fog swallowed the sound, dulling it until it bounced back at her in distant echoes.

"Do not become a murderer for your brother's sake! Revenge will not bring you peace!"

"Will it not?" Marcello whispered in her ear, the words barely audible above the crackle and roar of the fire, creeping ever nearer them. "Perhaps you are right. But won't it be fun for us to find out together?"

He was strong. His arms wrapped around her like chains as he hauled her forwards towards the fires still licking at the damp grounds, the embers burning like the rubies and golds of the autumn leaves. She kicked and screamed, but it made little difference as he wrestled them both inexorably forwards.

"Let me go! We will both die!"

"Good! Let us go out together, let it end once and for all." Marcello was laughing again, a manic, hysterical noise. Charlotte thrashed and screamed, panic clawing up her throat, and he shifted to put his hand over her mouth, clamping it shut. *Nobody knows I am out here. Nobody is coming to help.*

The irony did not escape her — let it finish as it had begun.

His fingers tasted like ash and sweat, she noticed distantly, and the strangeness of that tiny detail helped ground her a little.

No, it is not finished yet. I am not finished yet.

She bit down hard on the hand smothering her mouth and elbowed him hard in the gut as he released her with a yell. She pushed him and went scrambling out into the night. She felt fingertips clasping around her bad ankle and went fumbling down to the ground, the fog swallowing her whole as she fell.

He wrestled his way up until his body was pressing hers down to the ground, his hands like claws around her wrist.

She thrashed and kicked, but he was too heavy, too strong, pushing her down to the soil beneath, as if the grave were just waiting to swallow her whole.

"Julia!" she screamed. "You have a niece! Giuliani had a daughter!"

The pressure lessened slightly as Marcello paused, shocked.

"Giuliani is dead," she pressed on, desperately, "but his daughter still lives. You are not alone. I know what it is like to be alone and unloved, but you still have family waiting for you, Marcello. You still have someone who needs you. Do not abandon yourself to grief when there is still hope."

"Julia," he whispered uncertainly, and she seized hold of his hesitation eagerly. She kicked up and felt her knee connecting hard. He rolled off her with a soft *oof* and she scrambled up and out into the gaping darkness of the gardens. Footsteps hurried towards her, voices yelling and screaming, but she could not tell who they belonged to. She scrabbled forwards desperately, tripping on her own skirts, twigs and leaves scratching at her hands as she fumbled forwards alone.

Where are you Edward? I need you.

There was a call behind her, and she glanced desperately over her shoulder to see the gardeners and house staff were forming a bucket-chain from the lake, seeking to douse the flames. She could not see Edward or Albert amongst them. One of the footmen was wrestling Marcello to the ground, it looked like they were dancing together by the fire light, their shadows thrown up against the sky large and demonic. The smoke hissed, and she fled away from the destruction hounding her.

She ran for home, but the mist and muddle lingered in her mind and she found herself turned about in the dark. She thought she had turned left through the azalea terrace, but found herself in the middle of the magnolia trees instead, their blossomless branches knotted amongst each other.

A light – there. Another fire? More destruction?

Drymote was being stolen out from her feet and there was nothing she could do. Fear tasted like madness in her mouth as she plunged desperately towards the light, and found . . . Ursula's Abbey? Long streams of chilly, bright light streaming up through the glassless windows out into the sky.

The door was open a breath, spilling light out amongst the fog from a soot-clouded lantern balanced there upon the stone altar. It tinted the flickering light a deep and musky yellow, and the shadows which surrounded it danced eerily.

There was a woman within, wreathed in shadows and night, pacing before the altar, the hem of her dress hushing against the ground. She was talking to someone, or perhaps just to herself, for Charlotte could not make out any other figures from the darkness. Her voice was little more than a whisper, caught in the echoing recesses of those mist-shrouded vaulted halls, and it sounded strangely distorted and unrecognisable.

"You're right, the parade will be the perfect distraction. It has to be tonight. We must steel our nerve for one last night. For better or for worse it will be done by tomorrow." The thought seemed to amuse her. "For better or for worse, yes, it will all begin tonight . . ."

Charlotte leant forwards against the door and it groaned all too loudly as it crept inwards. The woman turned towards her and Charlotte let out a little mewl of fear. The stranger's cloak was pulled up high over her head, so that there was nothing but darkness within and, perhaps it was just the whispers of the night creeping into her mind, but it almost seemed as if she had no face at all. As if there was nothing left within that shroud—nothing but darkness coming to claim her. The figure took a step towards her, and Charlotte fled screaming out into the night once more, abandoning all reason behind her in that cold stone building.

CHAPTER FIFTEEN

Her heartbeat pounded. She could feel it everywhere — in her thumping head, in her fizzing fingertips, in her thick, stumbling legs, even throbbing upon her tongue, coppery and metallic. The night howled about her, the darkness tangling in her hair, snapping at her shadow as she fled. She dared not look around to see if the woman was chasing her — terrified lest she should see it once more — terrified lest she should not, for then where would it be? She did not know if she wanted it to be real or not — to be haunted and hunted was an awful thing — to be mad was a worse one.

The trees in the night beyond called for her, beckoning her outwards with their malevolent fingers, waltzing her about in nightmarish shadows and grim grey hues. The lights were already starting their small, bobbing procession out in the far, foggy darkness, like will o' the wisps calling her onwards to her doom.

She slipped and slid across the night-soaked grass, scrambling on all fours up the stone steps which led to the front doors like a wild woman possessed, her feet catching in the hems of her petticoats, making her stagger and fall. Maud stared at her as she slammed her way through the door, stumbling like a drunkard through the candle-lit hall. The shadows flickered and danced as she passed, following her, swaying around her, binding her round with their amorphous touch. She thrashed her arms, tripping for the stairs and grappling her way up them madly.

Edward caught her in his arms before she had even reached the top step. His face and shirt were soot and sweat stained, his hair disarrayed, his eyes panicked.

"Charlotte! Where have you been? I have been searching all over for you. I have been calling your name! Could you not hear me? I thought — the fire — Marcello — I thought — "

But whatever he had thought, he did not seem strong enough to put it into words. His face was pale beneath the soot, she noticed distantly. His hands found her face and tilted them up to face his.

"You're so cold." He swore. "Did Marcello hurt you? If he hurt you, I will see him hanged. I will never forgive myself."

He pulled her into his arms again and she rested her head against his chest, and the panic that had been driving her forwards exploded all at once. She wept copiously.

"They have caught him now," he murmured into her hair. "They have got the fires under control and they have taken him away. He cannot hurt you any longer."

Her legs went out from underneath her and he swore again. His arms swept around her and he lifted her off her feet, carrying her as gently as if she were a child, through to her own chambers and laid her gently down upon the bed.

"I will go for a doctor," he said, but she clutched at him desperately.

"No, stay — I cannot be alone right now — she is looking for me."

"She?" Edward frowned. "Charlotte, you've had a shock. Rest."

"Stay," she commanded again. The tears did not stop falling. He wiped them away with a gentle thumb. His hands were warm about her cheeks and they seemed like the only solid thing left in this swirling night.

"I saw a figure down in Ursula's Abbey." She could not keep her voice steady. It trembled as much as her frozen fingers still did. He wrapped them up in his own, warming them through.

"A figure?"

"Something. *Someone.*" She caught sight of his expression and a surge of fury washed over her. "I am not mad! I know what I saw — a lady where none ought to be."

"You are the only lady of Drymote, and, if I had my way, Charlotte, the only lady there would ever be."

She snatched her fingers from his. "Do not tease me, Edward, I am serious. I am afraid."

He just wrapped his arms about her and pressed a kiss into her hair. She closed her eyes tightly, her skin shivering and fizzing, her head thumping, panic still sparkling before her eyes. *I must stay here. I am only safe here.*

She looked up, her eyes so close to his, dark enough to reflect her own frightened face back at her like tiny mirrors, as if she were trapped inside him. Her hands clawed at his face, her lips finding his urgently. He let out a small half-breath of surprise, leaning back slightly.

"Charlotte, what are you doing?"

Something foolish perhaps, but tonight is the night for foolish decisions.

She just kissed him harder. She squeezed her eyes tightly shut, feeling Marcello's phantom hands grappling about her still, rougher than Edward's reassuringly solid ones encircling her. That dark-faced hood still turned to her from the abbey — Ursula, come to haunt her for her impropriety? *Emily, Emily, Emily.*

She bit back a sob.

I must stay here. He is the only one who can protect me. She pulled him down to the bed beside her and ran her hands up his thighs, reaching all the way up for the buttons at his waist. His breath hitched again, and his hands dropped from her back, clenching onto her wrists like manacles.

"Stop, Charlotte. Not now. Not like this."

He forced her hands away, trapping them in his own. His breath was coming out ragged and rough, his eyes still squeezed together tightly. She licked her lips. They were cracked and dry, and her voice, when it came through them, was a stranger's, prickling with the fear still beating upon the windows with the dark.

"Love is no crime. It was you who said so."

He laughed bitterly, his breath still jagged and rough. "Do not wound me with my own words, Charlotte. My defences are low enough as it is."

"I do not understand. Why will you take the maids to bed, but not me?"

"I've never taken a maid to bed!" he exclaimed furiously. "What on earth put such a thing into your head? Where are these thoughts coming from, Charlotte?"

"I just —" *I just thought you liked me.* It sounded foolish even to her own thoughts. She scrubbed her fists into her eyes hard. "Why will you not let me find comfort in your arms?"

"Because you would regret it." He forced his fingers under her chin and tilted it up to look at him gently. His eyes were more earnest than she had ever seen them before, as they glimmered into hers and she found she believed him. "I know what it is like to seek solace in the body of another. It is a fleeting and ephemeral comfort in the night, and you would regret it bitterly in the morning. I *never* want to be anything you regret."

The words hit her hard, like being run over by a carriage. *Surely, he ought to be taking me regardless?* If all he wanted was the thrill of the chase, he would take her now and glory in his victory.

Albert was wrong about him! The thought sang sweetly in her chest even as it ached there. Edward was more than just a hunter, more than a poacher or a thief. Ha! They had both judged him ill on that account. She found herself bursting into tears and was not entirely sure why. Edward looked at her in alarm, but she just buried her face in his chest once more.

Surely my tears ought to have run dry by now? Uncertainly, his hand snaked around her waist, rubbing small soothing circles into her back until she had sobbed herself calm again. The front of his shirt was sodden with her tears, but he did not mention it, not even to make some little snide aside or sarcastic joke about it. He seemed to sense that she was too fragile and vulnerable for his teasing right now. He just held her, held her as she needed to be held, until the world resumed its usual hues once more.

"Forgive me." She hiccoughed softly, wiping her face with the thumb. "I have made a fool of myself tonight in more ways than one."

"No. You cannot be strong all the time. A little weakness is permitted now and then." He smiled a gentle, teasing smile and she smiled tearily back. "Besides, I wish you to be weak with me. Give me everything, Charlotte, your weakness and your strength. I want all of you."

"Just not tonight. Not like this," said Charlotte bitterly. She rubbed her temples with a sigh, trying to scrub away the headache growing there with her fingertips. *He is right. I should not succumb to the same weaknesses as my mother.* Ursula's warnings echoed in her head. *It starts with disgrace, then the madhouse, then death. Emily, Emily, Emily.* Her eyes shot wide as the truth slammed home. She clutched at him, her hands turned to talons, certainty forming granite hard in her mind.

"I know who it was," she whispered. "Down there in the abbey. There is only one woman it could be, only one person who would wait for me—only one woman who would come to find me. I have been such a fool—John even told me, he told me I would find the truth down in Ursula's Abbey—how could I not have seen it before? It is my mother, Edward. She is alive."

The silence in the room was deafening. The crackle and hiss of the fire in the grate laughed at her as she blinked up at him.

"Charlotte." Edward's voice was careful, as though she might break if he spoke too loudly or too roughly. "Your mother has been dead for eighteen years."

She leapt to her feet, pacing the room as the idea took hold. He stood, too, watching her warily.

"That is what they wanted me to believe. She must have escaped Bedlam, she must have been hidden here all this time trying to come back to me. Or she was taken by force, kept as a prisoner down there for all these years."

"Is this some joke you are teasing me with?"

She ignored him, her mind whirring with the sudden revelation. Edward caught her chin, pulling it round to face his, staring deeply into her eyes and trying to find the truth there. "Charlotte, you are not serious? Surely you hear how unlikely that is?"

"Unlikely?" she muttered, her brow furrowing. "There is nothing likelier. It is all so clear to me now. It makes so much sense. I do not know how I have been so blind. They have been lying to me for years."

"Who has been lying to you for years?" He was still using that same, careful voice, and she found that it grated upon her nerves. She tore herself out of his arms, pacing the floor alone. The shadows paced with her, haunting her footsteps, creeping in on all sides in the darkened room.

"Are you being wilfully blind or were you just born foolish? Ursula and John, of course!"

"Slow down, Charlotte, you are exciting yourself."

But she could not slow down. Everything that had been missing finally made sense.

"She could not have any children of her own," she said. "She was jealous of her little sister. Ursula had done everything right. She had kept her virtue until marriage and had made a good match. My mother fell in love with a rascal and fell with child out of wedlock. It was not fair, and the jealousy ate Ursula up inside. She conspired with John to steal me, they hid my mother away in the abbey, and they told me she was dead."

"Does that sound like something John and Ursula would do?"

She felt her temper raising in reply to the scepticism in his voice. "John would have done anything for Ursula, he loved her so dearly. That must have been why he built Ursula's Abbey—to hide my mother in it. It makes sense, Edward. It makes so much *sense*."

"Charlotte, I cannot see the sense in it at all," he said gently. "I think you are tired and over-wrought from your attack. You loved Aunty Ursula and Uncle John dearly and I know well how fond they were of you. I cannot think they would do this to you."

"You are in on it, too!" she screamed at him suddenly. "You have hidden her away—you have stolen her from me, like you stole everything else from me."

A look of pain and panic flickered across his face and she took it as an admittance of guilt.

"I trusted you!" she screamed.

"Charlotte, stop! Listen to me, you will do yourself a damage."

He grabbed her, holding her tight as she thrashed. Her head had begun to pound once more, flashing colours before her eyes, and she rubbed it with tingling fingers. She tried to pull herself free, but her limbs were weak, and Edward was strong. He held her firm, pulling her against his chest.

The door banged open behind them, and Charlotte looked up with a gasp of triumph, but it was not her mother standing there. It was not a woman at all. Albert stood silhouetted in the doorway with a look of fury on his face.

"Will someone kindly tell me what is going on here?" he roared.

Chapter Sixteen

Edward looked helplessly over at his father, his hands still full of the struggling Charlotte. Maud was lingering smugly by Albert's elbow, Charlotte noted. The maid's expression wavered halfway between horror and vindication.

"You should not be out of bed, Father. You are not well. You need to recover."

"You are right, I should not be out of bed! But I must if my son is fool enough to earn such disgrace in my own house. Do you really think the gossiping servants will not carry this scandal down to the village tomorrow? What do you think will happen then? Charlotte will be shamed, and you will be considered the worst kind of cad, hardly a fit candidate for parliament."

"I am not going to parliament!" roared Edward in exasperation, still trying to hold Charlotte still. "Charlotte, quiet yourself, please. Father, help me with her."

Albert's stare grazed over her and Charlotte felt herself chafing under the sceptical glare.

"What is wrong with her?"

"I hardly know. She was attacked tonight, and the fear has over-exerted her. She thought she saw someone down in the folly."

"I did not *think* I saw someone down there, Edward," she said hotly. "I saw my mother!"

"Your mother?"

"Charlotte," Edward was murmuring into her hair, his voice pained. "I am not saying you did not see *something,* but it was not your mother. It may have been a passing vagrant or some mischief-seeking children from the village, that was all."

"It was not a vagrant! Does a vagrant wear a fine dress and cape?"

"Did your mother?" sneered Maud quietly. "Wasn't she little more than a woman of ill-repute?"

Charlotte growled, an awful, feral sound, as if she had reverted to an animal, rather than a thinking, reasoning human, and lunged at the maid in her fury. Edward scarcely managed to hold her back.

"What is wrong with you, woman?" Albert roared, holding a sore-covered arm out to protect his favourite lady's maid. "Is this the way you thank us after all we have done?"

"Father, stop, she is not in her right mind right now."

"That is no surprise, Edward. It was always going to come to her in the end. She has the same weaknesses and fallibilities as her mother. A weak character has a weak mind, after all."

Charlotte thrashed and struggled in Edward's arms, and he could scarcely contain her anymore, though he was large and she was small. Her rage and fear and thundering emotions swam through her veins like electric eels, squirming under her skin, overwhelming her with their bite.

"Help me get her up to bed, and I'll send for Dr Mendle."

"Mendle is an old hack," sneered Albert.

"Well, Farringham then," Edward retorted sharply.

"I will not see a doctor — I am not ill! I will send for the runners! I will send for the magistrate! You cannot keep me here against my will!"

"I do not think Farringham will be qualified to help. I think, perhaps, she needs someone who specialises in such things," said Albert.

There was a moment of silence as this sank in. Even Charlotte ceased her fight as she stared at him in horror, the last of her fury echoing around the now still room.

"What are you saying, Father?" Edward asked carefully, his hands still grasping tightly onto Charlotte's shoulders, gripping firmly enough to leave imprints even through the fabric. His face was grim. Albert sighed deeply, shaking his head. When he spoke, his voice was unusually gentle.

"I know you do not want to hear this, but it is for the best. The poor thing is out of her wits. Let her be sent somewhere where they know how to deal with her. It would be the kindest thing. We can take power of attorney over her, we will see her well-treated until she is able to regain control of her own affairs, but until that time, she needs someone who can treat her as she needs to be treated, at a hospital designed for these kinds of invalids."

He gestured at Charlotte, as if she could not hear him talking about her over her head, as if she were some kind of idiot, unable to comprehend their conversation. She shook her head.

"I will not be sent away, I will die before I set foot over the threshold of Bedlam!"

"You must have seen the signs yourself, Edward. This is scarcely the first exhibit of paranoia she has shown. I know you have been denying it to yourself, but she has been getting worse lately."

"No!"

"My brother was worried about this," said Albert softly, his gaze still fixed on Edward's. "He knew madness ran in her blood, that was why he left her in my care and not in her own when he passed. He did not provide her with an inheritance because he knew that he could not trust her with an annuity. He knew that she was not able to make her own sound judgements and the time would come that the faculties she did have would disintegrate, too."

"That is not true! He left me an inheritance in his will!"

"He did not write a will, Charlotte," Albert said in that

same, long-suffering, patient voice.

"He did! Fletch said he did! Fletch *said* he did!" she repeated, turning to Edward instead.

"Did you hear Mr Fletcher say such a thing, Edward?" Albert asked, raising an eyebrow. Edward looked miserable and did not reply. She grabbed at his hands.

"I am not lying!"

"No one thinks you a liar, Charlotte. We know that you believe these things to be true, just as you have always believed everyone in the village hates you, I am secretly working against you out of spite, and the ghost of your mother haunts these halls, but believing it does not make it true. Go on, Maud, tell Edward what you told me this evening. You will not get in trouble."

Maud shuffled her feet, blushing slightly, wearing a much more modest, meek demeanour than she ever wore for Charlotte.

"I only said that I was worried about Miss Mayweather, sir. I've seen it before when a mind starts unravelling, I recognise the signs . . ."

"I am not unravelling!" shouted Charlotte, straining in Edward's arms, but he hushed her gently, holding her tight.

"Please, Miss Mayweather, you can't see it for yourself, that's what's so sad about it all. At first it was just confusion, losing things, forgetting things, that sort of thing. She'd ask me three times where the same item was and then she'd start insinuating that I took it instead, getting paranoid and suspicious."

"That's a lie!"

"Then she started trying to hurt herself. She'd start scratching herself with sticks and pebbles from the gardens, crawling around on her hands and knees until they became bloodied, hitting her head on the trees in the garden sometimes. We tried to restrain her, but if anybody ever caught her, she'd insist it was an accident. How many accidents can you have, sir? Have you never seen her crawling on all fours across the paths?" Maud asked wide-eyed and innocent. She looked down at her feet and shrugged. "And then it got even worse than that. She started getting violent, sir. She tried to drown me in the lake, and if you had not been there, she would have succeeded."

"I was rescuing you!"

"You were trying to hold me under the water! You were trying to kill me!"

"Edward, you cannot believe this!" Charlotte implored. "Maud is the one conspiring against me! She's working against me, they're all working against me!" she said urgently, her eyes wild. Edward looked down at her but did not speak. "You have to believe me!"

"Why would he? Can't you hear how you sound?" Albert sneered. "I knew something like this would happen, I knew she would get worse, but I did not believe she would fall this far or this fast. The fault is partly mine, I should have made preparations before now. I will send for an asylum keeper."

"No!"

She tried to thrash her way free, but Edward's hands were strong. The panic was choking her now, blinding her, fizzing in her eyes and fingers and brain, until the world felt close and claustrophobic and everything was messy and muddled and hot and she was screaming, her heartbeat pounded in her eardrums, rattling in her bones, resounding like taunting laughter.

The world spun, and the floor came crashing up to greet her in fizzing, swirling greys. She heard Edward cursing loudly, frantically calling her name out in the darkness, but she did not reply. *He wants to send me away. He wants to have me committed. Hunting me.* She never should have trusted him. She could not trust anyone any longer. She was alone as she had always been alone.

Strong hands lifted her up and deposited her gently on the bed and she heard a voice growling above her about smelling salts. An acrid, vinegary smell assaulted her nose and she found herself inhaling sharply, the dizziness abating slightly. She tried to move, but her strength had failed her.

It is over. She slumped to the pillows. Albert was leaning against the bedpost, looking grey but vindicated, and Maud was lingering by his elbow with a cruel smugness, but it was to Edward she looked, Edward sitting beside her, the bottle still in his hand, the haunted look still sitting there beneath the soot-smudges on his skin.

Oh yes, the fire. It had only been this evening. It had felt like a lifetime ago. She closed her eyes again. *I am so very weary.*

She felt the salt-water washing down her cheeks, but made no move to wipe it away. The pain sat like a stone in her stomach, heavy and hard, and her chest ached with the weight of it, so that every breath she stole ground tightly against her ribs. Edward said nothing. There was nothing that he could say. The fates had been unkind to her and he could do nothing at all to fix it.

Perhaps I belong in Bedlam. Perhaps I deserve the same fate as my mother. It would be best for everyone. I am nothing but a burden.

"You are no burden, and even if you were, it is one I would gladly bear."

She blinked at him. She had not realised she had said it aloud. He stroked her hair away from her face again, his thumbs lingering upon her cheeks, and for a moment she thought—hoped—he was going to kiss her, but he retracted his hand with a sigh. "This is just a trial we will have to learn to face together. I am up for the challenge, if you are. I have finished running away from my problems. From now on I will face them head on, hand in hand with you, my darling." He grinned at her wickedly, but his eyes were soft and wistful. "Marry me, Charlotte."

"Edward!" Albert blustered angrily from behind them, but Edward ignored him, his gaze still fixed on Charlotte's.

"I love you, foolish woman, and nothing will ever change that. Marry me, and we will face whatever comes together, come madness or mayhem, or even Marcello Antinori. Marry me."

"I will not condone this! I refuse to give my blessing to this union!" shouted Albert, his face red and blotchy, his hands shaking. "She is a mad-woman! A penniless, witless, reputation-less madwoman!"

"She is mine, and she will be my wife with or without your blessing, Father. If she will have me?" he added, a small, almost uncertain look upon his face as he glanced back towards her. Charlotte found she was crying again and could hardly say why.

She just held out a hand towards Edward and he gripped it tightly. The bottle of smelling salts slipped from his hand and rolled across the floor. He winked at her.

"I guess I'd better put those back before someone gets hurt, hmm?" He scooped them up and strode past his quivering, cursing father with all the arrogant, swaggering blasé she loved about him. But as he approached her dresser to replace the smelling salt bottle back in the ornament box, he hesitated. He looked at Charlotte. He looked at Albert.

He scooped the vitamin bottle out of the ornament box and held it up to the glow of the candlelight. He frowned. He looked all over for a label, and, not seeing one, he unstopped the bottle and shook out one of the little white tablets in the palm of his hand. He raised it to his nose and sniffed it, and his frown increased.

The world went still and silent for a moment, then, in a voice that was dangerously quiet, he said,

"Why are there mercury tablets in your pill bottle, Charlotte?"

Chapter Seventeen

Charlotte stared in confusion. Edward had gone very still, like a predator waiting to pounce. Albert had stopped his cursing. He, too, had stilled, though he looked more ready to flee than to fight. Charlotte shook her aching head.

"They are not mercury tablets. They are vitamins prescribed by Dr Farringham for strengthening my ankle. I will go lame without them."

"Mercury weakens muscles, not strengthens them," he said with that same intense quiet, but as she looked over to him, she found he was staring at the reddening Albert now, not at her. "It also creates numbness in the extremities, headaches, extreme mood swings, and paranoia. I know, because when my father was first prescribed it, I read up upon the side effects to prepare myself. Tell me that these are not the symptoms you have been experiencing lately, Charlotte. Tell me that I am wrong."

She knew she could not. She felt her temper rising, fear and panic clawing up through her throat. "It is not mercury," she insisted.

"How did Charlotte get these tablets, Father?"

Albert began blustering again, his face red, his hands twitching, but Edward just slammed the bottle down upon the dresser, hard enough to shatter it. Little while tablets went skittering over the polished wood, mingled with the crystalline fragments, sharp enough to cut. Albert went pale, stuttering into silence.

"Is that who you are, Father? A murderer?"

"I do not know what you are talking about, Edward." But his voice was unconvincing.

Charlotte felt herself swaying uneasily as the truth at last set in. She had not believed it until now. She had not wanted to believe it. She sat up dazedly, even as the world began to spin around her.

Albert began to stumble unsteadily for the door. "It is late. I am tired. I will go to my chambers now, and we can talk in the morning."

"You loosened her mind on purpose! No wonder she has been seeing conspiracies everywhere. You have not succumbed to madness, Charlotte. You were being poisoned!" he added in her direction. A shiver ran through her, and she did not know if it was relief or horror. Edward did not notice.

"You're being ridiculous," Albert said, still edging towards the exit.

"You're not going anywhere," Edward snarled. "How could you?"

"I do not know —"

"Stop lying! You were the one who gave Charlotte those tablets — your own tablets, I'd warrant, that's why you stopped taking them. You were the one trying to convince me she was mad so that you could ship her off to an asylum. Why?"

"He could not risk you falling in love with me," Charlotte said faintly. "He could not risk you marrying me."

"Let me pass, Edward. You are not in your right mind tonight." Albert darted for the door and Edward lunged at him, but Maud threw herself into his path, blocking the younger Cotterhugh man from leaving.

"Move!" he snarled at her as Albert scuttled away, down the winding stairs into the hall. Maud did not.

"Edward, please, leave it," Charlotte called futilely, scrambling out of bed and tottering unsteadily towards him, but

Edward had already pulled Maud out of the way and was chasing Albert out into the hall. The front doors banged shut — Albert had not fled to his chambers, he was trying to make his escape out into the night.

Edward hurried out after him, stopping only to grab a lantern, and Charlotte followed after as quickly as she was able. The lantern threw a circle of light out onto the path, which wobbled as they ran. Albert seemed to have disappeared entirely. How he could see his way through the gardens in this pitch black was anybody's guess. The moon rose high above them, but its light was too dim to clear the paths. The far off glow of the lanterns returning to the chapel, in a bobbing, swaying line, glinted in the distance down at the bottom of the hill, tiny pinpricks breaking through the darkness, until it seemed that the stars had fallen from the sky and were swaying through the valley instead. Charlotte almost felt like she might be floating. *Is this just the mercury still poisoning my mind?* Edward did not seem to notice.

"Where is he? He must be here somewhere! He cannot have gone far!"

"And what will you do even if you find him, Edward? Please, it is the middle of the night, come back into the house. We will summon the law in the morning."

"And give him a chance to escape? No! There he goes! Look!"

He whirled the lantern wildly and a glint of light fell on the fleeing, stumbling figure, all but tumbling down the hillside into the waiting fog.

"Come, quickly! We can cut him off if we make haste."

"Edward, you are not thinking rationally!" This was ironic from her, she knew, but there was danger in the air tonight and she could not shake the feeling some terrible calamity was hovering over their heads — that something which could not be undone was about to come crashing upon them.

Edward was not listening to her, however. He was charging wildly down the gardens, leaping over flower beds and through shrubs with a careless abandon which would have made Uncle John wince. Charlotte went hurrying after him as fast as she could, but it was scarcely fast enough.

Edward slammed into place before the gates just as Albert came panting up to them, and Albert reared away in fear.

"Let me pass!"

"You will pass these gates with the magistrate, Father, and with no one else," Edward snarled. He lunged towards Albert, trying to grab him, but Albert dodged out of his hands with surprising agility, turning on his heel and fleeing back up the winding pathways.

Edward cursed as he dropped the lantern and spent precious seconds trying to retrieve it. He looked up, scanning the dark pathways, as he vainly tried to follow the disappearing figure and then hollered with victory.

"There! In the abbey!"

The door was left open, swinging in the wind, and even from a distance, Charlotte could see Albert's shadow whipping into it.

Edward ran into the abbey at full speed, and Charlotte limped after him as fast as she could. Even now, her ankle hadn't healed properly. *Mercury weakens muscles, not strengthens them,* Edward's voice reminded her in her head. She cursed under her breath. It was a vicious circle — the more she took, the more reliant on them she would become, a plot both diabolical and cruel. She staggered into the abbey and leant against the door, breathing hard, barring the exit with her body.

Albert held up his hands as he backed away into the shadows, Edward stalking towards him, a look of inhuman fury etched on his features. The wind howled through the glassless windows and the door to the vestry creaked open to the left of them, exposing a slither of darkness within.

"You do not understand, Edward. You have gone mad. No one will believe you anyway. It is the middle of the night, please, let us talk about this in the morning."

"Do you have any other excuses, Father?" sneered Edward, still striding purposefully towards him. Albert stumbled backwards, his hands still raised. He bumped into the stone bench his brother had so often sat upon, throwing out a hand to catch his fall. His whole weight fell upon the large, square stone behind the altar, and it shifted, falling to the ground with a thunk. Every set of eyes turned towards it as it lay there upon the ground and, propped up against the wall in the alcove it had left, was a large envelope, sealed shut. It fluttered to the floor and for one timeless moment everyone watched it drift, and then Albert snatched at it with surprising speed. He tore it open, and, before any could stop him, ripped it through with a shout of triumph, shredding it into pieces as Edward and Charlotte just stared at him in shock. Then he slumped at last against the stonework, all strength apparently fleeing from him.

"Do as you will now," he said. "It is too late." He opened his hands and the pieces fluttered to the floor like autumn leaves. Charlotte bent and picked one up, tilting it to the moonlight streaming through the high windows, trying to pick out the words.

It was in Uncle John's familiar, crabby handwriting.

"This was the will," she realised aloud. "This was where he had hidden the will."

She looked at the loose stone on the floor, the alcove it had hidden, and the fragments of paper which held all hope of her independence. Her hands tightened around that crumpled fragment in her palm as if she could somehow save it even now.

"Yes." Albert said with a satisfied sigh. "Only my

ridiculous brother would think of hiding a will in the folly. Only John would be fool enough to hide his will at all—but he knew I had help within his lawyer's firm. Clerics are so underpaid, you know. They will do almost anything for a small consideration. I was ready to have it destroyed when it reached the legal office, but it never arrived. Then I thought perhaps he had left it with that garden fellow he was so stupidly fond of, but he hadn't, nor did he leave it in his study or his safe or his chambers. I should have *known* he'd left in the garden. Obvious, when you think about it." He chuckled softly. "I have been searching for it since he wrote it. I knew it would turn up eventually. I knew we would not be safe until it had been destroyed."

"Because he left me some money in it?" Charlotte whispered incredulously.

"No, you foolish child, because he left you Drymote."

Charlotte staggered. She felt her stomach plunging, her head spinning wildly, her throat closing up.

"I thought Drymote was entailed," she whispered.

"No, no. It was never entailed," he said impatiently, waving his sore-covered hand. "John inherited it through our mother's line. But that does not matter anymore. Without a will, the estate goes to the nearest next of kin and through me to my wonderful boy." He stared lovingly up at Edward, who only gaped down at him in horror. Albert seemed to be talking more to himself than anyone else now. "At last, my son, your future will be safe."

"And how do you think my prospects at parliament will look once everyone knows I have a criminal for a father?" Edward asked. He tried to sound sardonic and careless, but pain and the horror streaked through his voice like veins.

Albert seemed surprised at Edward's tone. "I did this all for you, Edward. I had to. John would not give me any more money to secure your place in parliament and your future prospects. When I found out he was going to give this estate to that ridiculous, illegitimate spinster, I had to do it."

"Uncle John had been giving you money?" Charlotte said dazedly. "Is that why Drymote is in financial straits?"

But Edward was talking over her, still staring at his father. "What do you mean you had to do it? You had to do *what*, Father?"

Albert did not reply, he just chuckled softly to himself, slumped against the ground. "It does not matter now," he said gently. "I am dying, and you will be safe, my son."

Edward knelt before him.

"Tell me this and tell me it truly — did you kill Uncle John? Did you murder your own brother?"

Albert smiled serenely up at him, his eyes paling with the last of his strength. "I did what I had to, Edward, that is all."

Edward cursed long and loud, the sound of it echoing up into the vaulted ceilings. He rounded upon Charlotte. "Send for the magistrate," he commanded.

But Albert just laughed weakly. "What would be the point, Edward? It is your word against mine. John is long in the ground, they will not dig him up now, and even if they did, any trace of poison in his blood would be long since gone. Without the will . . ." He gestured around at the scraps of paper already fluttering away in the wind, "You have no proof. No one will believe you."

"They will believe me," said a voice behind them, and Charlotte and Edward whirled around. Mr Harris was walking resolutely forwards from the side chamber, his face pale but determined. He was dressed in travelling clothes and had a small bag in his hands. Clutching onto his arm, also dressed in travelling clothes, was Georgiana.

"Georgiana and I are witnesses to your confession, sir," Mr Harris said grimly. "And I will do my duty by the law, even though it costs me dearly." He glanced at Georgiana, and she nodded, even though tears were streaming freely down her face.

"Georgiana? What is going on here?" Charlotte asked. Georgiana smiled at her weakly.

"I am afraid you have caught us at a scandal, rather. Henry and I were planning to elope tonight, you see, whilst everyone was distracted by the All Hallow's Eve parade. We have been using this folly as a meeting place, for my guardian watches far too closely over Langhorne Estate, and I recall how you said this was the best place for privacy. Tonight, we were finally going to wed. My guardian has threatened to make me a ward of court. He has said if I marry unwisely, he will keep every last farthing of my inheritance, but I love Henry. I do not care if he is penniless, I will marry him, I will!" she cried passionately. Mr Harris patted her hand.

"We must do the right thing, Georgiana," he said grimly, his eyes dark as they stared down at Albert, slumped upon the floor.

"We will not get another chance," she whispered. "If we do not go tonight, it will be too late."

"We cannot go like this, not with the truth left unheard. Love is not selfish, Georgiana, my own. We must yet be brave."

"You were the lady I saw in these ruins." Charlotte realised with a gasp. "That shadow that has been haunting me here — it was you, Georgiana, it was always you."

"Will somebody go for the law?" snapped Edward, but Charlotte just placed a hand upon his arm, gazing down at Albert, wheezing upon the floor.

"I think it is not the law he needs, it is a doctor. Look at him. He is dying."

"Yes," croaked Albert. "I am dying, but you are safe at last, Edward." He slumped sideways, his strength abandoning him and all four of them stared at him for a moment as his chest rose and fell in pitiful, shallow wheezes.

"Go," Charlotte said at last, breaking the silence. The others turned to look at her. She smiled back at them even as tears filled her eyes. "You two should go. We will take Albert back to the house and send for the doctor and, should he survive the night, we will send for the magistrate. You cannot prosecute a dead man anyway. You two should wed whilst you have the chance. We will still be here when you get back as Mr and Mrs Harris," she added reaching out for Georgiana's hands. Georgiana grasped them gratefully, turning wide, imploring eyes to Mr Harris. He chewed his lip, looking torn, staring between his bride-to-be and the two Cotterhugh men kneeling upon the abbey floor — his desire and his duty.

"Charlotte is right," Edward said brusquely. "There's no reason why one of us should not marry the woman we love. Go. You can give your statements to the law when you return. Go!" he snapped impatiently, and Mr Harris held out his arms to Georgiana with a sheepish grin. Georgiana tumbled into them gratefully, her lips finding his face, smothering them with eager kisses despite the audience. Mr Harris' hands curled around her waist, kissing her fervently back with a passion Charlotte had not thought possible from the staid and upright clergyman. He laughed, so clearly delirious with joy, and the two of them fled from the abbey hand in hand, their happiness over-spilling around them, as if it were a light which shone out from within them. Charlotte watched them go with a deep sigh, and when she turned, she found Edward staring at her. He caught at her hands, his eyes troubled and torn.

"Charlotte, I . . . I am so sorry . . ."

"This was none of your doing, Edward. Albert is responsible for his own actions."

"He did all of this for me, you heard him say so."

She pressed a soft kiss upon his lips. "You did not ask for

any of it. Do not take the world upon your shoulders."

"He murdered John! He tried to murder you!"

Charlotte felt a flare of anger bursting through her at the thought of it. She nodded grimly. "I know it, and the law will bring him justice, but his crimes are his own."

Edward rested his forehead upon hers. He shook his head bitterly.

"But *why*? If he knew John had given you Drymote, why was he so desperate to keep us apart? Surely he should be encouraging us to wed?"

"You heard what he said, he has been taking money from Uncle John for years. The heir of Drymote, whomever that might be, needs to marry into money to save the estate from foreclosure."

Edward stared at her for a long moment and then took a few steps back. "I suppose it doesn't matter much now anyway," he said. "You were hardly going to marry the son of a murderer, were you? Like father like son, eh?"

"Edward —"

"You stay here with him, if you can bear to. I'll go fetch a servant to help haul him back to the house. Not that he deserves even that much consideration," Edward spat out bitterly. Charlotte called after him again, holding out imploring hands, but Edward had already stridden away.

Charlotte slumped down onto the floor besides Albert, suddenly exhausted. She glanced down at the man beside her. His breathing was laboured, rattling out through his chest in strained exertion, and every now and then he would twitch in feeble convulsions. She felt strangely numb, hollowed out of everything except disdain and exhaustion. She could not even summon the energy to hate him yet, though perhaps that would come later.

"You made me believe I was mad," she told him. He did not hear her, slumped unconsciously, but it made her feel better to say it aloud. "Uncle John trusted you, he loved you. He only ever tried to help you, and you punished him for it."

She glanced upwards towards the ceiling far above, though she could not see it in the darkness, and she wondered distantly if Uncle John and Aunty Ursula were watching them both, and if they were, what they might make of it.

"You are dying, Albert. You are going to meet your maker and face His judgement. Do you think this all was worth it? And what have you done to Edward? How do you think he will cope with all this? He has carried enough guilt on his shoulders for Giuliani's death, and now he will blame himself for John's, too, knowing you did it for his benefit. You have done that. You have broken the very man you were trying to save. So I ask you again, Albert, was it worth it?"

Of course, Albert did not reply.

"I believed I was mad," she whispered once more. "But I am not. I am still here. I am still sane — and I — yes, Albert, *I* will be the heir of Drymote when we have buried your body in the cold, dark ground and the sod grows green above it. The worms will eat you, and the flowers will grow, and all the darkness you have wrought here will be forgotten as the seasons turn death into new life again." She glanced down at him and nodded silently to herself. It was enough.

CHAPTER EIGHTEEN

The funeral was a quiet affair. Edward had wanted it that way. It was probably most fitting in the circumstances, but Charlotte couldn't help but think that Albert would have hated it. He would have wanted a bit more pomp and ceremony.

She stared down at the freshly churned earth in the graveyard as they few gathered around it. *Is this what it has come to? Is this what it was all for?*

At her insistence, they had not sent for the law. What would be the point? It would only cause unnecessary scandal and, as Albert himself had pointed out, they had no proof. Even with Mr Harris' testimony, they still had very little to go on. They could not prove Uncle John had been murdered, they could not prove there had ever been a will that was destroyed, they could not even prove that Albert had been giving Charlotte mercury — Edward had destroyed the bottle it came in, in his rage. Seeing as Albert was dead now, and past the reach of even the long arm of the law, there seemed little point.

Still, she had been feeling better now, and that was something. She had not realised how ill she had been feeling until it passed. The shadows no longer held terrors for her, she no longer doubted the evidence of her eyes or the strength of her mind. It was terrifying still to realise how close she had come to being robbed of her sanity permanently, shut away in the stern confines of a sanatorium and left to rot, all so that Albert could advance his son.

She felt a gentle touch on her arm and looked up to see Georgiana lingering beside her. The graveside service had ended, but she hadn't noticed, her gaze still fixed upon the ground which covered Albert's coffin, her mind still churning with unspoken thoughts.

Georgiana was very modestly dressed today, as befitted a poor curate's wife. It had been quite the scandal in Birchton when news broke of their elopement, and Charlotte was secretly, selfishly pleased for it. In between the arrest of Marcello Antinori and the scandalous marriage gossip ricocheting around the village, hardly anyone was talking about Albert's passing. She was sure the news would take root once they waded through the legal battles and tried to get Charlotte officially reinstated as the mistress of Drymote, as Edward was still doggedly trying to do, but for now, the world outside the gates of the estate did not know of the madness that had occurred within it.

"Are you all right, Charlotte?" Georgiana asked gently. "I know you have been through a lot lately."

"Oh yes, I'm fine. I am doing much better than I was, thank you. It is Edward I worry for."

He was not talking to anyone, save in curt commands or low mutters. He barely ate or slept, he would not stay in the same room as Charlotte if he could help it, shame driving him away whenever she tried to reach for him. He was falling apart before her eyes, and there seemed so pitifully little she could do to help him. She sighed, long and deep. She would have to leave it in the hands of providence. There was nothing else that could be done.

"Yes, Henry wants a word with him, when Lord Cotterhugh is available."

"Call him Edward, dear Georgiana. He winces every time someone calls him by his new title. And I wish that Mr Harris would speak to him, for he is desperately in need of some spiritual guidance."

"Now, if I must call him Edward, then you must certainly call Mr Harris *Henry*. After all we have been through together, I think it is a little late for formalities, don't you? And it is not just spiritual guidance Henry is offering." Georgiana pressed her lips together with a smile, and leant forwards, her voice dropping low in the quiet afternoon air. "He has found the child," she confided. "Henry has found Julia Antinori."

Charlotte's hands flew to her mouth. "Oh! Edward will be so pleased." *So will poor Marcello.*

Marcello had been dragged off to a sanatorium to regain his sanity, and it had only been through Edward's intervention that it had been the mad-house and not death row that the man had been taken to. But when he was released, at least he would have something to look forwards to — some family left to comfort him.

"It will be a great burden off Edward's shoulders to return that poor orphaned child to her grandmother, and a comfort to the old lady, too, I should think." She looked over to Edward, who was already waiting for her with a grim solemnity by the carriage door, and her heart wrenched within her. *We must find some money in the accounts to provide for little Julia.* Drymote was still heavily in debt, of course, but if they had found enough money to re-employ Fletch — returning at the end of the week and bringing his family with him, just imagine it — then they could certainly find some for the child.

Charlotte turned and found Georgiana watching her quietly, a small, sympathetic smile lingering there on her lips.

"It was kind of you to come today," Charlotte said earnestly. "I appreciate it. You are looking very well. Being a wife suits you, I think."

The newly-wed wife could not help but beam. Even in sturdy, practical clothes, she glowed fresh-faced and dewy. She was still the most beautiful woman in all of Birchton, and Charlotte was sure that Henry Harris counted his blessings twice each morning.

"I think it would suit you, too, Charlotte, if it is not impertinent to say so," Georgiana said archly, her gaze darting towards Edwards lingering at the carriage in a sullen silence. "I don't know if this will help that endeavour . . ."

She thrust out an envelope towards Charlotte, who took it curiously. Inside was a thickly gummed piece of paper, fragments and scraps of paper stuck like a mosaic onto a larger sheet.

"I went back to Ursula's Abbey. I found all the pieces I could," Georgiana said quietly, but Charlotte scarcely heard her.

Charlotte's throat was dry. The paper blurred before her eyes as tears sprang up, smudging Uncle John's familiar hand from view. Charlotte wiped her tears away quickly, scanning the dusty legal terms hastily.

Being of sound body and mind . . . hereby bequeath . . . my niece, Charlotte Mayweather . . . sole owner of Drymote Estate and all its environs . . .

Charlotte hugged the fragmented paper to her chest. *It is true. It is all, really true, there, written by his own hand. He did not forget me.*

"I don't know if it's still legally binding . . ." Georgiana said awkwardly, but Charlotte shook her head hard, blinking back tears.

"It doesn't matter even if it is not," she said. "To see it here in black and white in his own handwriting, to know, without a shadow of a doubt, that he intended to leave Drymote to me . . . it is *everything,* Georgiana. I cannot thank you enough."

Georgiana's face lit up in a bright smile.

"Nonsense, it is what friends do for one another, is it not? And I would not be married to Henry now if you had not urged us to leave when we did. I think our debts of gratitude cancel each other out. But if you ever need any help, if there is ever anything I can do . . ."

Charlotte squeezed her hand tightly. "I will recall it," she said, and she meant it. She tucked that precious paper back into its envelope and slipped it into her pocket for safe-keeping.

She began to hurry over to Edward, but stopped, as a black clad figure caught her eye. She frowned, her heart racing as she wondered whether the mercury lingered in her system still to send such apparitions to her, but no, the woman seemed real enough. Charlotte felt her temper flaring. She clenched her fists and turned her footsteps towards Maud, standing there on the edge of the graveyard, a small black veil covering her face.

Maud did not try to leave as Charlotte approached her, and Charlotte saw to her surprise that tears were flowing unchecked down Maud's face.

"What are you doing here? I thought we told you that if we ever saw you again we would call the law."

Maud just shrugged wearily and Charlotte felt the heat go out of her anger. There was something so pitiful about Maud's tragic resignation. Charlotte shook her head.

"Why did you do it, Maud? What did I ever do to you?"

"Why should you have everything? You are no better than I am," Maud spat out.

"I have never made anyone believe they were mad. I have never sought to damage your reputation."

"He promised me he would value my help," she whispered, her gaze still fixed on the gravestone. "He said he would pay me, but I didn't believe it. Not really. It wasn't even about the money. I just . . . I just wanted . . ." The tears flowed fast now, streaming down her plump face. She did not try to wipe them away. "He never kept any promises to my mother, I do not know why I believed he would keep them to me, but I so wanted him to be proud of me, just once."

Charlotte stared.

"Are you saying Albert was . . ."

Maud shrugged furiously. "My mother was just a maid in his household. He never claimed me, but he got me this position, a good position for an illegitimate woman, and he said he'd leave me something in his will, enough to make me independent for the rest of my life. And . . . and . . ." Fresh waves of tears burst from her. "Why should *you* get everything?" she spat at Charlotte. "You were born in infamy just the same as me, and John Cotterhugh was my uncle just as much as he was yours. Why should you be the heiress and I be the maid?"

"Uncle John didn't know about you," Charlotte said with bedrock certainty. "He'd have done something to help you and your mother if he did." She looked over to Edward still lingering at the carriage. Edward, she realised all in one moment, who was Maud's half-brother. *He did not even know he had a sister.* She had been under their noses all the time, and none of them knew.

"I used to take your things all the time," Maud confessed distantly. "I used to steal your jewels, your ribbons, your shawls and hide them down in the boat house where I knew no one ever went. I even took your ball dress to try on once. I used to use your hairbrush and your old rose-waters and your jewellery, and stand before your looking glass in your bedchambers and pretend it was all mine. I would pretend my life was different. I would pretend my life was *yours.* And whenever you noticed that anything was missing, I would pretend to help you look for it, knowing all the while that it was down in the gardens, and I would tell people that you had gone mad, that you were muddled in your mind, losing things, confusing things, accusing people. It was a bitter satisfaction, but it was all the satisfaction I would get. I was ever so pleased when Albert asked me to help him confuse you and spread ill rumours about you. I didn't know about the mercury. He told me to make sure you took your tablets, but I never knew what they were. He should have told me. I could have helped. He could have trusted me. I wanted you to be mad. I wanted you to be locked away in an asylum like your disgrace of a mother and never released again. It would have been justice."

"No. It would have been vengeance. They are not the same thing," Charlotte said softly. Maud turned to look at her in surprise, as if only just remembering that Charlotte was there. Charlotte sighed. She was still Edward's sister. She was still Albert's daughter. And Charlotte herself could so easily have been in Maud's place . . .

"I wish you had died that night and he had not."

"Maud," Charlotte called, but Maud was already striding away between the granite gravestones and out of sight.

Charlotte looked over to Edward once more, wondering anxiously whether to tell him.

Yes, I must, no more secrets between us. But not today. He is grieving enough over Albert's actions already, let him not grieve for his sister, too. There will be time enough later.

She hurried over to the carriage, and Edward handed her in to it without speaking. It was ridiculous, really, it would be quicker to walk over the fields from the chapel to Drymote Estate than it would be to take the carriage around, but there should be some ceremony on an occasion like this, and it was the only concession Edward had made to it. That, and the sombre black outfit he wore. They were not having a wake.

He sat opposite her on the plush seats and withdrew his pocket watch.

"We should just about beat the lawyers home," he said. She started. It was the first conversation he had initiated with her in a week or more, practically the first thing he had said that was more than a grunt or a monosyllabic reply. "Harris has the tendency to go on, does he not? Even in funeral sermons.

I confess, I like him a grand deal better as Georgiana's husband than I ever did on his own account. I don't mind his prattling half as much, when I know you will not be hanging on his every word over the breakfast table. At least it wasn't raining, I suppose." He smiled, but it was bitter and twisted at his mouth. He stared out of the window.

"Why are the lawyers coming today? Edward, you should not be doing business on the day of your father's funeral."

"He was a murderer."

"Yes, but he was still your father. You are allowed to grieve him, even after all he did."

Edward's mouth contorted further, but he did not argue with her. "I just wish to get it all sorted. I do not want to linger through this mess any longer. I wish for it all to be behind me now. I wish to start again."

Charlotte felt her pulse quickening.

"You are planning to leave Drymote?"

"I think that would be best in the circumstances. I think our best option would be if I were to just draw up a legal exchange, giving Drymote into your hands irrevocably. It is unconventional, I realise, and I am sure it will draw much speculation and gossip, but honestly, I do not know how else to do it, and that Drymote is yours by right is not under any question in my mind."

"Edward," she said gently, but he continued, still refusing to look at her.

"It will take a little while to get such documents ratified, I fear, and I hope you will allow me to continue here with you until I can put my signature to such things, but as soon as I am able, I will be out of your way."

"I do not want you out of my way. You belong here."

"I belong anywhere I can earn an honest living, as indeed, I will have to now, it seems. I fear my father did not leave me anything that was not ill-gotten. I have been living all these years on the assumption of wealth, and now I must make my own way. Ha. Well, it is the making of a man, so they say. It will not do me ill."

"Stay."

"I cannot. Mendle has offered me an apprenticeship in town, and I confess, I did consider taking it. You always said I had a penchant for medicine, Charlotte, but there are more opportunities for work abroad. I will go to Canada, I think. I have heard that they are looking for surveyors out in the wilds, and I have a taste to put my hand to it."

"Edward, you do not know the first thing about surveying, or, indeed, Canada. Stay here where you belong."

"I cannot, Charlotte." He met her gaze at last, and his eyes were racked with pain. "I cannot stay and watch you marry another man, and if you had any heart within you would not ask me to."

"Then stay and marry me," she said softly. He took a sharp breath in. He shook his head, as if he had not quite heard her.

"You would still marry me?" he whispered. "After all this."

"Yes."

"But Drymote—you need the money—"

"So take Mendle's apprenticeship."

"That will not cover all the debts my father accrued."

"No, we will have to make retrenchments and sell off some of the lower lands, but once the worst of the debts are paid and you have qualified as a doctor, the money will help keep Drymote afloat. Besides, it would certainly make things easier from a legal perspective. A wife's house is her husband's property by law. Why give me Drymote when you will just take it back from me by marriage? We can make things right without involving the lawyers at all. Stay, Edward."

"How can I?" he whispered. "How can I ask you to marry me now?"

"You are not asking me, I am asking you," she teased him, grinning mischievously, and he let out a breath of laughter. "Nothing has changed, Edward. You said you would marry me in sickness or in health. Well, I will marry you for richer or for poorer. Does it matter who the estate belongs to, as long as we are both here together?"

"There is a wide berth of difference in asking the penniless ward to wed you and asking the heiress."

"Only to your pride. I am still the same woman."

"Everyone will think me a fortune hunter. They will think I wed you for your inheritance."

She slipped her hands into his. "They will not, for there are very few left living that know Drymote is mine anyway. Only Fletch, who signed the will, and Henry and Georgiana Harris, who will not speak if we ask them not to. As far as the world knows, Drymote is yours. Let me be yours, too, Edward, and we will share this burden together."

His expression was a mixture of hope and torment, as if he could scarcely believe it even now. "Truly?"

"Of course, you foolish man. How could it be any different?" She stretched up and pressed a gentle kiss to his cheek. He closed his eyes, his breath flickering across her face.

"You have already saved me once, Charlotte. How can I bear to be indebted to you further?"

"How could you bear not to be?" she whispered back, a smile lingering on her lips. "Say you will stay with me."

And the words, so sweet, so dream-like in her ears came whispering back, hesitant and faltering, vulnerable, free from his usual confident swagger, but melodious all the same.

"Yes, Charlotte. I will stay, and you will be Lady Cotterhugh of Drymote."

Charlotte Cotterhugh. A smile burst across her face and she could not help it, she leant forwards and pressed a kiss to his lips. He laughed, the first time she had heard him laugh in days, his hands clutching urgently to her, his forehead resting against hers and she quietened him with yet more kisses.

"Kissing in the carriage? In the middle of the day? What if someone should see?"

"Let them," she murmured playfully against his lips. "You care far too much for the world's opinion, Edward, I have always said so."

The carriage rounded the final corner, and they rattled through the gates and up the driveway to Drymote together.

Godshollow
Catherine Price

Excerpt

"Mrs Evans, this is my niece, Miss Annabelle Knight. Well, she's not exactly my niece. My husband is her maternal uncle. You know what I mean. Anyway, Annabelle is accompanying us to Bath for the season."

"Oh! How wonderful," Mrs Evans cried loudly, turning to her daughters. "Look, girls, how sweet she is. How lovely, look at her curls. Oh, just darling." She didn't pause for breath, reaching out and grabbing a ringlet of Annabelle's hair. Mrs Evans' tone was the kind one might adopt with regard to a small puppy, which, to these large women, was the way Annabelle must have seemed. They were practically as wide as they were tall, and they loomed over Annabelle. The girl let out a small, nervous laugh.

Oblivious to Annabelle's discomfort, the ladies continued with their assessment. Mrs Evans' daughters, who had been tittering behind her, giggled at their mother's appraisal and added their own.

"Just wonderful," said one.

"So darling," chimed in the other. They both regarded Annabelle with the same shrewd eye with which one would appraise cattle at a market.

While the girls had clearly inherited their looks from their mother, from the brown eyes to the light dusting of freckles over their noses, their accents most definitely came from a Welsh father. It was strong and thick. Annabelle had never heard anything like it, and it took her a considerable amount of concentration to discern what they were saying.

Their mother spoke with a softer English accent that was peppered with small Welsh moments, indicating a good amount of time spent in the country. "These are my twins," Mrs Evans announced. "Carys." She gestured to the girl on her left. "And Gwennyth." She motioned to the other. Annabelle wondered how she was going to remember which twin was which. They were identical, even, unhelpfully, down to their choice in clothing. Both girls dutifully curtseyed.

One of them leant forward and added, "Most people just call me Gwen."

Right. Annabelle noted. So Gwen is the one with the beauty spot beside her right eye. She curtseyed again to each girl as she searched for other unique identifiers.

"Don't you just love Bath, Miss Knight?" Carys asked as though she thought every young lady in the world should have an intimate knowledge of the place.

"Actually, this is my first time," Annabelle admitted timorously.

The twins looked at each other in horror.

"Your first time!" Carys exclaimed, completely aghast, her tone bordering on offended.

"We go every year," Gwen continued, shocked.

"It's just the best place."

"Oh, the very best!"

"Especially for eligible young ladies." At this, both girls dissolved into giggles, laughing at their own insinuations.

Annabelle nodded along, though she couldn't truly

empathise. She knew that Bath was, aside from London, the best place for a young woman to be. But her parents had strictly forbidden her to travel there until she attained the age of eighteen because of its less than sparkling reputation.

"I can't believe you've never visited," Carys said contemptuously.

"How is that possible?" Gwen questioned.

Annabelle made the quick assessment that Gwen was definitely the nicer twin. While that didn't help her immediately, knowing that would help her distinguish which one was speaking.

"I've never had the opportunity to go before now," Annabelle replied simply. "It's something I've always wanted to do. I'm very excited to be visiting. I've read everything about it. There are so many things I would like to do while I'm there."

Gwen seemed satisfied with the answer, though Carys looked more sceptical. Suddenly, the sterner twin was seized by an idea, or at least Annabelle hoped she was—that, or she was having a fit. Carys turned to her sister and began to whisper theatrically. More giggling ensued, and they finally faced Annabelle.

"We have decided," one twin—Carys?—said, with much grandeur.

"That, as it's your first time in Bath . . ." the other added.

"And you'll need someone to show you around . . ."

"And we've been many times before . . ."

"We are the best people . . ."

"To take you under our wings . . ."

"And show you how to do Bath." They nodded in unison and eagerly awaited Annabelle's reply.

Annabelle was so confused by all the sentence-sharing and the back and forth that all she could do was smile weakly and say thank you, though she didn't know exactly what she'd agreed to.

"What a clever idea," Mrs Evans exclaimed, reminding the

young girls of her existence. "Don't you think, Moira?"

"Marvellous." Mrs Daniels nodded. "Of course, Colin and I know the area substantially," she added quickly. "We know it better than anyone, but I'm sure Annabelle would prefer some younger companions to keep her company. Though, of course, she adores us. Don't you dear?"

Annabelle nodded vigorously. Her aunt didn't like to be contradicted and hated even the remotest implication that she wasn't the best at everything.

"Well then, it's settled," Mrs Evans beamed. "Girls, tell Miss Annabelle about the ball."

In the deserted inn, it wasn't difficult for the young ladies to find an empty table. Once they were sat down, Gwen began to tell Annabelle about the upcoming event.

"Oh, it is the best ball," she announced, her boundless enthusiasm giving away her identity. "They have it every year and it is the most wonderful thing. There's tea, and dancing, and card tables, and so many eligible bachelors." Gwen began to giggle girlishly then stopped suddenly. "I know!" she declared. "We must all get ready for it together. Where are you staying? You may be closer than we are."

"I think my uncle said it was St James' Square," Annabelle replied when Gwen stopped to draw breath.

Carys looked disdainful. "Hmm . . ." She paused, her nose turning up at the thought. "It is closer to the ballrooms, but I'm sure it's nowhere near as comfortable as our accommodation in Sidney Place."

Annabelle quickly decided that arguing with Carys would be a bad choice and instead nodded her head in agreement. "I'm sure." she said sweetly. "But we risk less damage to our dresses if we are closer to the halls."

Gwen's head bobbed enthusiastically. "Quite so. And"— she spun on her toes to face Carys—"St James' Square is rather lovely."

The other twin gave no response to this. Instead, she raked her gaze over Annabelle's appearance. "What will you wear?" she asked in a belittling tone.

"Well, I have one dress that's my favourite. I've worn it for years," Annabelle replied fondly. "It's yellow with—"

"That will never do," Carys cut in harshly. "This is the ball of the season, you know. You can't go in wearing old clothes!" She said this with such a tone one would have thought Annabelle had suggested she would make an appearance wearing just her under-things.

Annabelle was too stunned to make an intelligible reply. Luckily, she was saved from having to find a rebuttal by the arrival of Mr Daniels.

"There you two are. I've been searching for you. Bath is still a fair way away, and we really should get going."

Annabelle nodded and rose from the table, happy to escape this odd, insulting conversation. As she left, Carys fired her parting shot.

"Don't worry," the Welsh girl called out. "We'll look through your clothes to find the least terrible gown. And if there's nothing suitable, I'm sure Gwen has something you can borrow."

Annabelle curtseyed politely and followed her uncle out of the room, trying to stop the flush she felt rising in her cheeks. She sat in solitary embarrassment whilst her aunt bid farewell to Mrs Evans and they made plans to meet for lunch the next day.

Annabelle waved from the carriage as the Evanses shrank into the distance, but as she sat back in her seat, once they'd completely disappeared, she wondered just exactly what her aunt's introductions had gotten her into.

About the Author

Beth Fuller lives just outside of Aberystwyth in Wales with her husband and two young children. She is currently studying for her PhD in Victorian literature. Heir of Drymote is her first foray into romance novels.